Black Cordite, White Snow

Crooks' Haven Series Book 1

Venator Media Solutions LLC

In loving memory of Sue Kortum,
owner of Royal Shade and Awning
and dear friend.

And for my great-grandfather,
Pvt. Christian Christophersen of the 131st Infantry,
whose story I will never fully know.

Equanimity

A.380-caliber pistol had the tendency to maim, not kill. The caliber was designed for concealable handguns, the sort carried by military officers doling out battlefield executions or tucked inside women's hand muffs to thwart muggers and rabid dogs. Its bullet—a trivial-looking thing—was nudged along by only a few meager grains of cordite, leaving many of its victims to live out their days in agony, the slug anchored indelibly into bone, its path covered by a puckered scar the size of a pencil eraser. But anemic as it might be, such a little bullet had still proven enough to deliver Archduke Franz Ferdinand and his considerable mustache from his motorcar to an ornate Viennese burial chamber a decade before. That sliver of lead ignited a war that claimed the lives of twenty million people—and very nearly his own. So as Niklas Kristofferson stood, fingers pressed tightly to the icy brick of the derelict warehouse behind him, body tense as the muzzle of a Colt Pocket Hammerless pressed decisively against his forehead, any doubt he may have had about the deadliness of such a weapon promptly vanished.

The distant thrum of traffic and streetcars mumbled from the city center across the Mississippi River, a subtle reminder that they now stood in a desolate place where gunshots would not be heard and would-be witnesses were both scarce and taciturn.

"What are you doing here?" The gunman was portly, gone soft in the middle. His bloated belly strained against his heavy wool coat, the buttons just one good sneeze away from taking flight. Still, he sported a large frame and posture that radiated a boorish inclination toward violence—which his spongy, punching-bag of a nose confirmed. Beneath an ungroomed mustache, his mouth reeked of cheap tobacco and garlic, which emerged in splenetic huffs of warm vapor that hung on the cold air. His baleful eyes darted around the vacant, snow-covered street, hunting for others. "Piss off."

"We're here to see Nunzio. He's expecting us." Niklas tried to keep his voice steady and calm, hoping his composure would prevent his younger brother from doing anything rash that would get them both killed.

It didn't seem to be working: Kessler had gone from calmly smoking his briar pipe a moment before to thumbing open his coat buttons, easing a hand inside to retrieve the Bergmann-Bayard pistol wedged inside his leather shoulder holster.

Raising an open hand toward his brother, Niklas said, "No need for gunplay. Let's give diplomacy a try, first."

The barrel slowly lifted away from his forehead, the pistol disappearing into the mobster's coat pocket. "You'll refer to him as Signor Barbieri. Only men of honor may address him as Nunzio." He turned and shouldered open the building's rusty steel door. Then, with the shambling gait of a lame horse, he stomped inside without waiting for them.

With the danger past, Kessler exhaled audibly. He passed a hand through his thick black hair, his usual insouciant grin returning. His eyes lost their fire, waning to the glowing embers of good humor. "Don't worry, brother. I had him."

"I wasn't worried."

He had been a bit worried. Kessler was an admirable shot and a proven marksman on the battlefields of France, but no amount of Wild West quickdraw skill would have outpaced even the meagerest twitch of a finger it would have taken for Barbieri's lackey to send him on an express voyage to Hades.

"What do you think he meant by us not being men of honor?" Kessler tapped the bowl of his pipe against the heel of his shoe. The dottle and embers fluttered to the snow. "President Wilson's secretaries even typed us a lovely note saying that's what we were when we left the service."

Niklas chuckled as he re-buttoned his brother's coat and swept a dusting of snow from his shoulders. "A lot has changed since then. Maybe our honor has tarnished a bit. Besides, I think our pungent new friend was referring to members of their *cosca*, not men with actual honor."

He stepped back and evaluated his brother's appearance. Kessler always dressed well, spending much of his meager income on fine haberdashery designed for those above their station. Niklas knew it stemmed from an impecunious childhood spent wearing only his worn-out, hand-me-down clothes, crudely patched and permanently dirt stained. But now they looked a bit of an odd pair: Niklas' well-worn leather Mackinaw coat and tweed scally cap lent him the appearance of a down-at-the-heels factory worker while Kessler's silk-lined Chesterfield overcoat and beaver-felt fedora made him look as though he owned the factory.

"Now, just like we discussed: I lead."

Kessler nodded. "And I hang back. Try to look intimidating. Make sure they don't garrote us."

"Exactly. I don't know what to expect with Barbieri. I've only heard rumors about him and most of those aren't flattering. But he's connected with the Genna family in Chicago, and they have deep pockets. Honestly, I'm surprised he was willing to give us an audience at all." It had taken Niklas weeks of chasing leads, persuasion, and bribery to work his way through the convoluted network that ultimately led to the Sicilian gangster. "He may be difficult to deal with. May try to intimidate us or talk down to us. But the word of the day is equanimity. Say it with me."

"Equanimity," they repeated together.

"That means calmness and composure, especially in a difficult situation," Niklas explained. "That's what we're going to have, right? No matter how difficult this situation may turn out to be."

Swallowing hard, Kessler glanced over Niklas' shoulder at the building with thinly veiled dread. "I'm not getting a great feeling about this."

"We make this sale, it will open up the door for more. The rest of the Genna family—hell, all the gangsters in Chicago and New York—will want to buy from us." Niklas patted his brother's shoulder reassuringly. "Once we've cleared everything out, we'll have enough money to buy half a county's worth of land. Tall pines and maple trees, a pasture for horses, and a lake to hunt ducks like when we were kids. We might even convince Dad to leave Denmark and move here to be with us."

His words seemed to galvanize Kessler's resolve, his brother's confidence returning. "That would be nice. Raise a few kids. Enjoy some peace and quiet."

"It *will be* nice. And it starts here." Niklas turned toward the door.

Picking up the leather trombone case at his feet, Kessler followed him inside.

The fetor of pigeon droppings and dried grease met them as they entered the warehouse. They followed a trail of snowy footprints in the dim, dust-diffused light. Hulks of rusty equipment too heavy to steal sat like gravestones in the sepulchral cavern, frozen in dying poses, their exposed blades, belts, and gears bridged by fine strands of dusty cobwebs.

The portly gunman loitered outside the foreman's office but directed them to enter with a wag of his chin.

Inside sat a table and a single chair, occupied by a young man, maybe mid-twenties, wearing a fur-trimmed ulster coat and a bored expression. His thick nest of dark hair had been smothered in an oil slick of pomade and combed with great care. He reclined, legs crossed at the knees. Delicate, feminine lips kissed at a cigarette slid through the loop of an ornate gold ring on his right hand.

"Good afternoon, Signor Barbieri. Thank you for seeing us." Niklas offered a handshake, which was ignored. Instead, Barbieri leaned across the table, like a cat stretching after a nap.

"Let's just keep it brief, all right? As cold as Chicago is right now, St. Paul is unbearable."

"In that case, let's begin. We understand you're in the market for—"

"You know,"—Barbieri's eyes narrowed and he wagged his cigarette holder at them—"you sound just like the fucking Huns I killed at the Marne."

Kessler, ignoring Niklas' original directive to remain silent, spoke up, his voice bitter. "We're Danes. We weren't with the Boche. Fritz felt the sharp end of our bayonets, too."

"Ooh, a feisty one, him. Your brother?" Barbieri stood slowly and leisurely approached Kessler, evaluating him like livestock at auction.

Nodding, Niklas kept his eyes forward, jaw set.

"You make quite the spiffy pair, don't you?" Barbieri reached a hand to Kessler's face and gave him a gentle slap. "Don't look much like brothers, though. This one tall and dark, and you—Niklas, was it?—you look like you coulda stepped off the bow of a Viking longship or somethin'. That jawline, though." He whistled through his teeth and shook his head. "Two of you look like you were carved out of marble. That's some noble breeding."

"Flattered," Niklas muttered.

Scoffing, Barbieri returned to the desk and wiped away the dust where he intended to lean. "Don't be. I don't do business with aristocratic types. Too soft. Weak. Probably inbred. I need hard, practical men. Men who aren't afraid of getting their hands dirty. Good Sicilian men like Vicenzo, there." He nodded toward the gunman in the hallway, who had taken to scraping dirt from beneath his fingernails with the blade of his pocketknife.

"We've had our share of hardships. We can handle anything," Kessler said quietly.

"Is that so? Good. You'll need to prove it to me before we can do business together." He sucked at his cigarette as he stared intently at Kessler. "But first, show me what you brought."

Niklas nodded to his brother, who hefted the trombone case atop the desk and clicked open the clasps. Inside, atop a velvet liner, rested a field-stripped light machine gun. The coal-black finish glistened like oil in the low light, whispering of unrealized violence and indisputable lethality.

"What the fuck is this?" Barbieri asked, palms held upright. "*Gesù Cristo.* I thought you were bringing me guns I can use. Not field artillery. A man would need a fucking team of horses to deploy this."

"Vicenzo looks like he might take to a bridle," Niklas deadpanned. "This is a Madsen light machine gun. You may have faced one down when you went up against the Krauts."

"What would I want with it, then? Maybe you don't remember, but they lost the war. You're trying to sell me guns from the losing side?"

"If you faced the Boche, you know that they didn't lose because of inferior weapons," Kessler said. "Besides, this is a Danish design. Even better than the Germans came up with."

"Fine, fine. But how is this better than a Tommy Gun? We can just buy those outright. No need for any of this sneaking around, meeting in abandoned warehouses in the fuckin' Arctic."

"This is more powerful." Niklas slipped his gloves into his coat pockets and began unpacking the case, reassembling the light machine gun on the desk with such certainty and precision of movement one might believe he had done it thousands of times. "Don't get me wrong: The Thompson is a fine piece of equipment. In close quarters, it's tough to beat. But if you want something that will send a message to your enemies that they can't ignore, something that will chew right through a car's engine block and obliterate whoever's hiding on the other side, this is the better choice. These will cost you a hundred fifty each. An out-of-the-box Thompson runs two hundred." Finishing the assembly, he jammed a magazine in place atop the ungainly rifle and tugged the charging handle rearward, the mechanism emitting a loud, mechanical *ka-chunk*. "We suggested meeting here because you can try it out. Test fire it. Experience what you're getting for your money. On this side of town, the few people who will hear the shots won't pay them any mind."

Barbieri flicked the cigarette from his ring and approached the rifle. "How did you get it and how many do you have?"

"A strong entrepreneurial spirit, and plenty," Niklas said vaguely, blowing warm air atop his palms after touching the icy steel.

Barbieri hefted the rifle in his hands as if to weigh it. "Test fire it inside, hmm?"

"There's a long hallway we can use."

"And you say no one will hear the gunshots?"

"Certain of it."

Examining the rifle for a moment, Barbieri swiveled the muzzle toward the door. Through the begrimed glass, Vicenzo noticed the gun aimed at him and froze. Terror seized his features.

A cruel grin blossomed on Barbieri's face as he pinned back the trigger.

Deafening reports and chest-punching concussions filled the confined space. Flame belched from the muzzle. Glass shattered. The brothers covered their ears and retreated to a corner.

After what felt like an eternity, the last round cycled, the brass casings tinkling onto the floor and disappearing into the room's dusty recesses. The thunderous roar faded to a shrill ring.

Dropping the rifle atop the desk, Barbieri let out a satisfied sigh. Slipping an abalone pearl cigarette case from his breast pocket, he fished out a fresh smoke. "I think you're right about this machine gun. Powerful. Very powerful. Eight millimeter, right?"

Vicenzo had disappeared, but a viscous pool of crimson flooded beneath the door like a spilled bottle of wine. His body rustled and tapped against the wall, twitching and spasming as his dying neurons fired hopelessly into the abyss.

"Why did you do that?" Kessler sputtered.

Barbieri lit his cigarette and leisurely took the first few draws. "Two reasons," he said. "One, my dear Vicenzo made the inexcusable decision to sell information about our organization to the Irish. The fucking micks! That's a betrayal of his family and his entire race. And two,"—he pointed a finger at Kessler—"you said you can handle anything. Your exact words. And I told you I would need you to prove that to me before we could do business together. Well, here's just the opportunity."

"What are you suggesting?" Niklas asked cautiously.

"I'm not suggesting anything. You *will* clean this up. You *will* see to it that I'm in no way inconvenienced by this. And when the deed is done, we will be much closer to each other. You will have something on me, and I will have something on you. That is the only way to properly do business, wouldn't you agree?" He pulled hard on his cigarette, closed his eyes as though in post-coital rapture, and exhaled a cloud of smoke and vapor toward the ceiling. "Forestalls any thoughts of blackmail by either party." He stood, suppressed a shiver, and walked toward the door. "Meet me at the Hotel St. Paul when you're finished. We can discuss the sale of your guns. Have a drink. Celebrate our partnership."

The brothers shrugged deeper into their coats as they watched Barbieri toe open the office door, smearing blood below it. He stepped gingerly over the puddle to avoid soiling his shoes.

"Equanimity," Kessler mumbled, eyes pinched shut.

One man's trash

When they were young—too young for Kessler to remember—one of their horses died in the night. It was January. The snow crunched crisply underfoot like broken glass as Niklas and his father, Milas, approached the stable carrying a stout rope and a block and tackle.

They paused outside the barn door. "This is going to be grisly work, Niklas," Milas warned him with a resigned sigh. "But it needs to be done."

Niklas cried at first. He fought it, wanting to impress upon his father that he was tough enough to be useful in this solemn task, but this horse had been his companion all his life. He spooled through memories of feeding him handfuls of grass while teetering on fence rails, the creature's broad lips nuzzling his palm, and of the gentle giant placing his head lovingly against Niklas' chest. Even in death he looked so familiar, as though Niklas had simply caught him sleeping in his stall. In his day he had been an admirable specimen. Built like a medieval knight's stallion, broad chested and powerful.

Hide as black as ink. He had been no less regal before a plow than under saddle. But the years had grayed his muzzle and swayed his back, and finally, the end had arrived.

At first Niklas handled him tenderly, reverently touching the body, gently wrapping the rope around the rigid legs.

Within an hour his tears had frozen upon his cheeks. The tenderness of his touch vanished. He stopped seeing the body as that of his dear friend and reduced it in his mind to little more than a heavy stone, uncooperative and resistant to movement. He and his father strained and struggled, hands chafed raw upon the abrasive fibers of the rope, slowly negotiating the body out of the stable and onto the icy dirt of the pasture.

The ground was too hard to penetrate with a spade, so they covered the corpse in snow, knowing in the spring they would have to deal with it again. Only, by then, the smell and the decay would make the job much, much worse. Assuming the weasels and foxes didn't get to it first. An ignoble end to a majestic creature that deserved better.

The lessons Niklas had learned then revisited him now. First: It was remarkable how quickly the human mind could go from seeing a corpse as an extension of the living to nothing more than an obstacle to move or burden to carry.

Second: A dead body is hell to deal with in the winter.

Vicenzo was a large man to begin with. The concrete block tethered to his legs with a coil of rusty wire and the dusty canvas tarpaulin—peeled up from the factory floor and wrapped around his body—made it a struggle to move him more than a few yards at a time. Sweat beaded on their foreheads and lower backs despite the cold. A sheen of ice lay treacherously upon the brick alleyways, causing them to stumble and slip, dropping the ungainly package to the ground with a dull thud, time and again.

After a particularly heavy drop, Kessler looked down at the body and winced as he rubbed his palms. "Well, if he wasn't dead before, he surely will be after we're done moving him."

After Barbieri departed for his hotel, the brothers had evaluated their situation. The body needed to be hidden in case someone had heard the reports of the rifle and came to investigate. Although unlikely on the city's south side, amongst the derelict warehouses, clamorous rail lines, and bustling freight depots, there was always a chance. They found an empty paint closet and dragged Vicenzo's riddled corpse into it. Then, the machine gun needed to be disassembled and returned to their apartment, concealed once again under the floorboards beneath Niklas' bed. Finally, they would wait for nightfall before returning to the scene, retrieving the body, and discreetly dumping it into the Mississippi. Thankfully the swift-moving river resisted freezing even in the most severe winters.

"We should have asked Oscar to help us," Kessler groaned, struggling with Vicenzo's legs. "He would have had a better way to handle this. Knows all the little nooks and crannies in this city where a body could disappear."

Shifting the weight to his opposite side as he steered around an overturned garbage can teeming with rats, Niklas grunted, "We are not involving Oscar in this. He's moved enough dead bodies for one lifetime."

Oscar Hole-in-the-Day was an Ojibwe. As such, he wasn't considered an American citizen. He couldn't vote. No one would hire him for anything but day labor. Still, when the United States entered the war, he promptly enlisted in the U.S. Army, eager to serve his country despite it having never served him. But even repeated acts of gallantry on the battlefields in France did little to garner him respect or acceptance among his countrymen. His superior officer frequently assigned him to burying bodies, cleaning latrines, repairing duckboards, and exterminating rats. These days, Oscar stumbled through a penurious and mostly sleepless existence, haunted by memories he endeavored to erase with gallons of whiskey and gin he made himself, bottled in old glass milk bottles and sold to anyone looking to pay bottom dollar for a drink.

"Why couldn't we just leave this guy in the paint closet?"

Niklas grunted, "Wondering that myself. Just trying to be thorough, I guess. If you leave him to be found there's always a chance it could be traced back to us."

Kessler eased his end of the body to the ground and panted, hands on his knees, bent at the waist. "Call me overcautious, but I'm beginning to think we shouldn't go through with this deal with Barbieri. If this is a normal introduction to him, we're in way over our heads."

"It's already more than we bargained for, I know." Adjusting his hold on the body by wrapping his hands tightly in the canvas, Niklas nodded toward Vicenzo's feet, signaling for Kessler to pick up his end and rest later. "Still, in for an inch, in for a mile. And we don't have any other leads."

The riverfront appeared ahead, illuminated by orbs of amber light cast by rows of electric streetlamps. Broad flakes of snow drifted like ash to the ground, obscuring the winding footpaths carved by pedestrians earlier that day. The serpentine oil slick of the Mississippi glistened below, sloshing rhythmically as it coursed its way through the city. Its offensive effluvia of decay and rancid offal reached them before it even came into view.

The brothers paused at the edge of the alleyway. They listened for footsteps but couldn't hear much over the sound of their winded breaths. Kessler stepped out and searched for passersby or police. "Looks clear," he panted, wiping his brow with his coat sleeve. "Let's pitch him in and go home. First round is on me."

They shuffled across the street to the water's edge, as quickly as their load would allow, weaving between shadows as they moved. With a grunt, they hefted their burden onto the brick bulkhead.

"You know, at one time, you could drink straight from this river," came a distant voice. It was high-pitched for a man, almost a whine. Adenoidal, too, as though congested. "I actually swam in the Mississippi as a kid. Would never dream of it now. The amount of trash and raw sewage in this water is egregious. Like ice floes of garbage and refuse." A thin man, so slight of frame he looked as though a strong wind might upend him, materialized from the shadows. He wore a fur-lined, double-breasted overcoat and fedora that cast a deep shadow across his face. Stooped a bit at the shoulders, he shambled toward them at an unhurried pace. He barely lifted the toes of his shoes as he walked, pushing aside little drifts of snow. Even from a distance, one could plainly see the heavy bags under his eyes and the prominent, craggy nose jutting from his face.

"Most of the meatpacking and chemical plants down here still pump their waste right into the river," Niklas shouted back, eyes wide as he looked at Kessler with alarm. He leaned against the bulkhead as though casually resting, but his hand still firmly gripped the canvas covering Vicenzo's body. "What's one more bundle of garbage, anyway?"

The man continued his approach, looking over the edge at the river without apparent regard for the brothers or their alleged garbage. As he neared, Niklas noticed a Smith & Wesson revolver held limply at his side. Standard police-issue Model 10 in .38 Special.

"Well, as they say, one man's trash. You mind if I take a look? Maybe there's a treasure or two hidden inside."

Suddenly finding it hard to breathe, Niklas said, "That's an unorthodox request, mister—"

"Eugene Stauss." The man said pleasantly, flipping open the lapel of his coat to reveal a timeworn, nickel-colored police badge. "Detective, St. Paul Police."

Niklas felt a tug as Kessler began pushing Vicenzo's legs over the edge.

"Please don't." The detective's revolver rose slowly. "Or I'll have to send you in to get it."

A sad clown

The row of detectives' offices at the precinct looked as though they had been designed by someone with a long career spent constructing military barracks while equipped with only a right-angle ruler and an apparent disdain for comfort. Detective Stauss found that distracting. Hard to focus on locking up criminals when he felt like a prisoner himself.

So he swapped the pitifully dim banker's lamp on his desk for one with a floral-pattern stained-glass shade that bathed the entire room in vibrant hues. He unrolled a thick rug on the concrete floor alongside a pair of cozy slippers, then scattered half a dozen throws over every horizontal surface in the room for when he got cold—which happened frequently thanks to the skinflint managing the thermostat on the building's boiler. On the open wall beside the door, he had even hung a painting one of his artist friends had made for him as a Christmas gift years before. Done with acrylics in long, playful strokes, it illustrated a sad clown in a policeman's uniform, shoulders slumped, a golden-yellow badge wilting on his chest like a dying flower. The few subordinate officers who had dared to enter Stauss' office gave it questioning looks. One of his fellow detectives had even been so bold as to say it was a disrespectful affront to the law. A comical assertion considering that same detective—and most of the others in the precinct—had been boldly padding his retirement with bribes and blackmail, a fact of which Stauss considerately reminded him.

Stauss thought the painting was ingenious. A subtle and well-deserved jeer at the integrity of the entire St. Paul Police Department. His silent protest to an organization that had gleefully abandoned any pretense of integrity, now rotten to the core with corruption, misconduct, and barefaced fraud, overseeing an ungovernable city that hadn't just accepted vice, but had doubled down on it, callously monetized it, and become a national refuge for criminals.

And him, still trying to salvage it.

Like bailing water from a sinking ship. With a shot glass.

Gently closing the office door, he eased into his chair, draping a throw around his shoulders like an elderly hospice patient. He lifted the conical earpiece from his phone. "Operator, put me through to Detective Bradford, Chicago Police Department." It rang for some time before someone answered.

"Bradford speaking," came a husky voice, one laced with exhaustion and a probable chest cold. Detective Walter Bradford was one of the few officers in the Chicago Police Department who could be counted on to dependably uphold the law. A black man who had grown up on the city's south side, raised in a dilapidated house on State Street, he had fought his way through the ranks of the CPD, battling racism from within and organized crime from without. Ragen's Colts, an Irish street gang with a reputation for violent raids on black communities in the city, had nearly ended him, leaving him with a patchwork of knife and bullet wounds. But they had failed, and Bradford received a promotion to detective once the flames of the Chicago race riot had died down.

"Stauss here. I've got some bad news on the Barbieri case."

"Well, no need to build the tension for a big reveal. It's late and my kids haven't seen me in three days. Let's have it."

"Your informant, Vicenzo Rossi? The one you wanted me to connect with? His corpse is lying on a cooling board in my coroner's office. Had more holes in him than a drunk's alibi."

Bradford let out a long sigh on the other end of the line. Stauss could hear the rasp of his thumb and forefinger vigorously rubbing his eyes.

"Do you know how long it took me to get an inside man in Barbieri's outfit?"

A dainty-legged spider, body as small as a broken-off piece of pencil lead, scampered across his desktop from some secluded nook. Using the end cap of his pen, Stauss herded his little friend toward the table lamp where a gauzy web draped across the inside of the shade like a delicate suspension bridge. "You make it sound like I'm personally responsible for this."

"Well everything was going pretty well until the first day he arrived in *your* city. Then this."

"All signs point to Barbieri getting wise to Vicenzo's communications with you. Is it possible he slipped up?"

The Chicago detective's voice took on a sharper edge. "Don't talk to me like I'm a fool, Stauss. Of course it's possible he slipped up. One overheard phone call and it would be curtains. Where did you find him?"

"Between a pair of Scandinavians about half a second from sending him back to Illinois by way of a free Mississippi River cruise."

That puzzled Bradford. "That doesn't make any sense. Barbieri's a racist to the core. He wouldn't have anyone in his outfit who wasn't Sicilian. Or at least Italian. Maybe Barbieri didn't whack him after all." Stauss detected a glimmer of hope in his voice.

"I doubt those two committed the murder," Stauss said. "Both are locals and military veterans without a criminal record. And we got an anonymous tip they would be there with the body, which is how I nabbed them. Seems to me they've been set up as patsies." He watched with satisfaction as the spider ascended the lamp base and settled into its web. It comforted him somehow, the simplicity of it, the sense that at least one small piece of the universe was where it was supposed to be in that moment.

"They sing when you brought them in?" Bradford asked.

"Not a note. They claimed they didn't know your man and just came across his body by coincidence."

"And just decided to toss him in the river instead of notifying the authorities, eh? Sure. Coincidence my ass. They know more than they're letting on."

"Agreed." Drawing his notepad toward him, Stauss began doodling around the periphery of his notes. "Strange thing about the body: It's no exaggeration to say he was filled with more daylight than a Summit Avenue sunroom."

"Someone probably wrote him a love letter with a Chicago Typewriter. Happens a few times a week down here."

"The wound channels were too big to have been made with a pistol caliber. These were caused by a rifle."

"That is unusual," Bradford admitted. "How many rounds are we talking?"

"Almost thirty."

"Christ. Either he got a firing-squad treatment from half a dozen men armed with hunting rifles, or someone got their hands on something that should have stayed in France."

Stauss jotted a line at the bottom of his notepad to look into that angle further.

Coughing away from the mouthpiece, Bradford spat audibly. "Look, Stauss, with Vicenzo gone I've lost my eyes on Barbieri. That's worrisome. You've gotta understand: This kid is demented. He doesn't have a mind for business or diplomacy. Not like the Genna brothers, with their bribes and their hooks in the police and the district attorney's office. Barbieri is just plain merciless. Earned himself a reputation as the attack dog of Little Italy. The kind the Gennas turn loose when they want things to get messy enough to make the newspapers and send a message. He's a blunt object. But he's clearly got aspirations to become something more, and whatever he's up to in Minnesota is gonna be a part of that. We don't need another player in this fucked-up game. Especially some wild card who doesn't abide by any conventions."

Conventions. That was Bradford's subtle way of referencing the tenuous agreements—spoken and unspoken—in place between the authorities and the various mobsters throughout Chicago. The Unione Siciliana, the North Side Gang, the Chicago Outfit, they were ruthless, sure, but they all tended to favor commerce over wholesale violence. Prohibition had unwittingly delivered them vast wealth. They didn't want to jeopardize that by carelessly terrorizing the locals or inviting the feds with gratuitous slaughter. But someone like Barbieri, whose only motivation was power and whose only tool was bloodshed, might upset the balance.

"I'll head down to the prison first thing in the morning to interrogate the two men from the riverfront," Stauss said. "And I'll see what I can do to get more intelligence on Barbieri while he's in St. Paul. I have some resources."

He could hear Bradford smile. "Looks like Barbieri has become both our problem. Thank God."

"Cheers." Stauss hung up the phone and stared at the sad clown on the wall.

His badge appeared droopier than usual.

Toe in the water

Anauseating earthiness, like moldy potatoes mixed with the acridity of stale piss, hung thick on the air. The chill of the prison cell's concrete floor leached into their bones like icy dew seeping up a dry pant leg, growing steadily more uncomfortable as the minutes plodded by. The brothers, now clothed in threadbare, loose-fitting black-and-white-striped prison uniforms, huddled shoulder to shoulder in a corner. The cramped cell had only two sets of bunk cots stacked against a wall, already occupied. They thought better of trying to flag down a guard to request a blanket and risk waking the inhabitants.

A few cells down, a drunk man maundered a feeble melody, of which he could only seem to remember a few lyrics. And so he repeated them over and over, his voice rising and falling, from flat to sharp, echoing lazily down the hallway as though spoken in a cave. *The whole world is a bottle and life but a dram. When the bottle gets empty, it ain't worth a damn.*

Finally, after what seemed an interminable length of time, the sun began to rise and dim light filled the cell.

"You get any sleep?" Niklas mumbled over crossed arms resting upon his knees.

"Not enough to brag about," Kessler replied, head against the wall, eyes closed as he suppressed a shiver.

Transitioning to Danish, Niklas said in a hushed voice, "I've been thinking about last night. It couldn't have been a coincidence that the detective arrived right when we reached the riverfront. He was waiting for us. Knew we would be there. We were set up."

"By Barbieri?"

Niklas shot his brother a look that said, "Who else?"

"Why would he do that, though? I thought he wanted to buy from us."

"The way I see it, there could only be two reasons to set us up to take the fall. The first: He's testing the St. Paul police to see if they're as corrupt as their reputation suggests. If he plans to do business in St. Paul—whether it's with us or someone else—he'll need to know just how much he can get away with. Checking the temperature of the water before he dives in." He shifted uncomfortably on the concrete and winced at the throbbing pain mounting in his lower back. "The second possibility is even simpler: He was testing us to see if we were as dumb as he thought."

"And we were," Kessler said resignedly.

"Seems so."

"Listen to those filthy Huns jabbering." A gaunt man, heavily tattooed and missing several teeth, slid from his bunk and approached them. He had small, cruel eyes and a liverish complexion—skin sallow, a braille of acne scars spanning his cheeks. "You know, my cousin went blind from German gas. My woman's brother lost half his face to a Boche artillery shell."

"And your childhood dog choked to death on a Vienna sausage, too, I suppose," Niklas muttered.

"You mocking me?" The man growled, puffing up his chest like a sage grouse.

Exchanging a knowing look with Kessler, Niklas rose to his feet slowly, his muscles tight from the cold. "Hardly seems worth the effort."

As he stood, the other prisoners hopped from their bunks, falling in behind their cellmate.

"You think you're clever, eh?" The tattooed man fished a crude knife from his pocket. "We'll see how clever you talk when I cut your tongue outta your mouth." Stepping forward, he tossed the blade from hand to hand.

"Made that out of a piece of, what, bed frame?" Niklas pointed to the knife. "You know, during the war, we got pretty creative with our hand-to-hand weapons, too. Needed them for night raids or when Fritz came over the top. My personal favorite was the trench mace. Everyone made theirs a little differently. Some added lead weights and nails to the end. Looked menacing. But I like the simplicity of a tractor spur gear mounted on the helve of an entrenching tool. Could crush right through a man's skull with a good swing."

Suddenly a bit uncertain, the man with the knife glanced away for just a second, ensuring his cell mates were still behind him. Niklas took the opportunity to drive his heel into the man's knee. Ligaments tore and the prisoner's leg bent backward at an unnatural angle. He cried out and stumbled. Closing quickly with the knife-wielder, Niklas planted one hand on his wrist and the other on his neck. His fingers closed tightly around the man's throat, the soft tissue yielding under his grip.

The smaller man wheezed, a rush of scarlet flooding his face and neck as he struggled for breath. His body writhed. Unable to break free of Niklas' hold, his hand continued its feeble effort to stab, the blade waggling harmlessly in the air.

Niklas leaned in and whispered sharply, "We're Danes, not Germans, you ignorant pig." He slammed the blade home against the man's leg, the blade plunging deep into his thigh. Eyes wide, the tattooed man's lips moved as though to shriek, but only a feeble rasp emerged.

Niklas let him slump to the floor. Turning, he stared at the other prisoners. "Well? What's it going to be?"

All at once, a frenzied skirmish commenced. Kessler knocked out a prisoner's front tooth with a right hook only to take a glancing strike off the top of his head that sent him reeling. Niklas drove the wind out of another prisoner with an uppercut but was taken to the ground by his bunkmate. Curses were exchanged in multiple languages. A mist of blood and saliva covered the walls as the dull *thud* of landed punches and the skittering of feet atop the concrete floor echoed inside the cell.

Regaining their feet, Kessler and Niklas backed into a corner, fists up. They panted heavily, faces red, snorting out blood and blinking away dizziness. The other prisoners hadn't fared much better, limping back in retreat, hands on bruised ribs, sucking air through clenched teeth.

A whistle sounded, booted footfalls echoing in the hallway. The combatants reluctantly stood down as half a dozen guards approached the cell.

"You two!" One of the guards hefted open the cell door and stepped inside, baton cocked back, ready to strike.

The brothers held their arms up defensively, anticipating an additional beating.

The baton lowered. The guard, nonplussed, surveyed the bloody scene. "You're free to go."

The other shoe

midst a chorus of jeers and whistles from the prisoners in the adjacent cells, the guards escorted Niklas and Kessler down the long, dimly lit hallway between the rows of cells, into a confined locker room. Two neat stacks of their clothing and personal effects had been left atop a low bench. Shivering from the cold and the adrenaline, Niklas slipped into his trousers. "You get the sense that was a little too easy? Just letting us go with no explanation...makes me think the other shoe is about to drop. Like back in the war, the stories about prisoners being told they were free to return to their lines only to get shot in the back, reported as attempting to escape."

Sliding his arm through his shirt sleeve, Kessler suddenly stopped and checked his billfold to see if the police had pilfered any of his money. "Gift horses, brother."

"Are usually lame but still eat the same amount of hay." Slipping his leather holster over his shoulders, Niklas reloaded his Steyr-Hahn pistol—a battlefield trophy he had taken from a German officer—using the loose rounds the police had dumped into a pocket of his trousers.

"You're starting to sound like Dad."

Niklas didn't respond to that. It was intended as a harmless jab, he knew, but the comparison to his father still triggered a flood of melancholy and remorse that hung in the back of his throat like a spoonful of bitter laudanum, with none of the relief. He tried to conceal it by focusing on winding his wristwatch. The timepiece, an Elgin housed in a metal guard that looked like a storm grate and protected the watch crystal from damage, was one of the few relics from his time in the service about which he felt any fondness. In an otherwise bleak and gray landscape where the days ticked by endlessly, the war's conclusion nowhere in sight, that watch gave him a sense of rhythm and normalcy. While they ate and slept whenever they could, often lost in a haze of exhaustion and hunger, boredom and terror, he found it comforting to glance down at his wrist to see when his mother would start buzzing around the house preparing for a church service. When his father would make the rounds to feed the horses or let them into their stalls for the night. It tethered him loosely to the outside world. To normalcy. To home.

Glancing at the clock on the wall, he adjusted the Elgin to match it.

"I still can't believe after all these years, the fistfights, the close calls with trench mortars and artillery, that thing still works," Kessler said, hopping on one foot as he wrestled on a loafer.

Niklas chuckled. "Talking about me or the watch?"

"Both."

"That makes two of us."

A man huffed into the room. He wore a three-piece suit: dark gray and expertly tailored, ornamented with a solid gold tie pin and diamond-studded cufflinks. His leather oxford shoes, somehow unbesmirched by the snow or dirt outside, glistened in the dim lights overhead. Although bald and wearing a pair of black-rimmed glasses, he did not appear bookish nor meek in posture. His height and build did not belong to an imposing man, yet he stood with an intimidating rigidity—chest out, chin up—as if challenging anyone to stand in his way or defy his orders.

The man was Ezra Abecassis.

They knew him as Uncle Ezra, the elder brother of their departed mother.

Uncle Ezra owned an iron ore business that employed a thousand men throughout the state, including Niklas and Kessler.

Uncle Ezra had money.

"Behold: The other shoe," Niklas mumbled under his breath. He briefly wondered how their uncle had even known they had been imprisoned, then surmised that an industrialist of his influence must have connections to authorities throughout the city, if only to make his business dealings more efficient.

Wasting no time on pleasantries or greetings, Ezra instead held up a single finger, gesturing for them to follow him down the hall, toward the exit. Every policeman they encountered on the way appeared far too busy filing paperwork or examining the cleanliness of their desk to look him in the eye or dare a greeting.

"I told them it was clearly a misunderstanding," Ezra said over his shoulder. "A couple of honorable war veterans like yourselves came across this unfortunate victim of a violent crime and sought to bring him some peace with a makeshift burial. Then I donated an obscene sum of money to their department, ostensibly for athletic equipment. Look at these fat fucks. They've never seen the inside of a gymnasium or lifted a barbell in their lives."

"Thank you, Uncle."

Ezra stopped abruptly, turning to face them. His expression was that of a man who had smelled something loathsome but, due to social doctrine, wasn't permitted to acknowledge it. "Don't thank me. This was neither a gesture of goodwill nor done due to familial obligation. You two are now indebted to me. That's where I would like to keep you. When the day comes when I need something—and rest assured, it will come—you will stand at attention and, without asking anything resembling a question, deliver to me what is owed. That said, I'm garnishing your wages to pay for this." He resumed walking down the corridor at a brisk pace. They began following him again, but he held up a hand. "You've embarrassed me enough for one day. I leave first."

The icy air hit their noses with trenchant sterility. Nearby, a young boy in a heavily patched tweed coat alternated between walking his bicycle and unsuccessfully trying to ride it through the drifts of snow the wind had blown onto the sidewalk. He would ramp up a little speed on the bricks not covered in ice, hop onto the seat, and quickly slide back off as the front wheel began to wobble and skid.

Wincing against the blinding sunlight, Niklas shielded his brow with his palm and scanned the surrounding buildings to get his bearings before setting off toward the south. "We need to get home and clean ourselves up, then connect with Barbieri tonight."

"But he's the one who got us locked up," Kessler protested as he followed. He paused to check his reflection in the front window of a barbershop, cringed at the damage, and began wiping at the dried blood on his upper lip with a handkerchief.

"Correct. So he needs to see that it didn't slow us down."

"I would like to slow him down—with a nine-millimeter in each kneecap."

"I would like that, too. But right now he's still our best bet for making our first sale. If we had a better option, I would gladly take it. But we don't." Niklas forced a smile and changed his voice to a more upbeat tone. "Hey, how about we grab a loaf of rye and some roast beef from Kroemer's on the way home? I'll whip up some *smørrebrød* for a quick lunch before we go to see Barbieri."

Clearing his throat uncomfortably, Kessler asked, "Before we do, can we stop by the theater? Kosena must be worried about me. I was supposed to see her last night."

Passing a hand beneath his hat, fingers coursing through his short brown hair before grabbing a palmful of it, Niklas cast a sigh and an entreating glance upward, as if beseeching the heavens for patience. "If we miss this chance with Barbieri, we are going to have an actual boatload of machine guns to hide while I start over tracking down another buyer with deep enough pockets to buy them. This has been months in the making. Kosena can wait."

"Please. Just for a little while. To let her know I'm all right."

Niklas plucked a stick of Clove gum from his breast pocket and unsheathed it. Chewing, he crumpled the wax wrapper and flicked it at his brother. "Do you think she even noticed you were gone?" It was intended as a joke but he immediately regretted saying it, the acerbic tone of it.

Kessler looked as though he had been slapped. Glowering, he turned and marched down the sidewalk, hands plunged into his pockets.

Groaning, Niklas jogged to catch up with him. "Wait. I'm sorry. That was below the belt." He planted a hand on his brother's shoulder. "Slow down."

Kessler stared sullenly at the passing traffic. "I know you don't like her. Not that she's ever done anything to you to deserve it. But would it kill you to just let me be happy?"

"You're right," Niklas said, forcing a contrite smile. "I was out of line. Of course I want you to be happy."

"Just because you got your heart broken—"

Expression instantly darkening, he stopped Kessler with a pointed finger. "Don't. You're about three words past losing the high ground in this conversation." He took a deep breath, forcing himself to soften his expression. "We'll go to the theater to see Kosena first. Barbieri can wait."

Peeping keyholes

I t was a regrettable compulsion he had inherited from his mother, one he strived to conceal whenever possible by wearing gloves or hiding his hands beneath the table. Glancing at his lap, Detective Stauss evaluated his unsightly fingers, chafed and cracked from the dry winter air, and the sorry state of his thumbs in particular—the skin scraped and chewed until it had become a patchwork of rough scarring and raw pink tissue. They were the unfortunate target of his anxiety. Whenever he became preoccupied with a case, sensed political pressure mounting and knew his job was in jeopardy, or noticed a boyfriend becoming emotionally distant in preparation for leaving him, the violence against his thumbs redoubled—like a neglected dog chewing on a table leg. He felt ashamed when he did it, which only exacerbated his anxiety. Heightened anxiety, more self-mutilation. And so the cycle continued anew.

Plunging his hands into his pockets, the fingernails of his pointer fingers fired another salvo against his thumbs. Sitting across from the desk sergeant in the prison, Stauss watched as he riffled listlessly through the blotter like it was an out-of-date magazine in a hospital waiting room. The sergeant had a slumped posture that seemed to fold onto itself like a pile of fresh manure. His mouth was crowded with stumps of amber- and coal-colored teeth, arranged at defiant angles atop necrotic gums. Not that many would see them, though. The sergeant didn't make a habit of smiling—least of all at Stauss— and the only time he parted his lips was to shove another cigarette between them.

"Don't know what to tell you, Stauss," he grumbled. "You know how the game is played. They had connections. So we did what we always do. Works out best for everybody. Pays our salaries and keeps the higher-ups looking the other way."

Uncooperative, as always.

Stauss wouldn't be much of a detective if he didn't find out what his colleagues thought of him and why. The sergeant, he had discovered without much investigation, took particular umbrage not with his rumored sexuality like many of the others, but with his education. Felt that Stauss was just an imperious toff whose high school diploma had wrongly furnished him with special rank and influence in the department. The detective's tendency to use words with more than a single syllable and bathe regularly just seemed to reinforce the sergeant's belief.

"So you're telling me you released two murder suspects, caught actually holding—in their very hands—the dead body of a man who was key to an ongoing investigation into interstate organized crime, and that doesn't strike you as worthy of concern or remorse?"

"There was nothing we could do," the sergeant said indifferently. He used the dog-end of his cigarette to light a new one, then stabbed the butt into a punji pit of others poking forth from an overflowing ashtray at the edge of his desk. "You know how things work in this town. And when someone like Ezra Go-Fuck-Yourself Abecassis strolls in here waving his checkbook around, you do what he says or you end up jobless. May not matter to you, but I'm not about to give up this gig just because a couple of rich kids got a wild hair to whack some bum."

Sighing deeply enough to take in a lungful of the sergeant's cigarette smoke—a noxious whiff that tasted like a mechanic's oil rag—Stauss asked, "Did anyone bother to question them before you released them?"

"Not our job. That's what you're here for, right?" The corner of his lips twitched into something resembling a smirk, threatening to reveal his graveyard of neglected teeth.

The detective felt a flush of anger wash over his face like opening an oven door. "That's true," he growled. "And I would have delighted in doing my job if you hadn't released my prisoners in less than twelve hours from when they first arrived."

"Save your fake outrage, Stauss," the sergeant said, reclining in his chair. "Just go back to ignoring extradition notices like the rest of us. Take a long lunch, then get back to peeping keyholes or whatever it is you flatfoots do to pass the time in this town."

Detective Stauss' thumb stung as he plunged deeply with his fingernail. He felt the stickiness of the blood as it wept from his cratered skin and soaked into the pockets of his slacks. Smearing it in circles with the pad of his finger, he stood to leave.

No lasting damage

An ornate headdress bestudded with fake diamonds glittered in the spotlight as it held Kosena's long, flaxen hair back from her face, her cheeks aflush as she gripped the edge of the grand piano on stage. Carefully rising into a handstand, face inches from the keys, she slowly curled her lissome form—wrapped in skin-tight sequins—into a C-shape. Her toes hovered above the keyboard. She began pecking out a simple song to energetic applause.

"Isn't she something?" Kessler whispered in awe, though mostly to himself.

"You said it," Niklas muttered, looking around for a place to discard his gum. He regretted throwing the wrapper at his brother before. The clove-flavored gum gave a pleasant hit of spice for about five minutes before fading to something that tasted vaguely like candle wax. He rummaged through his pockets for a scrap of paper.

"She plays the piano with her toes better than I do with my hands!" Kessler slapped his brother's chest, beaming.

Kosena Sashova was Kessler's obsession. Flossy in dress and personality, she had an inebriating presence that seemed to drive otherwise sane men to madness. That worked well for her professionally: Her contortionist performances still managed to draw a small crowd despite vaudeville wheezing its dying breaths, now little more than meretricious filler to distract the audience between flickers.

Kessler may have been enraptured by her vivacity, but Niklas saw through it. He recognized her for what she really was: a survivor. One who had figured out exactly what to say and do to bend men to her will with the same dexterity as she bent her own body. Her skills in manipulation had bought her passage from war-ravaged Bulgaria to the U.S.—likely on the arm of some wealthy businessman—then propelled her into show business. But if one caught her when she thought no one was looking, they could spot in the depths of her eyes her true personality flickering through like a distant lantern in a tempest. It was built of calculating guile and predatory avarice. Survival at any cost.

Kessler was little more than a handsome young toy with whom she could while away the hours. A temporary distraction who would gladly spend his last dime to treat her like royalty. Which was how she viewed herself—a princess deserving of a kingdom. The war and her circumstances had deprived her of luxury all her life and now she felt owed. But to Niklas, she was just like a child wearing play jewelry and a paper crown. She sashayed arrogantly through life as though her survival didn't wholly depend on the charity of her boyfriend and a few devoted admirers. Her contortionist act was at best a curiosity suited for a Barnum & Bailey sideshow, her personality like cheap perfume—artificial and noxious to all but the most callow.

She would soon tire of his brother, callously break his heart, and move on to the next opportunity with a fatter pocketbook. Of that Niklas was certain. He just wished she would hurry up and get it over with. The money Kessler continued to squander on gifts and lavish meals for her was more urgently needed elsewhere.

And he was tired of floating him on rent for their apartment.

"The things I would do to that woman," slurred one of the male bystanders nearby. Niklas glanced at him. The man's bullfrog neck met the lower half of his face without the slightest hint of bone structure, his mouth a postage stamp on an otherwise blank letter. He let out a loud whistle, then shouted, "Spread those legs for me, baby!"

Hands forming fists, Kessler wheeled toward the heckler.

Placing a restraining hand on his brother's chest, Niklas pushed him back gently, giving him a reassuring pat. As Kessler's eyes returned to the stage, Niklas leaned toward the heckler and poked his shoulder.

The man looked at him with a glassy-eyed stare, so drunk he could barely stand. His breath smelled as though he had eaten a juniper tree.

"No talking in the theater," Niklas whispered, peeling back the lapel of his coat to reveal his Steyr, hammer back as it rested in his leather shoulder holster. "It's rude."

It took him a few seconds to process, but the man soon understood, nodding timidly. Niklas smiled at him, plucked the spent gum from his mouth, and tucked it under the collar of the heckler's shirt, giving it a firm press before patting his shoulder. The man withdrew to the back of the crowd.

Niklas leaned toward Kessler. "I still can't believe you're sleeping with the enemy. It's bad business, little brother."

"She's no more the enemy than the Russians were allies," he replied, eyes still transfixed upon Kosena's lithe body as she writhed and twisted into a human knot, then raised a wine glass between her toes, pretending to take a regal sip.

"True enough. I didn't even know the Bulgarians were in the war until they surrendered."

"They requested an armistice. That's not surrendering."

"You sound like a Bolshevik sympathizer, tovarisch." He elbowed his brother playfully. "Better be careful. Never know who's listening."

When Kosena had finished her act and The Great Bakari—a kerosene-guzzling firebreather—had taken the stage, the brothers slipped backstage to meet her. They followed narrow, brick-walled corridors lined in curtains and ropes that disappeared into the darkness overhead, negotiating ladders and scaffolding, dodging set builders and seamstresses. Passing through a huddle of half-dressed performers helping one another change costumes, they approached her dressing room at the end of a long line of vibrantly painted doors. Pausing before one painted cardinal red, Kessler took an audible breath, teased his hair along its part, straightened his coat, and knocked.

"Come."

It was little more than a closet. Kosena sat atop a stool before a distorted mirror fringed in lightbulbs, half of them burned out, reapplying her lipstick. In shadowy corners lay vague piles of fabric and props: Japanese hand fans and a silk kimono, plastic fruit glued inside a shedding wicker horn of plenty, and a convincing skull of Yorick.

Kosena turned to face them. She had an objectively pretty face, with high cheekbones and a pair of full, pouty lips in between. But her eyes didn't fit the rest of her visage. They were haunted eyes, alert and distrustful, like those of a wounded animal listening for approaching footsteps. Like a pair of gemstones crudely pried from stolen earrings.

Upon seeing Kessler she stood and began fussing and cooing, kissing his cheeks and neck as though he had just returned from war. Their actual homecoming from the front had been far less theatrical. Or welcoming.

Niklas hung back near the door.

"Oh, look at your face. Did someone hit you?" she crooned. "You look like a piece of overripe fruit."

"Actually, several people hit him," Niklas noted. "But with a head that hard, no lasting damage."

Kessler rolled his eyes and smiled, basking in her attention.

"And brother Niklas, always good to see you." She said it a little stiffly, approaching him and placing her cheek against his, making an exaggerated kissing sound with her lips.

"You look well," he said.

"Oh, I look dreadful. This was the third time I've performed that act today and the second week of our tour. I'm exhausted."

"You've earned some rest and relaxation. Any chance I could take you to dinner tonight?" Kessler asked hopefully.

Setting his jaw and crossing his arms, Niklas stared upwards at the deteriorating plaster ceiling. They had discussed the budget—the need to save money for the various bribes and transportation of their guns—exhaustively. Repeatedly. Recently. Apparently none of that had stuck.

"I'm not available tonight, darling. I have a prior engagement." Seeing his downtrodden expression, she stroked his wrist and added with a wink, "But I'm home for a few days and I'm sure I can swing by your apartment later tonight for a tipple and a cuddle."

The dressing room door swung open. A man in a tuxedo shoved his way inside, shouldering into Niklas. "Oh, damn sorry, pal. Didn't know Kosena had guests." He was a tall man, broad-shouldered and handsome in the manner of someone never exposed to hard work outdoors, the skin of his face and hands unblemished by sunshine or dirt. He had a suave affectation, mustache rigidly waxed, his hair—a fiery red—neatly swept to a side with a pint of pomade. His accent placed his origins somewhere south of Kansas City. The redolence of his cologne placed him somewhere in a higher tax bracket.

Niklas immediately disliked him.

"Oh, Julian, these are dear friends of mine, Kessler and Niklas. Boys, this is Julian, the director of the Palace Theater."

"Damn nice to meet you." He offered them a rapid handshake each before turning back to Kosena. "Are we still on for dinner tonight, darlin'? I got us a table at this little place in Minneapolis—Jax Cafe. *Très exclusive.*" He butchered the French pronunciation with almost willful malice. "Supposed to have the best desserts in the city." He glanced at Kessler. "Our sweet Kosena does love her strawberry cheesecake," he added affectionately, pinching at her arm while she batted his hands away playfully.

Niklas didn't need to look at his brother to sense Julian was about three words away from losing his perfect front teeth.

Straightening the rose boutonnière on the lapel of Julian's tuxedo, Kosena said, "Julian's working on a plan to make our show even more incredible. Imagine: Bigger sets, dozens—no, hundreds—of dancers, acrobats, even indoor fireworks! He's got the attention of producers in New York. He's going to give them a run for their money. Reinvent vaudeville. The Palace Theater will be known worldwide."

"It's good to have big plans," Niklas said blithely, nodding to his brother that it was time to leave. "We'll leave you kids to your schemes. Enjoy dinner."

As he followed Niklas out of the dressing room, Kessler gave Julian's shoulder a vicious squeeze that drew a sound like a dry heave from his gut, his knees buckling.

Sitting in Allah's lap

That evening, sheltering on the leeward side of the Hotel St. Paul to avoid the gusting snow, the Kristofferson brothers discreetly checked the chambers of their pistols by the dim glow of the illuminated scaffold sign perched on the rooftop. It beamed *Hotel St. Paul, Light - Heat - Power by Consumers Power Co.* in golden yellow, barely visible through the snowfall. Flakes fell heavy and thick—all business, with none of the delicate tranquility one might see on a holiday postcard. The narrow tires of passing vehicles forged ruts of slush and slurry, cascading the mire onto the sidewalks of St. Peter Street.

"He tries anything funny this time, I say we shoot him straightaway," Kessler grumbled. "No more games." He had been in a foul temper since meeting Julian at the theater.

"Maybe we keep that in reserve as a last resort. I doubt Uncle Ezra will be in a hurry to bail us out again if we're caught with another corpse so soon after the first. Besides, if Barbieri is dead, he can't buy our guns."

Ramming his pistol into its holster and adjusting his coat to minimize the outline, Kessler gave a disapproving grunt. His younger brother was affable toward everyone at first, always seeing the good in people, slow to anger. But once someone had betrayed him—or if he felt he had been betrayed—there could be no reconciling afterward. He took it as an unpardonable personal attack. And so a lifelong grudge was born. That was where he would fail in business, Niklas knew. Business transactions—especially illegitimate ones like theirs—needed to be void of emotion. They were strategic. Tactical. Mercenary in their pragmatism. The goal was to win. It wasn't a matter of mutual benefit so much as it was total war. Leveraging every advantage to gain the upper hand and walk away the victor. Barbieri knew this better than most. Certainly better than they did. But in a way, it made him easier to understand. He was manipulative, sure. Creatively so, even. But his objective was unchanging and obvious. To win. To get more from them than they could possibly get from him. As long as they kept that in mind and maneuvered accordingly—letting Barbeiri think he had gotten the better of them to satisfy his ego—they could succeed. Niklas just needed to make sure Kessler kept his resentment buried deep and didn't let it affect his judgment.

The two men pushed through the hotel's revolving doors and stomped the snow from their feet atop the entryway carpet. A welcome warmth enveloped them. They paused in awe: The lobby was a thing of such grandeur and eloquence as they had never seen. Parallel rows of gold-gilt pillars, thirty feet tall, summoned them toward a distant staircase that looked as though it had been purloined from a European castle. Chesterfield couches of fine, pillowy leather reposed atop marble tile, illuminated in aureate tones by stained-glass lamps and grandiose chandeliers. Garnet-colored taffeta curtains draped from ceiling to floor, flowing and shimmering like the sweep of a luxurious evening gown. Filling the air like a subtle perfume arrived a gentle, sweeping melody played by a tuxedoed man at a gloss-black Steinway in an adjacent lounge.

The socialists and the anarchists and the labor unions all gnashed their teeth and cursed the wealthy sort who would stay in a place like this, regarding their opulent lifestyles with resentment and hostility. But Niklas viewed them with undisguised envy. How wonderful to be nestled comfortably away from hardship and privation, secure amidst one's riches, the entirety of the world eager to accommodate your every whim in exchange for a few paltry coins.

He didn't hate them. He wanted to be among them.

And if they played this correctly, he would be.

A bellhop spotted them from across the lobby. Hopping to his feet, he advanced in a flurry of heel-toe clicks from his polished black leather oxfords, his white-gloved hands eager to grab their bags and solicit a tip. Finding them empty-handed as he neared, he abruptly detoured toward a distant vestibule, as though suddenly recalling some other more urgent task.

They approached the receptionist, a young man with a smooth, practiced smile and a hat that looked like he had stolen it from an organ grinder's monkey. The smile vanished the instant they asked for Nunzio Barbieri's room number. In its place emerged a distressed expression—a startled cocktail of dismay and anguish, as though his finger had been caught in a drawer and he was too embarrassed to cry out. "Is he expecting you?" His voice quavered.

Kessler looked at Niklas with humor in his eyes. "No, he most certainly is not."

The receptionist nodded slowly as if to buy himself time, no doubt praying for the roof to collapse so he wouldn't have to answer. After a sustained silence, he mumbled, "I'm afraid we cannot share our patrons' information without their consent. Hotel policy."

"Our request trumps hotel policy." Discreetly drawing his Bergmann as he leaned across the desk, using his coat to shield his hand, Kessler placed the pistol atop the varnished walnut. He swiveled the barrel back and forth, sweeping the man's waist.

Gesturing for the receptionist to slide over his reservation log, Niklas said, "Maybe you didn't tell us. Maybe you stepped away from the desk for a moment to help another guest and we happened to see the room number in your book." Eager to accept a way out of this sudden life-threatening dilemma, the man nodded and spun the leather-bound ledger around so they could see it. He tapped his finger on a line before withdrawing into a back room.

Leisurely making their way to the elevator, still awestruck by their surroundings, they nodded to the elevator liftman and boarded. The elderly Arab man's uniform draped off him as though he had withered and shrunk inside it, the exposed skin on his face covered in dark sunspots like a speckled egg. Pulling the gold-gilt cage closed behind them, he sat down heavily upon his stool as though that simple movement had been the limit of what he could endure.

"Eleventh floor, please," Kessler said.

"You'll like the view from up there," the liftman said sincerely as he eased the lever upward. The elevator lurched, rocking and creaking as the floors spooled by. "Can see the entire city on a clear night. Like sitting in Allah's own lap."

"Something tells me no god is anywhere near this hotel," Niklas muttered.

They tipped the liftman and disembarked the elevator before starting down the hallway. They were met by the rasping hiss of a record player—entangled with the honking of trumpets and a woman's sustained, tremulous vibrato, belting out a song in Italian. It grew louder as they approached Barbieri's room.

"Would you listen to that obnoxious squawking," Kessler muttered, poking a finger in each ear. "How can he stand it?"

"He's doing it to keep anyone from listening in on his phone calls and conversations. Mobsters rent out suites in this hotel all the time. Stands to reason the authorities do, too."

They knocked. The door opened a few inches. A young Asian woman, black hair pinned up neatly atop her head, peeked out. She had kind eyes, innocent eyes. The sort that belied the environment she found herself in and the company she now kept. "Yes?" she asked suspiciously.

"Signor Barbieri in?"

"I'm afraid you've got the wrong room." Her eyes darted about the hallway nervously. "There's no one by that name here." She nibbled at her thumbnail and began closing the door.

"It's fine. Let 'em in," Barbieri called out over the music.

She complied without protest, opening the door and standing aside. Her short, red sequin dress glittered playfully in the lamplight. She met Kessler's eyes and gave a meek smile. Clearing his throat, he evaluated the tops of his shoes.

Lounging on a sofa before a tall row of windows, Barbieri puffed contentedly at the cigarette on his ring. Behind him lay a sweeping canvas of city skyline, veiled in white as the snow continued falling with unrelenting ferocity. Barbieri had unbuttoned his shirt to his navel, sleeves rolled carelessly to his elbows. A tall crystal champagne flute sat empty beside him, one of a dozen glasses that had been filled, half-consumed, and forgotten on various surfaces throughout the room. "Gentlemen! Welcome. Come inside and warm yourselves up. Care to dip the bill?"

"No thanks."

He ignored them and waved a couple of fingers at the young woman. "Drinks. Sorry kid, what's your name again?"

"Maya," she said sadly, eyes downcast.

"That's right," he drawled. "Maya, fix us a few Manhattans."

"I'm a pro skirt, not a bartender. I don't know how."

"Fine. Gin and tonics, then. You can add two ingredients together, can't you?"

Resignedly, she turned toward a spread of bottles and glittering decanters on an ornate credenza.

"And turn the music down a bit, will you? Can't hear myself fuckin' think." He kicked his feet up on the coffee table and crossed them at the ankles, his toes wriggling playfully inside his socks. "So! I hear you ran into a little trouble disposing of my dear Vicenzo. Yet here you are. Must have some impressive connections. I find that intriguing."

"We have friends in this town," Kessler said indignantly.

"Maybe it's time you make friends in another town, too. A friend like me could be a powerful asset."

"I think we are quite some distance from becoming friends, Signor Barbieri," Niklas replied placidly.

Contriving an injured expression, Barbieri asked, "What have I done to make you say this?"

Niklas accepted a glass from Maya and eased into a nearby chair, back arrow straight, as if he had taken a seat before a board of directors. "I would say tipping off the police that we were disposing of a body—the body of a man you killed—qualifies as an adequate reason for our distrust."

A mischievous grin crept across Barbieri's features. He had been caught. "So it is. But cheer up, boys. You really can't take it personally. Consider it a professional appraisal. Proof of competence." Maya held a glass toward him and he grabbed it from her carelessly, gin spilling over his fingers. He took a long drink and flicked his hand, scattering droplets across the ornate floor rug underfoot. "I really can't say for certain if I've acquired that proof, though. After all, you did get caught."

"We're here now, aren't we?" Kessler asked. "I'd say that's proof enough."

Wiping his hand on his trousers, Barbieri smirked and made an impressed chuckle in his throat. "I like you fellas. Maya, you can't help but like these guys, can you? I mean, they seem all polite and easygoing, but they're tougher than a boiled steak. You can practically smell it on 'em. Couple of real hard numbers. I bet they got that way battling it out in the big one like me. Hell, we probably even passed each other in the trenches without knowing it." He sighed thoughtfully as though recalling a pleasant family vacation. "I've got a dozen notches in my buttstock, if you know what I mean.

How about you gents? Any Huns sent to hell with your pretty maps being the last thing they saw?"

"We mostly just fixed guns," Niklas said. Kessler stared vacantly ahead, jaw set.

"Eh. Well, we can't all be killers."

Niklas noticed Maya discreetly slip a hand into Barbieri's coat, draped over a chair near the credenza. He caught a flash of banknotes as she drew them to her chest and tucked them into her brassiere. He sipped his drink indifferently. Whatever Barbieri had agreed to pay for her company that evening could never be enough to make it an even exchange, not that it was any of his business either way. Pouring a drink for Kessler, she glided across the room and handed it to him gently. They smiled at one another. Taking a seat beside Barbieri, she crossed a leg delicately over her knee and swiveled a foot in time with the music.

Kessler's eyes followed the movement as though they were attached to the pendulum of a metronome.

Placing a hand on her bare thigh, Barbieri squeezed so hard she flinched. "I hear all these soft-ass men complaining about how hard it was to go to war,"—his voice took on a mocking tone—"how tough it was having to fight and kill. Can't hold down a job because of their nightmares. I didn't get none of that. Still don't. I grew up on the streets of Chicago, where killing ain't such a big deal. That's just part of life. You want to live, you've gotta fight for it. Hell, I'd already blipped off a couple of cats by the time my balls dropped. So Uncle Sam calls me up and puts me in the trenches. I get to work, you know?" He made a *cack cack cack* sound and swept an imaginary submachine gun around the room. He laughed, then took a long, careless drink, the gin spilling down his chin and dripping into his lap. He came up for air and wiped his face with the back of his hand. The booze seemed to work like gasoline on a fire, making him more animated, his gestures more feverish, the volume of his voice rising until he was almost shouting—booming over the music intended to conceal his words. "I tell ya, the key to killing?" he continued with a broad grin, now really getting into his story. "Conviction. Don't hesitate. Most of the Boche were just farm hands and altar boys, raised to say their prayers every night and never, ever kill. So they get to the moment when it's you or me, and they pause—just for a second—hands shakin' while they try to override their instincts and the years of their mommas reciting Bible verses about deadly sins and heavenly condemnation. But when you're like me and your instinct is just screamin' 'kill 'em quick,' well, you can imagine who won that exchange."

"It's a messy business," Kessler said quietly, threading his fingers together atop his knees.

"Nothin' messy about it! Just leave 'em where they drop and let the crows and rats have 'em." Barbieri cackled loudly and slapped the armrest. "Speaking of battlefields, I've gotta know: How the hell did you two end up becoming gun smugglers? Hmm? Most guys like you end up working in mines or factories."

Guys like you meaning poor immigrants, Niklas thought to himself as he cast a knowing look at his brother. "Yeah, we knew that was where we would end up if we didn't do anything to avoid it. So we started planning for the future."

"By squirreling away guns. Clever. That must have been tough doing it without getting caught."

"Not as hard as you might think. When the Americans arrived in France, we came eager to fight. Everyone else had already been beaten down by years of war. They just wanted to finish it and go home. Meanwhile, the politicians, whose sons were safely out of harm's way, fixated on filling their treasuries and shuffling borders on the map. Everyone—from the prime ministers and tsars to the lowliest private—ignored the most obvious treasure. And it was so accessible no one thought for a second to grab it." He took a measured breath and studied Barbieri's face, looking for signs of intrigue or skepticism, finding instead only a wavering attentiveness behind an unfocused gaze. Maya shuffled uncomfortably in her seat and appeared preoccupied with picking the lint from the couch armrest. Niklas continued his explanation. "Everyone had become so disillusioned with the war, so disgusted with the tools of bloodshed, they never saw them as valuable. They would bury them or toss them all in the ocean, if given the chance. We took the longer view." He slapped his brother's arm lightly with the back of his hand.

Nodding, Kessler continued. "We took everything we could. Mostly gun parts or rifles in such disrepair that no one would care if they were lost or destroyed. We traded rations and favors to have it all smuggled home to Denmark. No one noticed. The war machine rumbled on."

"Then, one day, abruptly as it had started, the war ended," Niklas said. "Everyone returned to their homes and their jobs. Grass grew over the gravesites and the battlefields. Old rivalries were renewed. Petty squabbles and political movements surfaced."

"And suddenly everyone wanted their guns back," Maya said softly, her eyes sorrowful.

Niklas nodded. "They longed for the familiarity of their Remingtons and Brownings, Springfields and Colts. Now they're seeking out men like us, men who saw opportunity in the bloodshed. And here we are, ready to reap the rewards of that forethought."

"And rewards you shall have," Barbieri assured, drawing a fresh cigarette from a carton on the coffee table and rolling it vigorously between his thumb and forefinger as if trying to start a campfire with it. "I spoke to the Gennas about your rifles and they were, shall we say, deeply intrigued by the possibilities these tools could afford us. They're looking to put together a few hard-nosed chopper squads with your bean-shooters and give it to O'Banion and his little mob of Paddies." He snickered cruelly. "I like that Madsen you showed me. I'll take a dozen like that. And throw in a few heavier guns for garnish, if you have 'em. Something belt fed we can mount on a truck. I've got plans for those."

"How about half a dozen Portative Hotchkisses, same of the Madsens, and three Vickers?" Kessler suggested.

"Is that Limey shit?"

"The Vickers? Yes."

"Good. The Tommies made good shit. Give me all that, plus the ammo for everything. Extra magazines, ammo belts, the works. Whatever you recommend."

"You would be looking at nearly three grand for the guns. Plus another five hundred for the ammo," Kessler said, a hint of incredulity in his voice.

"Eh, ain't nothin'." Barbieri lit his cigarette and melted into the couch, his drink tottering dangerously in his other hand. With as many nefarious activities as the Gennas were involved in, it didn't surprise Niklas that money came easily and meant so little to Barbieri.

Niklas glanced at the time, eager to conclude their meeting and return to the apartment before Barbieri had a chance to change his mind about the deal—or try to rope them into staying and getting drunk with him.

Barbieri noticed. "Hey, that's a nice watch. Waltham?"

"Elgin."

"Nice. Real reliable timepiece. I appreciate reliability." The mobster turned to look at Maya. His expression slowly transformed from a blithe confidence to a searing contempt, his eyes narrowing until they had nearly disappeared behind his long lashes, his lip twitching. "Maya, you know anything about reliability? Being dependable? Trustworthy?" He leapt from the sofa and slapped her face. Gin cascaded upon the wall and the carpet. His cigarette sizzled into the cushions. "You think you have fast hands, huh? Didn't think I'd notice you lifting my bankroll?" He slapped her again, harder this time. As his arm rose above her, his fingers curled into a white-knuckled fist.

Niklas and Kessler both stood to intervene, but Maya held up a hand to stop them and shook her head. Her hair was disheveled, the marks of Barbieri's fingers glowing red on her cheek. Still, her expression was one of defeat and acceptance, not fear.

He licked his lips and bared his teeth like a feral dog as he stood over her. "You think I'm some kind of chump? You have any idea who the fuck I am, you worthless bitch?" He jammed a finger against his sternum. "Look at me. I'm a first-class button man. I've filled so many saps with daylight it's become as easy as takin' a fuckin' breath. Do you really think knockin' off a little chippy like you would keep me up at night? Huh?"

"Easy now. No need for that," Niklas said, voice steady and low. "No one is getting knocked off tonight." He made a beckoning gesture with his hand. Maya pulled the cash from her brassiere and handed it back to Barbieri without looking at him.

He made a big show of peeling off one of the bills from the stack, crumpling it, and throwing it in her face. "Now drift."

Collecting the money, she rose from the couch, fixing her hair, chin up with as much dignity as she could scrounge. Kessler found her coat and helped her into it. "Be safe out there," he said.

With a small, appreciative nod, her eyes low, she left.

Agitated, Barbieri paced before the bar as he lit another cigarette. "These chicks, I tell ya. Won't even put out until you take 'em to some clip joint where their pimps can mug ya or the house can take your money. When that don't work…." he wafted a hand toward the door. "I shoulda killed that bitch. Tossed her off the goddamn balcony."

Acting as unperturbed as if their conversation had simply been interrupted by a phone call, Niklas said, "We have an agreement, then? Six Hotchkisses, six Madsens, and three Vickers. Should have them ready for you in the next couple of weeks. We'll call you when they're ready."

"Yeah, yeah, good," Barbieri mumbled without looking up, his anger still bubbling near the surface. Tipping a decanter against the rim of a glass, he poured himself a fresh drink. Tonic water flooded over the tabletop, streaming like a miniature waterfall onto the carpet. "See you around."

Better than French beer

In the lowlands south of downtown St. Paul, scattered atop the marshy floodplain of the Mississippi like flotsam, lay a huddle of slums known as the West Side Flats. There was no point in building a decent house there; the river flooded every spring and coffee-colored water filled the unpaved streets like a cattle trough, staining the siding and washing away any attempt at gardens or landscaping. It was a place for the city's poor, immigrants, and undesirables. Depending on who you asked and on what day, the Kristoffersons met all three criteria handily.

Their apartment was cramped but tidy, and thankfully on the second floor, above the reach of the seasonal floodwaters. That didn't stop melting snow and rain—trickling through the outworn asphalt shingles—from discoloring the plaster ceiling. It had a single bedroom and a small kitchen with an icebox and a woodstove. They shared a water closet down the hall with three Jewish families and one young Irishman training for priesthood at the St. Paul Seminary. He was certainly getting some firsthand experience with the realities of a vow of poverty. The few pieces of furniture they had scrounged or purchased secondhand bore threadbare fabric and wood accents worn smooth from years of handling, those that weren't cracked or missing altogether. Despite it all, the place had a welcoming warmth and intimacy about it, especially on a frigid night such as this. A fire crackled cheerily from inside their soot-stained fireplace, casting long shadows against the opposing wall. "We did it," Kessler said, his broad smile aglow in the firelight. He thumbed a pinch of tobacco into his pipe, then flicked away the errant ribbons that had fallen into his lap.

"Not yet we haven't," Niklas said. His Steyr lay disassembled in his lap; he dabbed at the parts with an oily rag. "When we have the money and the Gennas have the guns, I'll agree with you."

Lighting a match and tipping it into his pipe, Kessler sank deeper into his chair. He crossed his long legs at the ankles, angling his feet toward the fire. "You think Barbieri is going to try something?"

"I've never been more certain of anything." Niklas sighted through the barrel of his pistol using the light of the fire to check for dirt or rust. "He thinks he can outsmart anyone. Those he can't outsmart he bullies or kills. Despite what he said at the hotel, he doesn't respect us. He's already gotten us locked up once. But worse than that, he sees us as harmless. While he has an entire regiment of hardened men ready to kill for him at the drop of a hat, we have, well, you and me. What can we do to him in retribution if he decides to double cross us?"

"We have Oscar, too," Kessler noted.

"Hardly an army, brother."

Kessler puffed thoughtfully on his pipe. "I don't know. I would put my money on the three of us against any number of tough-talking *mafiosos*. Besides, we still have our heavy guns. That's a force modifier if ever there's been one."

"Correction, dear brother: We have *one* machine gun—disassembled and hidden under the floorboards—which was recently used in a murder. The rest are floating somewhere just south of Greenland about now. Not much help to us yet."

Grunting in grudging agreement, Kessler blew a blue-gray smoke ring toward the ceiling and took on a contemplative air. "Do you ever catch yourself wondering if we're doing the right thing with this? You know, selling guns to people like Barbieri?"

Expeditiously reassembling his pistol, Niklas said, "No, I don't wonder. I know perfectly well it's not the right thing." He racked the slide back and released it with a loud *clack*. "I watched entire villages of men trying to do the right thing at Amiens. And at the Somme. And in Saint-Mihiel. I watched them drown in mud, get blinded by gas, and end up shot to pieces while ensnared in barbed wire. Doing the right thing has brought very little comfort to them, their widows, or their orphans."

Brow knit, Kessler shot him a doleful look. "At least they did it for honorable reasons. That's a long way from arming men who will use the guns to kill innocents."

"You just described our government. Or any of them, really. How many men were in the trenches against their will? Slapping a label like patriotism on it doesn't change the fact that the same guns we're selling today have already been used to kill innocent people. And at scale. Unlike the war, in the scope of human history, our little operation here won't even make the footnotes. The gangsters get our guns, the police will bring more guns to deal with it. Or the feds will roll in and take care of the issue. They may deploy the National Guard for all we know. But the outcome will be the same whether we sell our guns or not. Humanity trundles on. We may as well take advantage of the opportunity to guarantee our own futures. No one else will, and I for one will not spend the best years of my life working for pennies just so Uncle Ezra can get a little richer."

He could tell by the way Kessler chewed on his pipe that he didn't like Niklas' reasoning nor fully accept it, but he had the good sense not to belabor the point. The prospect of making a fortune and never again having to work in the sepulchral back offices of Uncle Ezra's freight department held strong appeal.

Niklas changed the subject. "Speaking of the man, what do you think of our dear uncle's gift?" He nodded toward the telephone perched on the hall table near the door. The men who had installed it spent twenty minutes trying to determine if they had gotten the address wrong: dubiously evaluating the confined apartment with its primitive furnishings, discussing among themselves in hushed voices, scrutinizing their typewritten work order, then starting the process over anew.

"I think it's typical for him to give us something so useless when he can't be bothered to pay us a decent wage."

"Couldn't bother bringing it by himself, either. God forbid he be seen in a neighborhood like this."

Drawing smoke through his pipe and exhaling two streams of blue-gray smoke from his nostrils, Kessler asked, "Why did he think we needed that thing, anyway?"

"So he can reach us at his convenience. Remind us that we're forever at his beck and call."

"Not much of a gift, then. Now, what Cillian left us, that's a proper gift," Kessler said, referring to their neighbor, the priest-in-training across the hall. "He baked a loaf of sweet bread for every family on the floor. Called it Barmbrack. Used his dear mum's recipe from the old country."

"Sounds delicious. You leave any for me?"

Kessler mustered an injured look. "Of course I left you some. A full slice, in fact."

"Your generosity astounds me, brother."

A heavy knock at the door was followed by a sloppy jiggle of the doorknob. Niklas drew a stripper clip of nine-millimeter cartridges from his vest pocket and jammed them home inside the action of his pistol, swinging it toward the door just as it opened. A man best described in all features as sturdy—sun- and wind-weathered, broad-featured and broad-shouldered—staggered inside. Niklas let the pistol drop toward the floor and lowered the hammer gently with his thumb.

"Comrades," Oscar croaked. His voice was pure gravel, as though he had swallowed a handful of rusty nails. He shook the snow from his long, raven-black hair; then, from beneath his coat, he withdrew a glass milk bottle full of amber liquid and placed it lovingly on the fireplace mantel. He proceeded to dump his coat in a careless pile by the door before approaching the flame to warm his hands.

"How are we feeling this evening, good sir?" Kessler asked, nudging Oscar's knee with his foot. Hastily, he tapped out the half-burned tobacco from his pipe atop a glass tray nearby, smothering the ember and waving away the smoke with his free hand. He knew tobacco smoke irritated Oscar's damaged lungs and did his best not to smoke near him.

"Cold. Cantankerous. Like an engine that won't start in the snow."

"I see you've brought some starter fluid, though," Niklas said, nodding toward the bottle.

Oscar smiled. "It'll start a fire in you—that I promise. This is my best coffin varnish yet."

Niklas stood, offering his seat to Oscar, who flopped into the chair and angled his toes toward the fire. Picking up his friend's coat, Niklas gave it a gentle shake before hanging it on a hook atop his own. "You always say that."

"This time I mean it."

"Change your recipe?"

He contrived an insulted expression. "Never."

"But is it better than French beer?" Kessler asked playfully.

That always agitated Oscar. "French beer? That swill? You'd drown in it before you felt a tingle."

Kessler smiled but eyed the door expectantly, finger tapping out an impatient rhythm on his knee.

"I'm sure she'll show any minute," Niklas assured. "Have a drink while you wait."

Moving to the apartment's small kitchenette, Kessler retrieved a few glasses, blowing in them to clear any dust. He held one aloft toward his brother and raised his eyebrows. Niklas nodded. He didn't make a habit of drinking, but Oscar's homemade whiskey and gin were among the best around. As a child at a government-run boarding school in northern Minnesota, Oscar had been involuntarily leased out each summer to a local white family as a menial laborer. The father made whiskey and gin as a hobby and, noticing Oscar's interest, took him under his wing and showed him how. Oscar showed an aptitude for it and, together, they spent several summers working to refine their recipes.

Now, Oscar had a reputation as one of the best moonshiners in the city. He could have gone to work for any racketeer in the Midwest with an illegal distillery and made a small fortune, but he insisted on sticking to his own little racket, instead—if only to avoid taking orders from anyone ever again.

"What do you think of that Julian guy?" Kessler asked, trying a little too hard to sound indifferent. He began pouring whiskey for everyone.

"I think he's really swell." Niklas said it with exaggerated deference. "Strong, tall, handsome. He's the full package. Successful, too. Theater director. Gonna bring about a new age of vaudeville."

"Ooh, fancy," Oscar added with a husky chuckle.

"And he's got the mustache to match." Tapping his chin thoughtfully, Niklas said, "You know, maybe you should grow a mustache, little brother. A really big one—imperial style. Something to make old Emperor Josef proud."

Handing his brother a glass, Kessler punched his arm playfully. "You had better be careful—I just might. And I'll get myself a cowboy hat to match."

An hour passed with small talk and reminiscing about the few good memories they had of the war. Half the bottle of whiskey had vanished before the door swung open and Kosena sashayed inside, flinging around the sleeves of a rabbit fur coat several sizes too large for her slim frame, poorly dyed to look like more expensive fox fur.

"Darlings, I have arrived." She spun on a heel and cocked her head to a side as if to better capture the light and illuminate her features. She smelled strongly of cigarettes and perfume.

"Fashionably late, as always," Niklas chided, standing and retrieving a glass for her from the kitchen cabinets.

"I didn't realize I was expected at a specific time. Oh, Niklas, chilled please."

He adjusted course. With a heave, he slid open the living room window, the bloated wood frame groaning in protest. He swept the glass through a drift of fresh snow on the sill.

"I just finished dinner with Julian," she explained, shimmying out of her coat and draping it over the back of Kessler's chair.

A twinge of jealousy crossed Kessler's face as his mind no doubt played through a dozen salacious scenarios based on those few words.

Dropping into his lap with a flourish, she continued. "He wants to expand our group's acts and find ways to use our individual skills together for a more impressive performance instead of coming on stage one at a time."

Pouring whiskey into the snow-filled glass, Niklas passed it into her outstretched hand.

"No matter who is part of your act, you'll always be the star of the show," Kessler said sweetly, running a hand down her leg and squeezing her knee.

"Thank you, darling."

"What do you do in the show?" Oscar asked, fishing a piece of detritus out of his whiskey with a fingernail.

"I'm a contortionist," she said, arching her back over the armrest of the chair. "You simply must come to a show, Oscar. You would have such fun."

"Doubt I belong in a place like that." He took a sip and chuckled. "I'm not even allowed to vote."

"Don't be silly. The theater is for everyone." She sipped at her glass and shivered as the whiskey burned a path down her throat.

"Maybe you can get me a singing part in one of these big shows." He laughed at his own joke, which sounded more like a pneumonia patient's cough.

"Oscar dear, I've always wanted to ask: Why does your voice sound like that?"

Niklas shot her a disapproving look. The woman seemed to be magnetically drawn to controversy, asking taboo questions before playing them off as a product of her ostensibly innocent curiosity. She thrived on drama. Would have thought she got enough at the theater each day.

"Kosena, please," Kessler scolded gently.

Oscar waved a hand dismissively at Kessler as he slurped at his glass, downing half of it in one go. "The matron at the assimilation school they forced me into as a kid used to punish us for speaking Ojibwe by making us blow bubbles with lye soap." He looked at them with seriousness for a moment, then chuckled. "Just kidding. That isn't what did it. Though that did hurt something fierce." He tapped his throat. "The Boche gas is what got me. It settled in the low spots. The trenches, the shell craters. You go to ground to escape the machine guns, the artillery, the planes dropping flechettes and grenades on your head, but that's where it finds you. Your lungs catch fire, making you cough up blood and foam. Eyes dripping and burning, skin itching and bubbling. You pray for a quick death. But death is cruel, because she makes no promises and favors only some."

"Didn't you have gas masks? I thought everyone had gas masks." She looked to Kessler for confirmation.

"There was a lot going on," Kessler explained. "When you're fighting for your life, it's pretty easy to miss the signs of a gas attack. Only a second or two slow to get your mask on can make the difference between survival and death."

Standing behind Oscar, Niklas placed his hands on his friend's shoulders and squeezed. "Oscar here saved the life of a green soldier in his platoon. Kid didn't realize they had been gassed. Couldn't find his mask in time. So Oscar put his own on him. Barely survived. That one should have earned him a medal. Oscar should have been given lots of medals for what he did over there."

Draining his drink and smacking his lips, Oscar grunted. "Medals don't change anything."

"Seems like no one ever talks about the war, now," Kosena said in her insouciant way, swirling her drink, the ball of snow sliding along the sides of the glass like a small planet in orbit. "Like it's some big secret."

"I'll let you in on the secret, pretty lady." Oscar had a glassy, far-off look in his eyes as he clutched his glass. "Everything was wet. Always. The rain and the artillery turned the ground to mud. Inside our boots, weighing down our clothes, jamming our guns. And hunger—we were hungry all the time. Rations so small even a child would be hungry. The cold and wet seeped into the marrow of our bones. Made young men ache like their grandfathers. Always tired. Star shells that made the night bright like day, made you wince, turned you blind. Mortars and cannons that never slept. So we never slept. At least never restful sleep. Always noise."

"But that was France, Oscar. We're here, now," Kessler assured him. "Back home."

He seemed to return to the present for a moment. "Sometimes we are home. Sometimes it finds us. Most nights it grabs my neck and drags me back there. I live it all over again as real as the moment it happened."

Niklas refilled Oscar's glass from the milk bottle. "Maybe this will slow it down."

"Nothing strong enough for that." Oscar pressed a finger to the underside of the bottle and lifted to speed up the refill. He added cheerily, "But hey, it's worth a try."

Don't slip off the duckboards

It came to Niklas in a dream. He had fallen asleep in tall grass, beaded with dew, in a field just far enough from the trenches to avoid the attention of enemy artillery. Must have been after Amiens. Definitely before Meuse-Argonne. It was hard to remember for certain. Those days spooled together into one seamless reel of blurry exhaustion. Head resting on a discarded wooden ammo box, he dreamt of guns—hundreds of them rising from shallow graves in the muck and mire, slipping from the hands of soldiers, plucked from holsters and hoisted free of their mounts, then levitating above the battlefield like glistening pendalogues from a colossal chandelier. He began counting them. As he looked at each one, a number appeared. Dollars. He began adding them together, and then his pockets suddenly felt heavy. He plunged his hands inside to find them filled with gold coins. Overflowing. He started awake, a revelation dawning upon him like stubborn rays of morning sunshine filtering through the omnipresent pall of smoke and fog.

That he dreamt of guns was no surprise. He and Kessler served in a unit known as a mobile ordnance repair shop. Their job was to linger near the fighting and attempt a repair of every damaged or disabled machine gun brought to them so it didn't have to be sent back to an arsenal. Less downtime meant more units stayed operational. It also meant the Kristofferson brothers and their team of gunsmiths rarely slept, constantly troubleshooting, disassembling, and reassembling everything from automatic rifles to belt-fed machine guns. Piles of them lay on the ground beside their boxy repair truck in various states of completion. As new jobs arrived, they would pick through and cannibalize parts from the discarded guns to get others working. Everything came to them coated in mud, rust, and grime. The few times they reached a lull in their duties, they would begin work on restoring captured enemy weapons. They had no sense of how many they had repaired, nor how many had been discarded and forgotten about when they moved to a different location.

And that was the key. No one knew. Not their commanding officer, not the quartermaster, not John Pershing himself.

Whether those discarded guns got buried, destroyed, or shipped elsewhere, no one cared.

Which presented a unique opportunity.

"One we took advantage of," Kessler added to Niklas' explanation. "We boxed up those partial guns—barrels, receivers, stocks, you name it—stenciled the words 'tractor parts' on them, and shipped them home to Denmark."

The three men had moved to the apartment's small dinner table, leaving Kosena curled up in a chair near the fireplace, asleep under a knit throw. They picked at a plate in the center of the table, piled high with fried Medister sausage.

Oscar scratched absently at an eyebrow as he considered the information. "How did you ship them without anyone noticing? I couldn't even get a letter home to my mother without it being read and redacted."

"There was a Danish company that delivered canned meat to the lines. They liked us because we spoke Danish and chatted with them about the home country. We paid them everything we had—gave them all our cigarettes and spare rations—to load their empty trucks with our gun parts and return the crates to our father's farm. He stacked them ten feet high in the horse stables."

"So you got a bunch of rusty old gun parts."

Wagging a finger playfully, Niklas corrected him. "No, we got *thousands* of rusty old gun parts that we spent the better part of a year cleaning up and reassembling into fully functional guns after the war. And now we're ready to sell them."

"But that's not so easy."

"No, it's not. First, we need a buyer with deep pockets, which I think we have in Nunzio Barbieri—mercurial as he may be. Then, we need to transport the guns to the U.S. without getting caught by federal law enforcement. Finally, we need a place to discreetly store them until we complete the sale."

"Where do I come in?" Oscar asked. "I'm flattered you think so highly of my criminal mind, but I just make cheap booze and sell it to other poor people so I can get drunk for free."

"I'm getting to that. The plan is for us to meet the Danish steamship *Johanna-Rose* off the coast of Anticosti Island aboard one of our uncle's lake freighters. I've been communicating with the captain, and if everything has gone according to schedule, they should be underway already and set to arrive in Canadian waters by the end of the week. Once we move them aboard our laker, the cargo will be hidden under cases of canned pickled herring for cover. I've doctored Uncle Ezra's books and paid off the laker's crew for their silence."

Kessler had been nodding along with his brother's explanation and eagerly cut in with the rest of the plan. "We transfer the guns aboard at night, smuggle them back via the St. Lawrence Seaway, and unload them at the docks in Duluth. We'll load up a couple of Uncle Ezra's freight trucks with the guns and drive them back to St.

Paul. Offload the guns and leave the trucks at one of his distribution centers."

Oscar held his hands up and rebuffed him. "I don't do water. Or boats."

"How did you ever make it to France?" Kessler asked incredulously.

"Covered in gallons of my own vomit. That's how."

"Fine. Can you spend a couple of weeks in Duluth while you wait for us?" Niklas asked.

"Duluth is beautiful this time of year," Oscar said fondly.

Kessler laughed. "It's goddamn frigid!"

"Eh, it's cold here, too. At least Duluth has interesting scenery. Big water. Some hills for a change. And, most importantly, a couple of my old girlfriends." Oscar raised his eyebrows playfully. "Which reminds me, I may need to borrow some money for a hotel room—and incidentals. Things have been a little tight this month."

"Of course. We don't expect you to pay for this." Popping a piece of sausage into his cheek, Niklas continued, "So you'll wait for us in Duluth. Assuming everything goes well, Kessler and I will meet you at the docks to unload. The three of us will load the guns into the trucks and head back to St. Paul straightaway. But before then, I need you to find us a few obscure storage places in the city. Somewhere secure, monitored by people we can trust, and close enough that we can get to them quickly if we need."

"I know a few places that might fit the bill." Oscar wrapped the table with his knuckles. Ragged white scars on olive skin. "What kind of guns did you manage to drag home, anyway?"

"Plenty of everything," Niklas said. "All your favorites."

Counting off on his fingers, Kessler looked at the ceiling as he recollected their haul. "Madsens, Chauchats, Potato Diggers, Browning M1917s, BARs, Lewis guns...."

"Vickers, MG 08s, Hotchkisses, Mills bombs, stick grenades, Mk 1s, land mines, and enough ammo to restart the war," Niklas finished. "We didn't ease into this casually."

Oscar shook his head in good-humored disbelief. "Dove in face first, as always, I see."

"In for an inch, in for a mile. We get caught with even one of these guns, we'll have our own suite in Stillwater until we're gray."

Oscar nodded to himself, his eyes drooping with exhaustion, then stood from the table. "I'll see what I can find for places to hide the guns. Let me know when it's time to head north."

The men hugged. Niklas retrieved Oscar's coat and helped him into it. Nodding toward the mostly empty glass milk jug resting on the fireplace mantel, a shallow ring of amber whiskey showing at the base, he said, "Don't forget your coffin varnish."

"You boys can keep it. I'll make more."

"You know my rule," Niklas said softly. "You take it with you or it gets poured down the sink."

"It's a stupid rule." Kessler said it as though he was only joking but was unable to disguise the sincerity of his sentiment.

"No, it would be stupid to get caught with an ounce of illegal whiskey when there's a stolen light machine gun under your floorboards." Reaching into a pocket and pulling out a stick of Clove gum, Niklas waved it in front of Oscar's mouth.

Making a dour face, Oscar groaned. "You know I hate the taste of that stuff."

"Covers the smell of whiskey on your breath in case you run into one of the few cops actually doing their job on your way home."

He reluctantly accepted the gum and stuffed it into his cheek like a child grudgingly sucking down a spoonful of cough medicine, then grabbed the whiskey bottle and hid it beneath his coat. "I'll see you boys around town. Don't—"

"—slip off the duckboards," they all said in unison.

Niklas walked him to the door and slid a few coins into the pocket of his coat without him seeing. Oscar would never accept charity willingly. A survivor by nature, he could get by with nothing and would never utter a word of complaint. Still, Niklas felt better knowing he at least had enough for a decent meal.

They could hear his shoulder dragging against the hallway walls and the heavy plodding of his boots as he tromped down the stairs and into the snow-covered street.

Not an inch
Le Hamel, France
July, 1918

*A*soldier approached their repair truck, waving his arms and shouting. Even from a distance one could see he wasn't a day over seventeen, his face still cherubic and hairless. He arrived winded, cheeks and forehead beet red, a soft wheeze pouring between his lips as he rasped, *"The major is asking for you. You're needed immediately. Bring your tools—as many as you can carry on your back."* Confused by the request but recognizing the urgency, Niklas and Kessler complied. They arrived at the major's tent a short time later.

The officer stood before a large map, smoking a pipe and fidgeting with the brim of his peaked cap as though the fit irritated him. *"Ah, corporals, you've arrived. Just in time. We've received word that our men have successfully taken the village of Hamel from the Boche. Most of the resistance has been cleared out at this point and we've beaten the bastards back some distance from the town. Still, we're in a precarious spot, especially here,"* he pointed to the map before him using the mouthpiece of his pipe. *"The 44th Battalion's sector. The Aussies and* our men are up there holding the line, but they're waiting on reinforcements and resupplies. They have a few Lewis guns with them, but it will be a while before we can move the heavier Vickers and M1917s up to support." He tapped his pipe against his lower lip and stared upward as though deep in thought. "Someone mentioned that you two are exceptional talents when it comes to repairing machine guns—even Fritz's. That's precisely what I want you to do. Go to the front and repair as many of the German guns as you can. Show our boys how to operate them. That should help them repel any counterattack until we can prepare the supply tanks for another run to the front."

A sense of dread filled Niklas' chest. They were support personnel. Gunsmiths. They had no business being near the front, let alone at the very tip of it, in a sector held so tenuously. "Sir, with all due respect, we've not been to the front before," Niklas said quietly. "Normally we're well behind the lines."

"Quite, quite. Not a problem. I'll have someone show you the way." He shouted to one of his aides outside the tent, "Private Garner, find Private Hole-in-the-Day and have him take these men up to the 44th Battalion immediately." He paused and looked at them skeptically. "Do either of you have a weapon?"

"Just our revolvers," Kessler said, patting the leather holster at his belt.

The officer tried to disguise a cringe. "I'm sure those will be…adequate. Besides, you'll be among your comrades. Your focus should be on repairing the machine guns, anyway." He began fidgeting with the brim of his hat again.

"Is that all, sir?"

"Yes, yes." He smiled appreciatively at them as though they had just agreed to do him a personal favor rather than simply complying with an order from a superior officer. "Godspeed, gentlemen."

Outside the tent, a Native American man approached. His uniform was filthy—so much so it almost seemed deliberate. His rifle, though, appeared immaculately clean.

"You're to be our guide, then?" Niklas asked.

"Looks that way," the man said flatly. He didn't make eye contact with them, instead staring at their chests in deference—or resentment.

They introduced themselves and offered handshakes.

He looked at their outstretched hands skeptically, as though he thought they were joking. Seeing the earnest look on their faces, he accepted their handshakes and seemed to brighten immediately. "I'm Oscar. I'm going to keep you alive."

"We need all the help we can get." Niklas recognized the nervousness in his own voice.

They set off, Oscar in the lead, scrambling through the earthworks until they emerged into a woodline. Oscar moved quickly and decisively, as though he had taken this path numerous times and was confident in its safety. The distant crackle of gunshots and rumble of artillery didn't seem to have any affect on him at all, whereas every report within a quarter mile caused the brothers to flinch.

Heel to toe, stepping around loud underbrush and deadfall without even looking at his feet, Oscar moved through the woods with a fluidity and smoothness that could only have come from a lifelong familiarity with such terrain. Eyes always scanning for movement in the distance, he glided along effortlessly without making more noise than falling leaves on soft soil.

A horse-drawn tumbril approached along the trail, stacked high with khaki-clad corpses, arms draped over one another, English, Australian, and American alike. Chalk-white hands draped over the wagon sides, swinging like pendulums in time with the horse's steps. The driver, his eyes downcast, held the reins limply. The horse didn't seem to need any direction or urging to retreat from the front.

They stepped aside to let it pass and stood quietly as though in the presence of a funeral procession.

"Huns are tough fighters," Oscar explained. "Every inch of ground we take from them comes at a high cost. Let's not let them have any of it back today."

Emerging on the other side of the woods, they took in a patchwork of shell-scarred corn and hay fields surrounding the crumbling remains of the town of Hamel. Wood beams, fire-scarred and snapped in half like piles of used matchsticks, spilled into the streets amidst a rubble of bricks.

"It was a nice town a few days ago," Oscar said. "Then the Tommies leveled it with artillery. Thought that would drive the Boche out, but they just dug in deeper."

A droning engine wailed above the distant clamor of gunfire and mortars. The brothers dropped to the ground and sought cover as a biplane swept by overhead.

"It's all right, comrades," Oscar chuckled, helping them back to their feet. *"Those are our friends in the Australian Flying Corps. Taking photos to make new maps."*

"I've heard German planes drop steel darts over the trenches," Kessler said warily, watching the plane disappear into the low clouds.

"Flechettes." Oscar grabbed the straps of Kessler's heavy pack and helped center it on his back. *"They're no more dangerous than bombs or bullets. Just another way to die out here in the Wild West."* He patted Kessler's shoulders reassuringly. *"Lucky for you two, you have your own Indian guide!"* He laughed and guided them onward.

They picked their way through the wreckage of the town, moving slowly and calling out to ensure they wouldn't be shot by their own men. Finally, passing through makeshift earthworks, they reached the farthest position forward.

"Friendlies coming in," Niklas announced. *"I hear you have a machine gun that needs repair."*

They entered a hastily dug machine gun emplacement where half a dozen haggard-looking doughboys huddled together, peeking over the top at the distant tree line with distrust.

"Come on in. It's damn good to see you."

One soldier held up a hand as Oscar followed. *"Where do you think you're going? Get on back to the rear. We don't need a redskin here."*

"He's with us," Niklas said. *"If you want us to fix that gun, he stays."*

Realizing the desperation of their situation, the soldier reluctantly agreed. Still, Oscar hung back at the opening of the bunker without protest. Taking a seat in the mud, he rested his rifle across his lap.

"We don't know what's wrong with this damn machine gun," one of the soldiers said, slapping the water jacket shrouding the barrel. *"Doesn't look like the Krauts sabotaged it, but nothing happens when you hit the trigger."*

"Let's take a look." Niklas and Kessler offloaded their packs and evaluated the dysfunctional gun. They had repaired dozens of captured MG 08s just like this one.

The soldier was right: It hadn't been deliberately sabotaged. Niklas tried racking the bolt and depressing the trigger only to find no resistance. *"Probably a broken sear spring,"* he surmised. *"We should be able to get it up and running* again if we have a little time." He dropped to a knee beside the gun, and, together with Kessler, began field-stripping it.

The dull thump of incoming gas shells filled the air. Yellow-brown smoke billowed across the open ground toward their position, a wraithlike portent of death. The men scrambled to free their masks from the leather pouches at their sides and position them securely on their heads.

"Get ready. They're preparing an assault," Oscar said, his voice muffled behind his mask.

"Like hell they are," another soldier said dismissively. "We whooped 'em good before, sent 'em running with tails tucked. They'll spend the next few days trying to soften us up with gas and artillery while they regroup. We will have gotten relieved by then."

Oscar just shook his head knowingly.

Ten minutes later, one of the soldiers cursed, "Oh shit. Here they come." Over the top of the bunker they could see an approaching hoard of Stosstruppen, bayonets affixed to their Mauser rifles, their gray-green wool uniforms blending into the muddy landscape. They approached in ragged lines, marching steadily toward them, unaffected by the clouds of gas and smoke eddying around their legs. Their snout-like gas masks concealed their faces, making them appear altogether inhuman.

"Get that gun ready, dammit!" one of the men roared at Kessler.

"We're trying!" Kessler shouted back angrily, his hands full of small parts and intricate assemblies.

Frantic, Niklas dug through his bag in search of a replacement spring, but his sight was compromised by the gas mask plastered to his face. He felt panic seizing his chest and fought the urge to tear the mask off, knowing what the consequence would be.

"There are too many of them," one of the soldiers said, grabbing his comrade by the arm. "We can't hold this position. We're too far forward. Come on, let's fall back to the town." The others followed, scrambling out of the emplacement, staying low as they withdrew, leaving Niklas and Kessler alone with the disassembled machine gun. They looked at each other in shock and panic.

Taking a few steps forward and resting on a knee, Oscar joined them, staring unflinchingly at the approaching Germans. "We don't give them an inch, all right?" He raised his rifle, closed his left eye, and squeezed the trigger. A distant scream was followed by a cacophony of rifle fire as both sides engaged each other. The Germans continued their advance through the gas, slowed only slightly by the incoming fire and the shell-pocked ground. Rifle rounds snapped wickedly overhead and thudded dully into the sandbags before them.

Finding the part he needed, Niklas steadied himself, tuning out the sounds of war as he wedged the tiny spring in place behind the machine gun's sear. He nodded to Kessler and the two began reassembling the gun with celerity.

And still the Germans came. Before they breached their defenses, Oscar leapt atop the parapet, thrusting his bayonet into the chest of an enemy soldier. Using the heel of his boot to kick the body away, he wheeled and fired into another, then swung the buttstock of his rifle on a third.

Tugging a cloth belt of ammunition along the machine gun's feed tray, Kessler slapped the top cover in place while Niklas took a knee behind the gun. He stared down the sights through the haze of condensation cloaking the inside of his mask, aiming at the chest of one of the approaching German soldiers. He froze. It all seemed so surreal, as though at any moment he could suddenly awake in his bed at home. The air seemed too dense to breathe, too thick to pass through.

Kessler turned and shouted at him, something urgent yet indiscernible. A rifle round clipped the shoulder of his uniform—a gentle tug. Suddenly, the savagery of it all came crashing down on him at once and sucked the air from his chest, like being struck with a bucketful of cold water. He suddenly grasped the reality of the war that, until that point, had been distant enough to seem illusory. He had willfully accepted his role in this unnatural thing, this horrific machination. All those months of fixing guns, sending them back to the lines once they were ready without consideration for what they would be used for once they got there. He was just doing his part. Harmlessly tinkering with broken tools, no different than mending uniforms or replacing a horse's thrown shoe. The killing was a millstone about someone else's neck. Some nameless, faceless soldier would pull the trigger, not him. Never him. But now, here he stood, thumb slowly—almost unconsciously—depressing the steel tab at the rear of the machine gun before him, like pushing the catch of a mousetrap and waiting for the inevitable snap of the hammer.

Oscar reappeared in cover, setting aside his now-empty rifle and shouldering Niklas out of the way, taking his place behind the German machine gun.

He exhibited no such reservations. The gun bucked in his hands, hot brass spilling atop his boots as a line of enemy troops fell under the withering gunfire.

Kessler fed the cloth belt of ammunition into the machine gun with one hand, drawing his revolver with the other in case any enemy soldiers made it into their bunker.

After what seemed like an eternity, but what was in fact no more than a few minutes, the Germans retreated to cover and an eerie silence washed over the battlefield, save for the grumbling of boiling water inside the machine gun's cooling jacket. Cloaked in fresh mud and blood, Oscar ripped off his gas mask. Panting, he turned to the Kristoffersons with a toothy smile. "Nice work, comrades. Didn't give them an inch. Just like we planned."

Don a dead man's helmet

Gentle moans and the rhythmic rasp of a bed frame grating against a plaster wall filled the dark apartment. Kessler and Kosena had gone to bed after Oscar departed. The brothers had a tacit understanding that if either man brought a companion back to the apartment, the other should find somewhere else to be for an hour. But it was late, he was drunk, and it was too cold for an extended walk anywhere but up and down the hallway. Which he had done. But after making a few unhurried circuits, Cillian peeked his head out from his apartment across the hall, his eyes puffy and red hair disheveled. He gave a sleepy smile. "Ah, just you, then, brother Niklas. Trouble sleeping? Perhaps a cup of warm milk and a recitation of Psalm 23 would settle your mind. Always works for me." Niklas thanked him for the wholesome suggestion, taking the hint and returning to his apartment.

Tugging on a thick wool sweater, he dragged a chair to the farthest corner away from the bedroom, angling it toward the window where he could look out upon the vacant street. Wind gusted, swirling snow along the curbs and driving it into dark corners like dust in an abandoned home. Cold seeped through the thin glass, greedily drawing the heat from the room. The fireplace gave no succor, the dying embers now pulsing only a dim glow. Lighting a candle, he tried to ignore the lovers' soundtrack by burying his nose in a timeworn copy of Jack London's *The Sea-Wolf*.

As a boy, he had purchased the novel, used, for two kroner at a corner bookshop. He had long ago gotten his money's worth from it. The cloth cover had worn through in places, the rest dirty and discolored after accompanying him from Denmark to the States, and even into the trenches in France. As a boy, he delighted in the tale of high-seas adventure, castaways and mutiny, fistfights and shark attacks. He found the antagonist, Captain Wolf Larsen, especially intriguing. A Dane like himself, Wolf possessed almost superhuman strength and ruggedness, and despite having never set foot in a classroom, was a brilliant intellectual as well. Though volatile and merciless, Niklas couldn't help but to feel a certain sympathy for him: The captain had endured endless hardship and deprivation from boyhood. He had been born penniless and, despite his intelligence and strength, was doomed to a lonely life without purpose or peace. It had driven him to callously develop a view of human life as merely a cannibalizing ferment. A parasite wholly committed to making itself more powerful. As a younger man, Niklas hadn't understood that perspective. The world for him was still fresh, full of promise and opportunity, untarnished by exposure to the moral failings of humankind.

Reading it in the trenches changed his interpretation of the novel. He came to understand Wolf's position absolutely, even if that had never been the author's intent. He and his fellow soldiers clung to an ephemeral existence often measured in days rather than years. The value of their lives had been cheapened until even they began to see one another as so many dead flies in a farmhouse attic, soon to be swept into a dustbin or brushed into the fireplace. Disposable. Life—human and otherwise—had become the cheapest commodity in the world. The death of a soldier mattered only to him, the few friends he may have made, and a family so far from the fighting they seemed imaginary. Everyone else who witnessed it felt nothing beyond a fleeting pity and gratitude that they hadn't met the same fate. The dead men would be replaced within days by a fresh wave of ruddy-cheeked recruits. And back home, every day that passed brought with it another surge of callow young men, ready to don a dead man's helmet and shoulder his fallen rifle before marching patriotically into the same meat grinder that had claimed their predecessor.

Niklas' world had been transformed, revealing itself as a cruel and unforgiving place that favored the strong and the cruel and the lucky, feasting on the weak—just as Captain Wolf Larson had insisted. The war ended and others had forgotten that lesson, but he hadn't. The curtain had been thrown aside to reveal an ugly reality he could never unsee. Now, others might dismiss him as merely cynical, but to his mind he had gained clarity. He would waste no time praying for safety, for God or the government to provide for and protect his family. Freedom and security came from a position of power. Those who commanded that power hadn't gone to war. Neither had their children. They hadn't been affected by drafts or rationing. They lived apart from the rest of the world, safely above it, looking down at the seething masses from their rarefied strata.

And one only became powerful by one of two means: force or finances. Shooters or sterling.

Niklas would have both. Whatever was required to protect his family, his friends, and himself, whatever it took to secure their future, he would do it.

A whimper and a sustained groan trickled through the bedroom wall, then silence fell over the apartment. Niklas could envision the two of them entwined, sheathed in sweat, his younger brother effusing his adoration for Kosena in breathy whispers while she stroked his cheek and made cooing noises in her throat.

He didn't begrudge his brother his adoration of her, but he worried about what would happen to him when she inevitably moved on to another suitor. It would leave him devastated. And it frustrated Niklas to be unable to shield him from the heartbreak. Niklas had protected him on their long voyage from Denmark, from danger in the streets and trenches, from starvation and cold upon their return home. But love was another matter entirely. Something about which he could do nothing and would never fully understand.

A few minutes later, Kosena slipped from the bedroom, stepping quietly toward her coat, tiptoeing in the dim light.

"Goodnight, Kosena," Niklas mumbled without looking up from his book.

She froze as though she had been caught rummaging through the family silver. "You scared me." Approaching him slowly, she drew back a chair from the table and slid it beside him. Sitting, she leaned forward as if huddling against the cold. She hadn't bothered redressing. Her pale skin shimmered like pearl in the candlelight, a thin silk chemise resting lightly upon the gentle curves of her breasts. "I asked Kessler about his bruises. He wouldn't tell me. Just said that you two had been in a fight. Every time I tried to get him to talk about it, he refused."

He closed his book and placed it gently atop the table. "It's nothing to concern yourself with."

She wagged a finger at him. "You know, my father used to say that same thing to me when I was a girl. We lived in a little village outside of Plovdiv. My brothers would help him with the farm chores while I stayed inside with my mother, cooking, cleaning, doing laundry. I didn't want to be in the house all day. I wanted to be outside in the sunshine, working alongside the animals and the dirt. Learning from him. But he always told me the same thing: It's nothing to concern yourself with. Your place is in the home. Then, when the war came, he was sent away to fight. So were my brothers." She suppressed a shiver and goosebumps appeared on her arms. "Mother and I were left with the farm. Neither of us knew anything about how to plow a field or harvest a crop. Apparently, none of the other women left behind knew, either. Because the fields lay fallow and everyone starved. All because we were told it was nothing to concern ourselves with."

Letting her conclude her narrative, he nodded once and said, "This is different. Trust me: You are better off not knowing." Touching his thumb and forefinger to his tongue, he pinched the wick of the candle. The flame extinguished with a sharp hiss. Darkness flooded the room. Only a diffused glimmer of moonlight illuminated their faces.

She stood, hovering over him for a moment, her expression as austere as that of a bronze effigy. Then, she gathered her things and left.

Pandora's Box

The morning sun filled the enclosed streetcar with a pleasing warmth. Still, the heat never seemed to quite reach the painful chill entrenched in his very marrow. Although he had survived polio as a child, Detective Stauss had been beleaguered by the lasting effects of the disease. It had left him with weak muscles, aching joints, and a susceptibility to cold that seemed to worsen with each passing season. It took him a full half hour each morning to limber enough to get dressed. His few friends and fewer lovers had all recommended he move south. Seek a warmer climate like a migratory bird. But such was his lot in life. He felt no self-pity, no furious indignation at the injustice of his pain, his shambling gait, his stooped shoulders. Yes, he had been dealt a mediocre hand in life's crooked poker game, but he still had a seat at the table. Others weren't so fortunate. He, at least, had a purpose. A meaningful mission that surpassed his daily struggles and lamentations. His physical suffering was to him a penance, a cilice he wore daily with the weary acceptance and familiarity of an elderly monk.

He settled deeper into his many layers of sweaters and coats, nuzzling into his scarf and closing his eyes. The streetcar churned and clanked pleasantly as it trundled along the icy road, coasting between ice-glazed sidewalks begrimed with dirt and exhaust. The car slowed as it reached its next stop. A young Asian woman boarded, handed her nickel to the conductor, and scanned the passengers until her eyes settled on Stauss. Taking a seat beside him, she mumbled, "Eugene."

"Maya. How was your date with our friend Nunzio?"

"I've met barnyard animals with more manners."

"I'm sorry you had to endure that. I can only imagine what you had to do to maintain your cover."

"I knew what I signed up for."

"Did he realize you were a plant?"

She shook her head. "No. Once I had gotten everything I needed from him, I made sure he saw me stealing cash from his wallet. Made him think that was all I was after." She unconsciously raised a hand to her cheek, fingertips tenderly brushing the bruised skin. "He bought it."

"And the Kristofferson brothers?"

"They don't suspect a thing." She discreetly passed him a folded copy of the *St. Paul Pioneer Press* she had tucked under her arm. He would review her notes in the margins later. "I've got to say, everything you told me about Barbieri was true, if understated. He kept bragging about how many life sentences he's already received for murders he committed, but has gotten out on bail or released by a judge on the Gennas' payroll."

"But did you find out what he's doing in St. Paul?"

She nodded. "He's here to buy guns and set up a new cathouse."

"What, he didn't think we had enough VD factories up here already?" Stauss scoffed.

"He thinks Chicago is too crowded. Their city vice squad doesn't even have enough officers to field an amateur baseball team, let alone stem the tide of brothels, so there's one on every corner.

Barbieri doesn't think he can grow his prostitution racket in the shadow of the Genna empire, especially with so much competition. So he's looking north."

"And they're fresh out of guns in Chicago, too, I suppose. Surely he has access to the Genna armories. I would imagine they're sitting on enough small arms to kickstart a revolution if they were so inclined."

She chewed her lip and looked out the window for a moment. When she turned her gaze back toward him, her eyes were wide with thinly veiled fear. "They don't have anything like these guns, Eugene. It seems the Kristofferson brothers have access to light and heavy machine guns from the war. They smuggled them off the battlefield as parts and reassembled them afterward."

Leaning forward in his seat, he rubbed his eyelids. He felt as though he had been hit in the chest with a brick. "That explains Vicenzo's riddled corpse."

She nodded. "That was Barbieri. He thought Vicenzo was selling information to the Irish, not realizing he was actually a mole for the CPD. After killing him, Barbieri told the Kristoffersons to dispose of the body before he would go through with the purchase of their guns. He called in the tip to see if they would get caught. Considered it a test of their competence."

"More likely a test of the St. Paul police." Leaning his head back against his seat, he closed his eyes. These boys had gotten themselves in deep. Quickly, too. Their harebrained scheme to make a quick dollar would end up getting them both killed. Countless others, too, if Stauss couldn't figure out a way to stop them.

As though she could read his thoughts, Maya continued. "Barbieri has committed to buying more than a dozen machine guns. He told the brothers that the Gennas intend use the guns to get the upper hand against the Irish in Chicago, but I don't think that's entirely true. I think he's planning to keep the guns—at least some of them—for his personal crew. It would give him a huge boost in the

Unione Siciliana. Maybe even position him to start his own outfit apart from the Gennas. It's all he talked about the entire night. How he's been held down by the Genna family and it's time for him to gain the respect and power he thinks he deserves. If he gets those guns, no one will be able to stop him. He'll take over Chicago. Minneapolis and St. Paul, too, if he wants them."

Stauss chewed on his scarf and stared out the window. "I need to think about this. Even if we're sure the Kristoffersons have these guns, I can't arrest them without evidence, and there's no telling where they're keeping them. I've searched their apartment already—totally clean. Not even a bottle of booze. But even if they had an entire artillery battery staged in their bedroom, the best I could do would be a charge of embezzlement of government property. We can't do much to Barbieri, either, for much the same reason. I have no case against him, even with the body of one of his boys in our coroner's office and your testimony. The Chicago Police can't seem to pin anything substantial on him, either, assuming they would even be willing to try."

"I think our best bet is to speak to the brothers," she said. "They may still see reason. At first blush they seem decent enough. Misguided, maybe, but not the conventional criminal type. We may not be able to stop Barbieri, but we might still be able to convince them not to open Pandora's Box."

The trolley announced its arrival at its next stop with a cheerful ding. As the other riders disembarked, she stood and straightened her coat. "I don't need to remind you that if Barbieri gets those guns out of St. Paul, a lot of people will die."

Stauss nodded and held up the newspaper, giving it a grateful wag. "Excellent work, Maya."

Stepping toward the exit, she said, "Doesn't feel like it at the moment."

Minnesota 13

D etective Stauss was a private man. Outside of working hours he mostly kept to himself. Didn't go out much, didn't have many friends to speak of. But personal information about him—or anyone in St. Paul, really— still came easily and cheaply if one knew where to look and who to ask.

Information was ammunition. And Niklas would need plenty of it when he met the detective again.

Which, apparently, would happen quite soon.

That morning, he had found a note from Stauss, folded tightly and inserted into an open pack of Clove gum. Inside his coat. Inside their locked apartment. It invited him, very politely, for coffee at the Commodore Hotel the following morning.

So Niklas took a late-night stroll down to the Green Lantern on Wabasha Street, just blocks from the state capitol. The front side of the building appeared to be that of an unremarkable restaurant, with a sign in the front window that read Dapper Dan, The Hot

Dog Man. Below it sat a cold griddle and a few leftover franks the lunch crowd hadn't gotten to. A few patrons sat inside, enjoying a late sandwich and a soda. Niklas strolled into the next alleyway, steering past hustlers and bums, waving away huddles of sex workers trying to stay warm while soliciting Johns. There, he descended a short stairway to the building's basement entrance. He wrapped his knuckles on the door and a gated porthole slid open, revealing a pair of bloodshot brown eyes. A dozen overlapping conversations and the clacking of pool balls being racked poured through the narrow aperture.

"Password?" the doorman grunted.

"Very funny, Ralph. But it's cold out here. You mind?"

The door swung open, revealing a smoky, narrow, poorly lit speakeasy where patrons squeezed in close and the aroma of stale beer was supplanted only by the noisome fustiness of sweating bodies cloaked in cigarette smoke.

At least it was warm inside.

The Green Lantern was an epicenter of criminal activity in the city. Supposedly, Al Capone and Johnny Torrio had been spotted there a few months before with a coterie of criminal accomplices in tow. Niklas had never seen anyone notable while he had been there. But one could always count on a corrupt policeman or two paying a casual visit to the begrimed little bar for a cheap drink, a fried pork chop sandwich, or a lively game of poker.

The bartender, a balding Pole with long sideburns and an aggressively receding hairline, spotted Niklas as he walked in and tossed him a brisk nod. "Ah, the handsome young Dane returns to once again break the hearts of our poor working girls by only ever asking for information and never finishing his beer."

The bartender's name was Kowalski. The bar's regular patrons thought that had too many syllables and shortened it to Kow, which inevitably evolved into MooMoo, a moniker he openly despised. Which just made it more indelible.

Leaning over the bar, Niklas shouted to be heard above the ratcheting clunks and insistent bells of a slot machine in the corner. "Don't suppose we have any off-duty policemen joining us this evening?"

MooMoo glanced over his shoulder at two hulking Swedes, white-blond and built like draft horses, sitting at a nearby table.

"How much have they had?" Niklas asked.

"I'm not their mother. Not my job to keep track."

"More than a little, then?"

"I had to tap a new keg."

Niklas stepped toward the two men and placed a hand on their shoulders. "You gentlemen look thirsty." Looking back toward the bar and waving two fingers in the air, he shouted, "MooMoo, their next round's on me. As a thank you for your hard work keeping the streets safe." He tried to deliver that line as sincerely as possible, though it rang so hollow he couldn't see how it could be interpreted as anything but a joke.

Nevertheless, they gladly accepted his generosity. A pitcher of lager and a few shots of Minnesota 13 whiskey later, they were on their way toward revealing everything they knew, or thought they knew, about their colleague, Detective Stauss. Much of it was obviously bavardage and rumor. But some of it sounded too pedestrian or too bizarre to be false.

"I'm dead serious!" One of the cops slapped the tabletop with an open palm, his voice slurred and eyes glazed. "Women's clothing."

"And from a man of his station, no less." Niklas shook his head in mock disapprobation.

"A man of his station…bah. What does that even mean in St. Paul? Just that he's stuck around longer than most and got promoted for being the only one too weak to join the war."

"I heard he wasn't just dressing up, either," his partner added as though passing a secret. He failed to suppress a belch that Niklas felt against his cheek, warm and sour. "He's got a thing for other men."

Niklas took mental notes as the conversation continued. Ordering another round, he paid their tab, slapped his new friends jovially on the back, and departed for the apartment.

Detective Stauss beat him to The Commodore by at least half a cup of coffee. Without his hat on, features laid bare in the bright morning light, he had somehow become even more homely, or at the very least a great deal older looking without the shadows to conceal his wizened visage and graying hair, or to disguise the proportions of his nose—built like the prow of a battleship. An alpinist would be tempted to plant a flag on that nose.

Stauss flagged Niklas over to a corner table with a small wave. "What do you think of that painting over by the window?" he asked by way of greeting.

Niklas looked at him curiously, then turned and evaluated the painting. "It's nice. Colorful."

"It's sublime," Stauss corrected. "Henri Matisse's *Vue de Belle-île*. It really captures the beauty of a French island village in springtime. You can almost taste the salt of the sea breeze when you look at it, can't you?"

"Yeah, like I said. It's nice." Niklas eased his coat from his shoulders and hung it on the back of a chair.

"You know how the winter months here can become so bleak, so seemingly endless? When I start to lose hope of ever seeing green grass again, I like to come here and admire it. Envision myself there, the owner of that little cottage. Maybe lying in a hammock, taking in the smells of the flowers in bloom, lulled to sleep by the rhythmic crash of the surf."

The detective's lofty description didn't sound anything like the France that Niklas had seen.

Stauss continued staring at the painting longingly. "I've been trying to get the hotel owner to sell it to me for some time. He wants more for it than I make in a year. I don't begrudge him that: It's certainly worth it. So I come here occasionally just to pine for it."

"I suppose for the cost of a cup of coffee, that's not a bad deal."

The hotel restaurant bustled with activity, a steady thrum of clinking silverware, low conversation, and muted shouts from the kitchen staff. The earthy aroma of freshly brewed coffee blended pleasantly with the smell of warm bread and bacon grease.

Allowing a silent moment to pass between them, Niklas said, "A bit theatrical, your note asking me to join you here."

"I assumed you wouldn't come if I asked by any other means. I wanted you to know I was serious."

"I don't see how breaking into my apartment proves much of anything other than your willingness to risk getting shot in the face to pass a note you could have just as easily slid under the door or left in the mailbox."

The detective grinned. It was an ugly, pinched expression, eyes narrow and lips drawn back as though grimacing. Like a man who had seen others smile but hadn't quite practiced it enough himself to get it down. "Have you ever heard of counting coup? The Plains Indians, as I'm sure your friend Mister Hole-in-the-Day can attest, once practiced it in battle. It's a show of bravery. Touching an enemy with a hand or bow—not to inflict injury, necessarily—and escaping without being killed or injured himself. It's a symbolic victory to the warrior who succeeds."

"So this is your symbolic victory. Does that make me your enemy?"

"I believe you've positioned yourself counter to my responsibilities. So yes, in a way, you are." He finished his mug, then poured another from a carafe in the center of the table. Glancing expectantly at Niklas, who nodded, he filled the empty mug before him. "Are you a devout man, Niklas? The Danes I've known have all been ardent Lutherans."

"At one time, maybe."

"Not anymore?"

"I've found that the world makes much more sense when you stop looking at everything as preordained or orchestrated by a higher power. Accepting that our lives are shaped by chaos helps to make sense of otherwise indefensible things."

"War, for instance." The detective gently slid the now-full coffee mug across the table.

Slipping two fingers through the handle, Niklas raised the cup to his lips, sipping the steaming-hot coffee gingerly. "Yes. Like war."

"You've experienced that intimately, I understand. A newly minted American sent back to Europe to fight."

"We saw it as an opportunity to prove our allegiance. Show everyone we had earned our place here."

"You and your brother. How did that work? Earning your place here, that is."

Niklas smirked. "I could walk the street in a uniform covered in more flashy metal than a belly dancer's brassiere and people would still challenge my loyalty because of my accent."

"You're far too young to be so jaded."

"It's not the number of years I've lived, Detective. It's which ones."

"Indeed." Shaking his head knowingly, Stauss said, "Sadly, we are simple creatures. When faced with something new or different, our minds seek the easiest and most comforting answers—seldom the right ones."

"How about you?" Niklas asked. "You spend any time abroad?"

The detective ladled a spoonful of sugar into his mug, followed by another. "Fortunately, no. The one time in my life I've been thankful for having had polio as a child. My muscles and joints were in no condition to go over the top. So I wore my little exemption pin on my lapel and stayed behind, doing my part as I could. I will say it became pretty quiet in law enforcement while everyone was away. Clearly the solution to violent crime is to send all the able-bodied young men to another country." He laughed, but it sounded forced and humorless. "I understand you were a gunsmith in the service. That's a bit unusual, isn't it? Did you already know how to fix guns or was that something they trained you to do when you enlisted?"

"You seem to know an awful lot about me." Niklas didn't like the direction the conversation was going. Although Stauss appeared relaxed and his questions seemed sincere, he couldn't shake the feeling that the detective was dexterously lulling him into letting his guard down and saying something incriminating.

Stauss shrugged and pressed his back into his chair, crossing an ankle over his knee. "After our meeting on the riverfront the other night, I thought it might be wise to do a little research on you, so I pulled some records and made a few calls. I find it especially intriguing that you managed to gain your freedom in less than twelve hours from the time I had you locked up. That suggests intimate ties to powerful people. Or just one powerful person. Your uncle, Mr. Abecassis, is just such a figure. Surprising to me, though, that he was willing to pay for your release given your family's rather quarrelsome history."

Slowly rotating his coffee mug by its handle, Niklas smiled stiffly at the detective. He was trying to make him squirm, trotting out all the intimate details of his life that he thought no one outside his family knew. Annoyingly, it was working.

It was time to lay down a few cards of his own.

"I've heard a few things about you, too, Detective."

"Oh?" He raised his eyebrows just for show. His eyes maintained the same disinterested gaze that seemed to follow the conversation at the table behind Niklas as much as their own.

"For instance, your colleagues have noted your affinity for attending drag balls."

Stauss' hold on his coffee mug slipped and a spatter of the amaroidal brew discolored the white tablecloth. He hurriedly tugged a cloth napkin atop the stain. "Many prominent people attend such events," he sputtered. "The Vanderbilts have been known to observe frequently. They're great fun."

"Not just observing, though, are you?"

The detective's stare hardened, his posture stiffening. "Of what concern is that to you?"

"None whatsoever. Much as my business should be of no concern to you."

"That's hardly a reasonable parallel, my young friend." His voice dropped to a barely audible whisper. "I'm merely acting upon a God-given predilection."

"By that logic, the criminals you pursue each day are guiltless as well. After all, they're just acting upon their God-given predilections, too."

"Mine harm no one. Theirs do."

Satisfied he had adequately discomposed the detective, Niklas let the issue drop for the moment. They sipped their coffee in silence. A waiter delivered a slice of quiche to a table near the window, where a man with an unusual haircut—prominently parted in the center and swept back on either side to resemble a loaf of split-top bread— sat cradling his head in his hands, gingerly massaging his temples. He ignored the food placed before him, groaning softly at his cup of untouched black coffee. Other patrons seated nearby cast glances his way and whispered to one another.

"Should I know who that is?" Niklas asked quietly. "The gentleman with the hangover by the window?"

Stauss turned to look without the slightest concern for discretion. Recognizing the man, he said, "F. Scott Fitzgerald. Local novelist. Read him?"

"Never heard of him. Any good?"

Seesawing his hand, Stauss said, "Depends on your tastes. I find him a bit incoherent with plot, but he has potential."

"He certainly looks the part of the tortured artist."

"A gallon of gin will do that. Speaking of which,"—Stauss nodded toward a far wall—"watch that server for a moment. He'll pull a clever little trick."

Niklas glanced over his shoulder. The waiter backed up to a wood panel in the lobby and began looking around—shiftily, eyes not seeking anyone in particular. Within seconds, the man slipped a hand behind his back, lifted an unseen latch, and vanished into the wall as the panel swung inward.

"Speakeasy in the basement," Stauss explained, his voice laced with disgust.

"If you know about it, why don't you raid it?" Niklas asked. "You're a teetotaler, aren't you?"

Deflating a bit, Stauss flicked his coffee mug with a fingernail and said, "In addition to such *personnes illustre* as our author friend by the window, Chief of Police Crepeau comes here with his wife quite frequently."

Realization dawned on Niklas' face. "It would be career suicide."

"One of many pitfalls I've learned to avoid during my time in the department, even if it means standing by while my countrymen kill themselves with drink."

Nodding solemnly, Niklas leaned forward in his seat, whispering conspiratorially. "Detective Stauss, clearly we have few secrets from one another, so answer me honestly. You make one hundred seventy dollars a month as a detective. That's a modest salary for a man of your experience and talent. And from it, you are expected to furnish your own sidearm, coat, uniform, and boots. You work for one of the lowest-paid and most corrupt police forces in the country, one that has an openly permissive—one might even say downright accommodating—relationship with the most infamous mobsters and gangsters. As long as the politicians and police chief get a taste of their dirty dealings, and as long as they take their cons next door to Minneapolis or across the border, you have to turn a blind eye." He smiled cynically. "There's an underworld expression I'm sure you've heard before: If you're looking for a mobster you haven't seen in a while, you can find him in one of three places: in jail, in the morgue, or in St. Paul."

Playing his tongue across his teeth as if trying to pick out a piece of trapped food, Stauss asked vacantly, "Was there a question in there?"

"Despite all that, do you really think you're going to make a difference in this town?"

A wry smile spread across Stauss' face. "I believe it with great conviction, in fact. Too many otherwise decent men have been dissuaded from doing the right thing by convincing themselves they would be alone in doing so. I have the advantage of enjoying my own company and loathing that of others, so I don't mind being alone with my dogma. No matter how misguided you may believe it to be."

"I don't think it's misguided. Just futile."

The two sat quietly, leisurely sipping their coffee amidst the bustle of the other patrons and hotel attendants.

"You and your brother met with Nunzio Barbieri." Stauss didn't wait for Niklas to deny it. "My sources report he's here buying guns—machine guns, in point of fact. Given your military experience, it seems you're quite knowledgeable about weapons of that sort and had access to a great deal of military ordnance."

Niklas leaned back and chuckled. He meant for it to sound insouciant, but the strained undertones played through even to his own ear. "Your sources being Maya." He wagged a finger playfully at the detective. "She was working for you, wasn't she?" She had been convincing in her role. The stolen money was just an act meant to seal her cover with Barbieri.

Stauss didn't contradict him. He toyed with the edges of his napkin, rolling it and letting it unfurl. "Niklas, throughout human history, there have been men born with an insatiable lust for power. It consumes them, driving out or smothering the human desire for love and belonging. They have no real friends, only those they keep around to elevate their image or to provide them with something they desire. Money. Power. Access. Sex. They are blind to beautiful things. Such men don't appreciate art or music or love unless they can be twisted to sate their ego. They are not governed by laws of man or God, only by their own calculating methods to satisfy their ambition and give them control over their fellow man."

"You count me among them?" Niklas asked, looking puzzled.

Stauss chuckled. "You? No. But such are the people you're making deals with. The ones you are empowering. I want you to consider that. The game you're playing here isn't a harmless one."

Standing and smoothing the wrinkles from his slacks, Niklas drew a nickel from his pocket to pay for his coffee, pinning it to the table with the pad of his thumb. "Nothing in life is harmless, Detective. Merely drawing breath is robbing it from another's lungs."

As he collected his coat and turned to leave, Stauss called after him, "I dread to think what those guns could do on my streets or in Chicago. Surely some part of you hesitates at the thought of turning them loose upon your countrymen."

Pausing near the door, Niklas slipped on his coat and took a deep breath, savoring the warm air before he plunged into the stinging cold outside. "My countrymen have seen them before."

Mid-morning matinee

The day had not warmed up much since Niklas first entered the Commodore, but the wind had died down to a whisper, so he resolved to walk to the Abecassis Steel office rather than take the streetcars. He had a couple of things left to complete before he and Kessler took the next few weeks off. The lie had been delivered easily enough: Solemnly, he had informed his supervisor that they would be returning to Denmark to visit their ailing father. It wasn't a particularly clever deception, but it would hold up if it made its way to Uncle Ezra—which it undoubtedly would. Their uncle and their father had only ever exchanged hostile glances and snarls when Niklas' mother was alive. Now? The two men were as good as dead to one another. Ezra would never reach out to Milas to see if their story was true, and the few mutual contacts they once had were all dead or had chosen their side years before.

The sidewalks were mostly empty at this hour and the gelid air felt refreshing. It quickened his pace and thus his pulse, pumping more blood to his brain where it was sorely needed for contemplation. Detective Stauss reminded him of a cat with a wounded rabbit kit, batting it about, letting it run a bit—perhaps even enough to think it had escaped—before pouncing on it again. For now, he seemed simply curious about what Niklas and Kessler were up to, but the minute he thought he had the complete picture, the claws would certainly come out. There was something shrewd and dogged about the detective that suggested he was not someone Niklas wanted for an enemy. He seemed to make up for his lack of intimidating physicality, the kind often seen in other police officers, with a sharper intellect. Only a fool would underestimate a man like that.

So preoccupied with his thoughts, he nearly missed seeing the couple, arm in arm, stepping into the nearby Astor Theater. There was something familiar about the woman's swaying walk—a bit careless, somewhat exaggerated at the hips—her ill-fitting rabbit fur coat, and her long golden hair that grabbed at his subconscious and gave it a firm shake. He crossed the street and followed them inside, maintaining his distance and tugging his scally cap lower over his brow.

Entering the theater's atrium, he spotted them. Julian and his immaculate mustache told a joke that must have been among the funniest ever told, based on Kosena's reaction. Then he bought their tickets and a bag of peanuts, and the two went inside. Niklas slid a dime across the counter in exchange for a ticket and followed them in, taking one of the empty red plush velvet seats toward the back.

The house orchestra warmed up. The lights dimmed and the projector clattered, white light cutting through the haze of cigarette smoke and illuminating the screen between thick velour curtains. Rudolph Valentino strutted onto the screen, batted his hooded eyes at the camera, and the music rose in an excited crescendo.

Kosena leaned close to Julian and nuzzled his ear, her fingers playing amorously through his hair.

It would be so satisfying to approach them, right as their lips met, and whisper in her ear, "Caught you." He could give her the ultimatum that either she told Kessler the truth or he did. Either way, his brother would finally be free of her. They both would. Sure, Kessler would nurse a broken heart for a while, but then he could focus on their objective without distraction.

Or maybe that would just make the distraction that much more powerful. Losing her might just drive Kessler into a frenzied hysteria, causing him to fixate on his betrayal or scheming some kind of retribution.

Suddenly, Niklas felt an unusual anger building in him. It made his cheeks flush and fists tremble. He was not normally a violent man. Never one for arrogant posturing or outbursts of anger. Generally cool under pressure, thoughtful and deliberate when others gave in to panic or rage. But there was something about this situation that infuriated him in a way he hadn't felt in years. Perhaps it was the timing, right as they were preparing to take possession of the guns. A needless disruption that could make Kessler all but useless when Niklas needed him to be at his most focused and driven.

Or perhaps it was the futility of it all. This time, it wasn't a matter of strategically choosing the correct course of action; there was none. The sudden knowledge of Kosena's infidelity was a burden, an unwelcome secret he would now have to keep from someone he would otherwise never lie to or betray. Now he would have to choose between maintaining a lie by omission or delivering a devastating truth. Either way, there were consequences. Direct and immediate. And not just for Kessler, but for him, too.

And for that, he wanted to hurt her. Deeply, vindictively. Of course, he could never raise a hand against her physically. But Julian? He was fair game. Niklas felt a feral desire to choke the life from him, watch his eyes bulge and go red with burst blood vessels, his pomposity replaced by fear and desperation as his heels slipped and slid atop the peanut shell-covered floor in search of purchase, his soft hands outstretched impotently as Niklas delivered blow after blow, knocking loose his perfect teeth, knuckles smashing his perfect nose and leaving blood stains in his perfect mustache.

Most of all, he wished he had just kept walking—or had been distracted enough to never notice them at all.

Standing, Niklas moved to the aisle. Kosena smiled placidly as Julian whispered something in her ear, his hand stroking her lissome arm, their faces aglow in the light of the silver screen. A man grumbled from the row behind him, complaining that Niklas was blocking the screen.

Letting out a deep breath and loosening his fists, he turned toward the exit. He nodded to the theater attendant to open the door for him, blinking away the sunlight as he hastened toward the street.

Corporate sabotage

O ne of a dozen trifling cases Detective Stauss had been assigned in the past few weeks involved a fire at one of the Dale Street Shops in St. Paul's Frogtown district. The shops were mostly dedicated to servicing equipment for the Great Northern Railway. Although the work was dirty and tough, those who worked there were well compensated and such jobs were coveted. As such, a reported fire—one that occurred in the middle of the workday, no less—was almost certainly accidental. But the owner insisted it was arson. Blamed the good-for-nothing unionists and their Bolshevik comrades, claiming this was just the latest escalation in their unceasing demands for pay raises. He kept bandying about the phrase "corporate sabotage" as though such a title would warrant special consideration and priority by the police.

Stauss agreed to stop by. He would make a big show of questioning a few of the employees, then assure the owner in his most serious voice that he wouldn't rest until he had gotten to the bottom of this. And by that he meant the case file would inevitably end up at the bottom of a tall stack of others.

The owner had a few employees high on his list of suspects and demanded they be the first to face the detective's withering interrogations. To help amplify the intimidation, he insisted Stauss use his private office overlooking the shop floor. Below, a grid of oil-blackened workbenches lay covered in steam engine rods, links, and couplings, the floor a minefield of heavy trucks and massive pistons.

Stauss called his suspects into the office one by one, inviting them to stand beside him as he watched the workers through the window, talking to them casually as though they were both waiting for a trolley. He asked them each a few cursory questions before dismissing them. The fourth man entered the room with eyes downcast but wearing an expression of acceptance. He quickly admitted to knowing how the fire had started. It turned out one of the men on his shift—with twin newborns at home—had nodded off, his lit cigarette accidentally igniting a pile of greasy rags. Case closed. The man begged him not to tell the owner. His colleague didn't deserve to lose his job over an honest mistake. Stauss assured him he wouldn't say anything. Not that it would have mattered: The owner would never be content with such an explanation. Too neat. Not enough malice or nefarious scheming involved.

Donning his coat, Stauss tucked his notepad and pen into his breast pocket. As the end-of-day whistle shrieked and men began their shuffle toward the time clock on a far wall, two young men entered the office, coveralls smeared in black grease and orange rust.

"Sorry boys, I'm all done here. You're off the hook. No one gets to ride in the paddy wagon today."

"You're a detective, right?" the older-looking one asked. He couldn't have been more than sixteen. "I think...well I think we may have something important to tell you, sir."

"Fire away," Stauss said, donning his hat and slipping on his gloves. "I could use something to make my day more interesting."

"We got invited to a...a place with...well, ladies. See—"

Stauss interrupted, "Look, boys, just speak plainly, all right? You're not in trouble. I'm not a priest and I don't know your mothers. Just give it to me straight. I can't be here all afternoon while you try to find a diplomatic way to say you went to a bordello."

"Yeah, right. That's just it. We got invited to go to this can house. Some wop—er, Italian—guy told us his boss just opened up this place on the seven hundred block of St. Peter Street. Said it had the most beautiful women for cheap."

"Well, everyone has to make a living somehow. I hope you wore your rubbers, though. There are some itches that can never be suitably scratched."

"We didn't go through with it," the younger boy insisted, then immediately became self-conscious and quiet.

"Oh?"

"Well, we got there and they weren't all grown women. Some of them were young. Real young. My little sister's age." The older boy furrowed his brow and looked down at his boots. "They didn't look like they were from here. Didn't speak much English."

Stauss sighed and pinched shut his eyes. Despite his many years on the police force and the countless cases that had hardened him, calloused his very soul as they forced open his eyes to humanity's enduring flaws, days like today made him realize he had yet to fully witness the depths of human depravity. "St. Peter Street, huh? This place have a name?"

"'Little Italy,' I think they called it. We just thought someone should know."

"Thanks for telling me, fellas. I'll look into it."

"If you need someone to testify in court, I'll do it," the older boy said doggedly. "I'm not afraid. It's wrong what they're doing. Someone should stop them."

Stauss smiled. "You should consider joining the police force, son. You've already shown more backbone than most of the men I work with. But you need to be careful. The kind of people who run places like the one you described? They're not inhibited by any sense of right or wrong. If they find out you've spoken to me about this, it could be dangerous for you. I don't want to find your body in a ditch somewhere."

"I'm not worried. We're careful."

The detective tipped his hat to the boys and exited the office. He suddenly had a new case at the top of his pile.

Eggs and baskets

Half a dozen pigeons fluttered inside a crude wooden cage nearby, startling Niklas and Kessler as they approached a squalid brick building from the alleyway. Leaning down, Niklas knocked on the large wooden door that opened into the building's cellar. "Oscar? It's Niklas and Kessler."

"Comrades!" Oscar shouted jovially from inside. "Feed my birds before you come down, will you? Half a scoop of seed. No more— they're getting fat."

Kessler complied, shaking feed into a corner of the cage and watching with fascination as the birds cooed, hopping over one another to peck at it.

Hefting open the cellar door, Niklas stepped down the concrete stairs, holding the panel open for his brother. Inside, the ceiling was so low Kessler had to stoop to avoid hitting his head. A small stove glowed a cheery red from a corner, illuminating Oscar's bedroll in the corner. Surrounding it stood a palisade of boxes teeming with potatoes, fruit, corn, and rye; empty glass bottles; and several copper stills.

Oscar looked up from a time-worn table that appeared to have been pilfered from an old diner, its decorative feet chipped and dirt-darkened. A row of half-filled glass liquor bottles and a large glass carboy sloshing with amber booze sat on the tabletop before him. "Wasn't expecting you two so soon. Was hoping to get another batch bottled and stored before we set out for Duluth."

"No rush. Take your time."

Kessler took off his coat and hung it on a rusty nail head protruding from the building's rim joist. "Oscar, why do you keep pigeons? Would have thought you more of a dog person."

"Would love a dog," Oscar admitted, his tongue snaking out between his lips as he gently poured liquor from the carboy into a funnel and filled another bottle to the rim. "But I can't afford to feed one *and* myself." He examined a threaded rubber cork he had drawn from a pile nearby, found it didn't meet his standards, and tossed it into the shadows in the vague direction of the stove before grabbing another. "Birds are easy. If times get too hard, I can just let them fly away and they'll take care of themselves. They don't count on me for much. Just to bring them inside at night for warmth and keep the alley cats from eating them."

Kessler nudged his brother's arm. "Remember when that carrier pigeon decided to ride out the war inside the ordnance repair truck? One of the tank crews had sent it back to the lines with a message but that damn bird wanted nothing more to do with it and refused to leave."

"Kept shitting on my tools," Niklas grumbled.

"I named him Ezra," Kessler added with a chuckle. "Seemed fitting given the grief he brought my brother."

"Who will watch your birds while you're in Duluth?" Niklas asked.

"Upstairs neighbor said she would take care of them. Nice lady. Brings me leftover muffins most Sundays when she gets back from church."

With help from Kessler and Niklas, Oscar worked his way through filling and sealing the remaining bottles. Once finished, a few ounces of whiskey remained at the bottom of the carboy. Oscar hefted it to his shoulder. "Open wide, Corporal."

Kessler held up his hands. "It's nine in the morning. I haven't even eaten breakfast yet."

"Helps with digestion," Oscar insisted. "Full of nutrients. Fortifies the body and the mind." He approached his friend and carefully poured some of the remaining contents into Kessler's mouth. The younger man sputtered as it dribbled over his chin. Niklas and Oscar laughed.

"Feeling fortified?" Niklas asked, slapping his brother on the back.

Tree branches, encased in glistening ice like blown glass, bowed heavily over the sidewalks. By February in Minnesota, the eye forgot the notion of color; the world little more than a bleached tundra of insipid, achromatic hues. The sky, the passing trucks and cars, even the people themselves, seemed muted and gray.

"Are we walking to the train station or are one of you rich boys paying for us to take the streetcars?" Oscar shouted above the tumult of traffic and the *ahooga* of klaxon horns.

"Streetcar. And we're not heading to the train station," Niklas said cryptically.

"We're not?" Kessler asked, confused.

"You'll see."

As they moved along the sidewalk shoulder to shoulder, other pedestrians hastened out of the way, clearing a path, eyes downcast in wary deference. None of the men on their own were especially imposing, but the certainty in their step, the steel-rigid posture drilled into them at basic training, and the rhythmic cadence of their stride made for a formidable sight. And in St. Paul, one could never really be sure if the men marching toward you were bloodthirsty killers with connections to powerful people.

In a nearby alleyway, a man sat on an overturned onion crate, a small fire burning inside a coffee can between his feet. A shattered wooden cigar box sat beside it, from which he fed splintered pieces into the flames. His glass eye, nested amidst an unsightly web of scars that spanned half his face, stared out at the street emptily. His left leg to the knee and left arm to the elbow were gone. Although he shivered against the cold beneath a nest of ratty blankets, one could still glimpse his filthy Army uniform, a row of ribbons and tarnished medals on his chest. In his right hand he clutched a mess tin with a few coins inside.

Kessler patted his pockets, but coming up empty, nudged Niklas expectantly. Digging into his pocket, he passed over a palmful of coins. Kessler detoured into the alley.

"You bleeding hearts give money to everyone," Oscar chided.

"He's just helping a comrade," Niklas said. "We got out easy compared to some."

"We all left something in the trenches," Oscar said coldly. "Every one of us."

After a moment spent speaking with the veteran, Kessler dropped the coins into his tin, stepped back, and saluted him. When he returned to the street, he said in a hushed voice, "Lieutenant in the 150th Machine Gun Battalion out of Wisconsin. He was wearing a Distinguished Service Cross. They didn't hand those out to just anyone." He shook his head sadly and glanced back at the wounded veteran as he slowly rose, pain etched deeply on his face as he grabbed a crude wooden crutch and began hobbling toward a tobacconist a few doors down. "It's a goddamn travesty, a man like that reduced to just a pile of rags in the street."

"The politicians never considered what they would do with us after the war. Just tossed their little toy soldiers into a box in the attic and forgot about them entirely." Niklas sighed and tried to change the subject. "What happened to your medals, Oscar?"

Tugging at his belt to pull his trousers further up on his hips, Oscar said, "Traded them to some kid for a fiver and a bottle of

Canadian whiskey. I've seen him around since. He likes to show them off to women and pretend he earned them by storming Boche machine gun nests."

"That doesn't bother you?"

Oscar shrugged. "Anyone who was over there and did what we did? They're not bragging about it. And anyone who believes that kid's lies is a fool anyway. Those medals never did anything for me. Look at that guy back there. Clinging to them in hopes that someone will appreciate what he did, the sacrifice, and give him a break. But everyone has short memories. Especially the ones who weren't there. They'll forget about us until the next war. Then it'll be right back to ordering every able-bodied idiot to do their patriotic duty. If we're lucky, we'll be too old by then for them to pull us back in."

Half an hour later, the three men disembarked a streetcar. Niklas led them across the street where they stood before a large brick garage faced with a row of heavy oak carriage house doors belted in black steel and diamond-head rivets.

Kessler smiled. "I know this place."

"You mean you know *of* this place. You've never been here before," Niklas said.

"How do you know?" he asked indignantly.

"Because none of us would normally be allowed on this sidewalk, let alone inside." Niklas scanned the street, looking for anyone out of place, anyone who didn't appear to be in a hurry to get somewhere, who fit the profile of a hired security guard—a thug with a shave and a haircut.

"Then why did we come here?" Oscar asked.

"Come on," Niklas urged them along, guiding them into the alleyway behind the garage. He plucked a key from his pocket. Tapping a steel box on the outside of the building, Niklas said, "Alarm." He plunged the key into a keyhole in the underside of the device and twisted. A heavy mechanical *clunk* followed. "Wiley old Uncle Ezra spent top dollar for this security system. Automatically signals the cops so he wouldn't need to hire a full-time guard. But then he goes and leaves the key in his desk at the office." He clicked his tongue reprovingly. "It's always the little details that derail a plan."

"Your uncle owns this place?" Oscar asked. "The rich one with the anger and no hair?"

"The same." Niklas unlocked the door and pushed it open, bending at the waist and sweeping an arm toward the interior like a dutiful bellhop.

The garage smelled of motor oil and freshly conditioned leather. Every surface seemed unnaturally clean, as though Uncle Ezra had hired someone just to polish the floors.

Like museum displays, stationed before each wall stood a row of immaculate luxury cars. A Duesenberg Model A with a rich green paint job so glossy one could use the massive hood like a mirror. An Alfa Romeo RL in silver with cherry-red leather seats. A gloss black Mercedes 28/95 trimmed in chrome that wouldn't have looked out of place transporting the president. Under each vehicle rested a steel pan to catch any dripping oil. The men stood, hands on their hips in admiration.

After a moment had passed, Oscar asked, "Anyone know how to drive?"

"We drove the ordnance repair truck all the time, but not very fast or far." Kessler examined his hair in the side mirror of a Hispano-Suiza, toying it along his part.

"Compared to that, driving one of these should be easy," Niklas said with aplomb he didn't feel in the least. "At least here, no one is shooting at us."

"Yet," Oscar snorted. "The day is young. And if there's one thing I've learned about you two over the years, it's that you are both bullet magnets."

"You really want to steal one of Ezra's cars to drive all the way to Duluth?" Kessler asked doubtfully. "That's a hundred and fifty miles. And we'll have his car for weeks."

"It's that or the train," Niklas said. "I'd prefer to make it an adventure. For all we know, it might be the last time we see the outside of a prison cell if things go poorly."

Oscar chuckled and slapped his back. "That's the spirit. It may be iron bars or a shallow grave waiting for us, but we're free men now. Let's act like it." He leapt into the back seat of the Mercedes. "I like the color of this one."

"Even though it's German?" Kessler asked.

Oscar jumped back out of the car as though it had bitten him. "Knew it felt wrong." He pointed toward the Duesenberg. "Let's take that one, instead."

Everything short of death

Niklas' fingertips played along the delicate stitching of the Duesenberg's leather-wrapped steering wheel as the car loped along the gravel, winding through a dense tapestry of snow-frosted pines, white-trunked birches, and wiry tamaracks. This car felt regal, he thought. Richness permeated the enclosed cab like an expensive perfume. Driving it felt akin to sitting on a king's throne or reaching across a velvet rope and touching a marble statue in a museum exhibit—exclusive and forbidden. He appreciated all the little details, the glass-smooth polish of the gear shift knob, the flawless chrome of the knobs and gauges—the finery that the hasty eye would overlook but had taken months of meticulous work by artisans to complete. Men more skilled than most, disciplined in their art. They had crafted something sublime the public might only see in passing. Something meant to bring pleasure to only a few elite customers. And he got to experience that sensation—even if he was never intended to be among them.

Like sneaking into Uncle Ezra's wine cellar and taking a pull off the finest bottle.

He and Kessler had grown up with little, and the possessions his family had inherited or purchased were all crude, rugged, and practical. Their father valued that most. Tools, furniture, clothing, they were meant to be useful and to endure, not to look pretty. What use was a wagon with a fancy paint job? It would only fade in the sun or get covered in mud the first time they hitched it. Of what value was a hunting rifle with ornate scrollwork and a precise action when the slightest dirt would jam it up or mar the finish?

And that was why Niklas found this car so appealing. He loved it precisely for its impracticality. It wasn't really meant to be used so much as admired. Palming the gearshift, he downshifted and powered through a curve. The makings of a grin formed on his lips. Or he could admire it *while* he used it.

"Don't get too attached," Oscar cautioned, his cheek pressed against the window as he drew an engorged penis in the condensation with his index finger. "You're gonna have to bring it back. And he *will* notice you took it." He chuckled cruelly. "Oh, he's gonna be so mad. And he's not a nice guy to begin with. Remember that time I met you at the office so we could eat lunch together? He tried to have his security guard haul me out back and shoot me."

"Good thing you knew the guard."

"But think about that: He was ready to have me killed just for being an Indian and having the audacity to set foot on his property and breathe his air. But you—you actually stole one of his fancy cars. Imagine what he's gonna do to you when he finds out. Family or no, you're in trouble, comrade."

Glancing over his shoulder at Kessler, mouth open and arm draped over his eyes as he dozed in the backseat, Niklas whispered, "If this goes right, we won't be working for Uncle Ezra much longer."

"Something about eggs and baskets," Oscar warned vaguely as he used a fingernail to add a nest of hair to the pair of oversized testicles draping below his artwork.

"I can only afford one basket."

The car crested the hill overlooking the city of Duluth. They were greeted by a sprawling patchwork of brick houses and factories, cobblestone streets, and clay-colored smokestacks puffing black smoke into the air above the harbor. The harbor itself was mostly covered in ice this time of year, with only a few wide channels of open water forged by the reinforced hulls of icebreaker ships.

The air became noticeably colder as they descended toward the city.

"I've always liked this place," Niklas said. "It reminds me of home, a bit." They had grown up on an island where the North Sea met the Baltic. Surrounded by cold, clear water and lush rolling hills of a vibrant green. Ice floes crept along the waterfront, the white-capped water beyond stretching out for miles before vanishing into the distant horizon. "I used to wake up before anyone else and walk alone to the beach. The air tasted different—cleaner and richer, somehow. It felt like the only place I could really think clearly. I don't believe I've felt that way since."

"Why didn't you stay in Denmark after the war? You two went back there, right?"

Niklas felt a strange lump form in his throat. "We had other plans," he croaked.

During the war, he had dreamt about home constantly. He fantasized about the quiet, the calm. The comfort of the familiar. But when he finally got back, he realized the home he had remembered was just that—a memory. One past the reaches of nostalgia, even. Going back felt unnatural. Like putting on clothes that didn't fit anymore. That belonged to someone else now. Too much had changed...*he* had changed too much to ever feel the way he had once felt.

Shoving the shifter into neutral, Niklas let the car coast down the steep hill plunging toward the harbor.

Bored with his illustration, Oscar wiped his rough palm across the window, smearing a clear path that revealed a huddle of large ships in the harbor. "Are you sure you want to go through with this?"

"Don't tell me you're gonna start challenging my morality like the others."

Planting a finger on his own chest, Oscar looked at him with surprise. "Me? Never. I can't judge anyone on their choices. The worst you can think of? I've done it. Twice. With each hand and probably some other appendage. But I do worry about you fellows. You're heading back into the trenches with this operation you've cooked up. The stakes are just as high. It's one of those all-or-nothing gambits the officers used to pride themselves on. Never turned out well. Just a lot of dead bodies for a few yards of mud you couldn't grow a dandelion on."

Kneading the steering wheel, Niklas said, "We've got it handled. You worry too much."

He snorted. "I don't worry much at all. See, I was meant to have died back in France. I know that. The spirits got confused with so many men dying at once and they miscounted. So whenever they catch their mistake, it will be OK. I'll let fate take me and I won't say a word." His voice grew solemn as he turned to look at Niklas. "But you two have long lives ahead of you. I can sense it. And I don't want to see them cut short. The money isn't worth it."

But it was worth it, Niklas knew. Short of death, it was worth everything.

The lesser evil

Rudkøbing, Island of Langeland, Denmark
July 1920

*T*he family homestead hadn't changed since Niklas and Kessler left eight years before. The fighting had never reached Denmark, and to the stone buildings—furbelowed with moss and discolored from centuries of weathering—another decade meant nothing. But the effect of those years on their father, Milas, was anything but subtle. His hair had gone completely gray. The strong angles of his face had softened, the wrinkles near his eyes deepening.

Together, they had spent the day collecting and baling hay to see the horses through the winter. This was the final harvest for the year—the richest of the three cuttings—and the bales were dense and heavy. Now, with the sun radiating its final aureate rays of the day, they stacked the hay in the loft of the barn.

Easing himself down to rest on the tongue of the hay wagon, Milas dabbed at his forehead with a handkerchief, chest rising and falling heavily. One of the dogs approached and laid her head on Milas' knee expectantly. He smiled and rubbed her ears. "Seems like these bales get heavier every year. It's a relief to have you both here to help out."

"Happy to do it." Niklas hefted another bail onto the elevator leading to the hay loft, where Kessler—shirtless, skin glowing like bronze in the dying evening light—stood waiting to receive it.

"I think the work suits you boys, too. You take to it naturally, the way the horses do. It energizes their spirit when they have a job to do. You can see it in their eyes and in the way they move. Same with you. You're at home out here, doing simple, honest work."

Niklas shrugged. *"I don't think I could do this forever."* Although returning to their childhood home after the war had been therapeutic in its way, it hadn't taken long for restlessness to set in. To go from the terror and frenetic energy of the battlefields to the somnolent farm fields of rural Denmark proved a stark change, and now it had begun to itch. The day before, the elderly neighbor had shuffled over and spent the better part of an hour discussing soil conditions. Niklas and Kessler exchanged a knowing look, an unspoken understanding that they were nearing the end of their time here.

"Well there's plenty more you could do besides farming," Milas insisted. *"You know your way around a mill and lathe. I'm sure you could apprentice under one of the machinists in Svendborg. And they're always hiring down at the cannery."*

A towering Jutland horse stood patiently beside the elevator, tethered to a thick rope that, via pulley, would drive the elevator. Niklas gave a click of his tongue and tugged the big horse's harness, and the belt began to ferry the hay bales upward toward the loft. *"You know we don't intend to stay through the winter. We're heading back to the States as soon as we finish preparing the guns."*

Mention of the guns brought a pained expression to Milas' face. He seemed to get tangled up in his reply, his lips moving but no sound coming out. His face reddened. Finally, he shook his head and muttered, *"I thought teaching you a trade, to be a machinist, a gunsmith, a skilled hand in fixing anything that needed fixing, would be a benefit to you later in life. Give you something you could fall back on to make an honest living."* Milas swept the flakes of alfalfa from his trousers. *"I never thought it would lead you to doing something like this."*

"This could be our way out. We sell these guns and we'll never want for anything again. Neither will you."

His father laughed derisively. *"You think I need anything?"* He waved his hand around as if to showcase their surroundings. *"I've got the farm, haven't I? The* horses, the dogs. Plenty of firewood. An icebox full of food." He paused and chewed his lip. "But I won't have my boys. You'll be on the other side of the world again. And I'm worried sick that you doing this is going to rob me of you two forever. These guns were never meant to be in the hands of people on the streets, anyway. They're weapons of war. If the law doesn't get you, the people you're selling them to will. And I can't do anything to protect you."

"By that same token, these guns were never meant to be in the hands of children, conscripted by governments and sent away to fight in foreign lands to slake the greed of kings and emperors. But they were. Ours is a lesser evil."

"But an evil all the same."

Turning to face his father, hands on his hips, Niklas asked, "Then why are you helping us? You accepted these guns when they showed up on your doorstep, knowing full well what they were and what we intended to do with them. You stored them for us until we arrived. Then you fed us and put us up in your home for a year while we rebuilt them at your kitchen table. And now you tell me you don't want me to sell them?"

Milas gritted his teeth and looked away. "It's your life; I can't tell you what to do with it. I tried that before. As soon as you were grown you took your brother and ran away to America to live with your mother—God rest her soul." He stood slowly and gently placed a hand on Niklas' bare shoulder. His palm was rough, his grip firm. "Stay here with me. Forget America, forget about these guns. We'll drop them in the sea. Make structure for the fish. And there are dozens of beautiful young women who live not far from here, looking for a good husband like you or Kessler. You two could take over the farm, start families. Live a quiet life. Peaceful. Forget about what happened during the war."

Shrugging away from his father's touch, Niklas said, "No one forgets something like that."

"I just meant—"

"I know what you meant. You're content with what you have here. I'm happy for you. But this life suits you, not me. Don't ask me to abandon everything I've worked so hard for just to ease your conscience."

His father nodded sadly, staring out at the distant tree line. "As much as I don't want to push you away, I can't condone this. I don't know what happened to you in the war, what part of you got left behind, but the man I raised would never go through with this. Would never for a minute think this was acceptable."

Niklas sought his eyes, his jaw set. "The man you raised? When we left here to live with Mom we were still boys—just children. You can't fathom what we have seen and done since that day. Just to survive. And you know what I've learned that you never taught me? The world doesn't care about anyone's suffering, no matter how noble, no matter how decent a person they might be. So we can choose misery— do like you've done and scrape out a meager existence in some backwater town hoping to be lucky enough to avoid a cruel death—or we can choose to do something to protect ourselves. I've chosen the latter. These guns will guarantee our future. We'll have enough money to protect our family for generations."

"But at what cost?"

"Let that be my cross to bear, then."

"That's not how this works. You've made me and your brother complicit. If you go through with this, the blood is on all our hands."

"Then don't help us anymore." Niklas' voice took on a mocking tone. "Send us on our way back to America and sleep soundly at night knowing that your soul remains unsullied." He stormed off toward the house.

"Hey, are we calling it a day?" Kessler shouted from above, completely unaware of the argument that had just transpired below. He mopped at his brow with his balled-up shirt. "I'm starving."

Birch burns quickly

The Little Italy brothel case had troubled Detective Stauss for days, ever since he had spoken with the boys at the Dale Street Shops. There was no shortage of debauchery and sin in St. Paul; he knew that better than most. Much of it he was helpless to stop, assuming it had been sanctioned by the mayor's office. But the knowledge that children were being kidnapped off the streets and forced into sex slavery, in his city, kept him awake at night and made him impatient to take action. Theft of innocence and purity on that scale had to be stopped at any cost. He wasn't sure if he could bring such an establishment down. As yet he still didn't know who owned it or the political influence they might have. But that wouldn't stop him from trying. This one was worth going to the wall for. He didn't care if it cost him his career or his life.

He and Maya stood shoulder to shoulder before a jumble of irregular tenement houses in the Connemara Patch, buried in the marshy Mississippi lowlands. He had come here once before—years ago, at the height of the Spanish Flu pandemic. There, every face he encountered wore an expression of utter hopelessness, awash in sickness and poverty, yet bleakly accepting in a way, as though they understood there would never be a reprieve from their pain. No brighter future awaited them if they could just endure for another month or another year. They didn't cling to life so much as life clung to them, its sickly claws hanging on through some sheer primitive fortitude despite all of society and nature herself conspiring against them. A pall of infirmity and death had hung over this place then. He saw now that it had never really left, the memory seared into the very fabric of the neighborhood like a wine stain on a cheap tablecloth—blood red and indelible.

Maya slung her arm through the crook of his elbow and leaned against him for warmth. He had asked her to join him to help interview the madam of the Little Italy brothel. Long ago he had found that female suspects were often more communicative with a calming female presence like Maya to conduct the questioning.

"This the place?" she asked.

He consulted a slip of paper torn from his notepad and, without looking up, aimed a gloved finger at a primitive-looking building with asphalt shingles nailed to the walls for siding, the windows covered from inside with canvas and rough blankets to stem the loss of heat. "That one." Eager to be out of the cold, he made a beeline for the door and gave it an urgent knock. A young woman wearing several crude sweaters layered atop one another opened the door only slightly, half of her face hidden by shadow, the rest by the door itself. "Yes?"

"Is Miss—" he consulted his slip of paper again—"Alma Woolridge available?" He stamped his feet and rubbed his arms as another gust of cold air rushed by.

"She's not in today," the young woman said, slowly closing the door.

"Please. She's not in any trouble." Maya placed a mittened hand gently upon the door to keep it from closing.

The young woman chewed her lip for a moment, debating whether to believe them.

"There are young girls in danger," Maya whispered. "We need her help."

The woman behind the door seemed to contemplate that for a full minute. Then, with an accepting nod, she opened it fully. "Alma is upstairs. Second door on the right."

They thanked her and ascended. It wasn't much warmer inside. Connemara Patch, like many of the other poor communities in the city, lagged twenty years behind in technology and infrastructure. Indoor heat was still a matter of woodstoves and fireplaces, fed with coal if they were lucky, broken furniture and scavenged tree limbs if they weren't.

They knocked gently on the door. It swung open to reveal a middle-aged woman wrapped in blankets, her brown hair interspersed with gray strands as it hung down her back in a long braid. She looked them up and down, then sighed. "Police, right? Come inside. I knew you would be around sooner or later. It's a relief, really." She disappeared into the darkness of the room, the tiny apartment entirely cast in gloom save for the dim light spilling from a feeble fire inside a smoke-blackened fireplace. Laundry lines encumbered with women's garments traversed the shadows.

They followed her inside.

"Our apologies for intruding on your day off," Maya said.

"It's fine. Not doing anything on a day this cold anyway. Just drinking, trying to stay warm." Alma pointed listlessly toward a half-empty amber bottle on a chairside table. "Help yourselves. It's the only thing in here to drink that doesn't freeze when the fire dies down at night."

"No thank you. Neither of us imbibe," Maya said pleasantly. "May we sit, though?"

"Yes, of course. Where are my manners? Please do."

Maya and Stauss sat together on a threadbare loveseat, tufts of down coughing from the cushions as they lowered themselves.

Plucking a cigarette from a pocket-crushed cardboard pack on the mantel, Alma stooped toward the fire and ignited the tip with an ember.

Stauss, despite his heavy coat and many scarves, began to shiver.

Noticing his condition, Alma exhaled a cloud of smoke and cooed, "Oh you poor dear. I'm sorry it's so cold in here. I suppose I've gotten used to it after all this time. I'll put another log on."

"Please don't trouble yourself on my account. I'll endure," he said through chattering teeth, willing himself to stop trembling.

"It's no trouble. But I'm afraid most of what I have is birch. Burns quickly and doesn't keep the place warm for very long."

"Can you tell us what's been going on at your place of business?" Maya asked, unwrapping her scarf and tucking it around Stauss' shoulders. "'Little Italy' on St. Peter Street, right? Word has it that there may be some…unsavory things happening."

"Unsavory. That's a hell of a way to put it." Alma moved to a small stack of wood piled in the corner, picked through it to find a log to her liking, and fed it into the fire. She wiped her hands on her hips and took a long drag on her cigarette as the birch bark crackled and curled into flame. "Someone from out of town bought our brothel from the previous owner. They kept me on as madam of the house, but most of the other girls chose to go work for Nina Clifford down the street when they learned how much of their earnings the new owner planned to take. When I told him how few of my ladies would stay given the conditions he had set, he said it didn't matter. He would have them replaced in days." She puffed contemplatively at her cigarette and blew the smoke toward the fireplace. "He was true to his word. Pretty soon new girls begin showing up on our doorstep. Most of them weren't even teenagers yet. All of them were delivered by big, mean-looking men. The kind with dark souls, evil just leaching out of them like a rank cologne." She shook her head as if to clear it of an unpleasant image. "Most of the girls don't speak English and don't even understand what it is they're expected to do when they arrive. It's been…difficult. I can't protect them or help

them at all. Can't even explain it to them in a way they understand."
She leaned an elbow against the brick of the fireplace chimney and
rested her forehead in her palm.

"Can you tell me who this new owner is?"

She shook her head. "Some young buck from out of town. Very
suave. Handsome in a way, real snappy dresser, but with that same
darkness about him I was talking about—like a feral animal, almost.
As though the wrong word could set him off at any time and he
wouldn't stop until someone was dead." She paused, evaluated the
half-smoked cigarette between her fingers, and flung it with disgust
into the fireplace. "Rumor has it he's a big deal in Chicago."

Stauss cast a knowing look at Maya. "Do you happen to know his
name?" he asked, almost reluctant to hear the answer.

Alma tapped her chin thoughtfully. "It's hard to pronounce. I've
only heard it once. Something like barbed wire."

"Barbieri?" Maya asked.

Alma snapped her fingers. "That's it."

A long silence followed, broken only by the crackle of the fire and
the chatter of Detective Stauss' teeth. He began digging his
fingernails into the skin of his thumbs again.

An unceremonious end

E ven the rhythmic chuff of the lake freighter's enormous steam engine couldn't conceal the chatter of Kessler's teeth. The brothers stood on the ship's exposed observation deck, icy wind gusting in their faces. Rolling swells, twice the height of a man, crashed stubbornly against the ship's hull like a child beating inconsolably upon the floor in the throes of a tantrum. The lumbering ship rose and dipped, rolling and pitching sickeningly among the lead-gray waves. Along the distant horizon, the black shoreline of Anticosti Island loomed ominously. Few people lived on the craggy spit of land—only a few haggard lighthouse keepers and those who eked out a living harvesting timber or working at the island's fish cannery.

The brothers had spent a week aboard the lake freighter and both men needed a shower and a shave. The good news was, should they get stopped, the authorities wouldn't doubt for a second that they were genuinely part of the ship's crew. They certainly looked and smelled the part.

"I'm sick of this view," Kessler grumbled. His pipe bounced on his lips but he had long ago given up trying to keep it lit against the wind. "I'm sick of being cold."

"And six months from now you'll be complaining about the mosquitos and being too hot."

"Right now I would kill for a sunburn. Anything is better than this. And even the cold wouldn't be so bad if it weren't for the food. How is it possible that the meals they serve on this ship are worse than the rations we had in the trenches? I don't ever want to see herring or tuna fish again. When is this goddamn ship supposed to arrive?"

"Could be any minute, could be tomorrow. Depends on a lot of things. Go inside. Read a book or something."

"It feels colder inside. Got nothing to do or look at, so all I can focus on is being cold."

"You can stick with the complaining thing to pass the time."

"I just might." Kessler beat his shoulders with his gloved hands. Suddenly looking as though he had just remembered an additional point of criticism, he asked, "Why did we have to do this at night?"

"Couldn't risk being seen by the authorities. After all the planning that went into this, it would be pretty idiotic to get caught just because we were seen from shore. Like I always say: It's the smallest details that unravel the plan."

"Doing this in the middle of a winter storm that could capsize a ship seems like more than a small detail."

Sniffing and wiping at his running nose with the back of his glove, Niklas chuckled, "This is hardly a winter storm, little brother. Just a little inclement weather. You should be used to that by now."

Pacing across the observation deck, Kessler stopped and wheeled to face him, his frustration peaking. "It all just seems a little…overcautious. That's all. We have a legitimate ship and you've seen to it that we have documentation. Even if we get stopped, they've got nothing on us."

"They have nothing on us for the moment, but what if they intercept the *Johanna-Rose*? Or they board us after we've made the handoff? We only get one shot at this." Niklas looked back at the laker's funnel, huffing along steadily, belching smoke so black it could be seen against the overcast night sky. "The Great Lakes are a highway for contraband booze coming in from Canada. You remember Arnold Rothstein—the guy who fixed the World Series a few years back?—he's been running shipments through Lake Ontario and right down the Hudson into New York. Word has it the Mayfield Road Gang has a whole fleet of speedboats that cut across Lake Erie a dozen times a day, packed to the gills with Canadian whiskey. Trust me, prohibition agents are all over this place, and they're looking for anything suspicious. All it would take is a little bad timing and a boat full of armed cops to ruin everything we've worked for. And given our past luck, I don't think we should tempt fate any more than we have to."

Raising an eyebrow, Kessler asked, "How do you know so much about this stuff? Here I thought my big brother was such a nice guy. Innocent to the evil ways of man."

Niklas thumped his brother's shoulder with his palm. "Pays to learn from the mistakes of others, little brother. In case you hadn't noticed, we're criminals now, too. I'm just hoping we can be smarter criminals than most."

"Ship spotted off the port bow!" shouted the captain from the helm. Distantly, a single dim light bobbed atop the waves.

Grabbing his brother's arm, Niklas exclaimed, "There she is! One step closer." He hastened down the stairs to the deck, taking two at a time, then dashed forward until he had reached the laker's forecastle, as though moving fifty feet forward would somehow speed their arrival.

After an agonizing hour spent pacing the deck and straining to see if the *Johanna-Rose* had made any perceptible progress on its leisurely approach, the two vessels came abreast. The crews exchanged ropes and began binding the ships to one another as they rocked and dipped atop the increasingly turbulent waters. Niklas considered that perhaps Kessler had been right about the winter storm. But there was nothing that could be done about that now. If they waited, the weather could worsen. It might just endure for days. Their best bet was to get the guns unloaded quickly and get on their way back to Duluth.

He shouted greetings in Danish toward the crew of the *Johanna-Rose* but got little more than a few hurried nods in reply. Clearly the sailors, after the long transatlantic voyage, were eager to be rid of their illicit cargo and on their way home as soon as possible. He couldn't blame them.

The clatter of anchor chains sounded deafening even over the whistling gusts of wind biting at his exposed ears.

More of the laker's crew emerged from belowdecks, preparing to help transfer the cargo. A sailor from the *Johanna-Rose* approached and hefted a long wooden case across the bulwarks of the two ships. Niklas recognized the familiar black-stenciled words *tractor parts* and felt a warm glow in his chest, like being reunited with a lost keepsake. He lunged forward to grab it and bring it aboard. But just as his fingers wrapped around the rope handle, a deep rolling swell passed beneath the two ships, the crafts dipping downward and rolling apart. The crate slid free into the open space between the two ships and plunged toward the water below. Like being caught in the stirrups of a runaway horse, the weight heaved Niklas against the bulwark, his ribcage slamming painfully against the steel and robbing his breath. The weight and momentum of the crate dragged him over the side. Instinctively, he tore his hand away from the handle, letting the case fall into the sea as he scrambled frantically for a handhold. But his gloved hand couldn't find purchase on the icy bulwark.

No one was near enough to help him. He was going in.

His feet swung free in the open air. Only the ship pitching back the other way kept him from immediately plummeting to the water below, but the second it made its inevitable return, he would be gone.

A vision of him drowning flashed across his mind. First, he would strike the freezing water and the shock of the cold would make him take a sharp, involuntary gasp. Salty ocean water would flood into his nose and mouth, setting him sputtering. Beset with stifling paroxysms, each desperate, heaving breath would only bring with it more water. Then, his coat and heavy boots, reaching saturation, would pull him down like an anchor. The cold would make his muscles sluggish, and he would exhaust what little breath he had before he ever regained the surface. Assuming he wasn't crushed between the two ships' hulls as they rocked against each other. Regardless, it would all be over in seconds. An unceremonious and abrupt end to his life's journey, rewarded with an unmarked grave at the bottom of the ink-black abyss.

What of Kessler? Would he know what to do? Could he carry on with their plan alone, or would he lose hope? No doubt he would abandon the guns and accept a life of mediocrity in the perpetual employ of Uncle Ezra, reminiscing sorrowfully about his older brother, whose grandiose visions led him to an untimely death.

Just as the ship pitched downward again and his fingers began to slip, strong hands grabbed his wrists. Wedging his shoulder against the bulwark for leverage, Kessler struggled to drag his older brother back toward the deck. The soles of his boots slid against the slick hull. Reaching up, Niklas managed to gain a handhold and crawl back to safety. Shoulder to shoulder, the brothers sat back from the edge of the rocking ship trying to catch their breath. Their crewmates looked at them for a second with surprised expressions, then quietly resumed their work, if a little more cautiously. Glancing over the railing at the dark water below as if expecting to see the wood crate bobbing amidst the icy waves, Niklas asked his brother in Danish, "Which model was that?"

Kessler mumbled, "One of the Lewis guns, I think."

Shaking his head in disappointment, he said, "That's a damn shame. Made it from a factory in the U.S. to France, to Denmark, and almost back to the U.S. again before one unlucky wave sent it to the bottom of the drink." He sighed, slapped his knees, and stood, pulling his brother to his feet. "Looks like another life debt added to your side of the scale."

Kessler patted his back reassuringly. "Knowing our luck, you'll have that balanced out in no time. Come on. Let's finish up with this and head home. I'm sick of being on the water. Starting to think Oscar's a lot smarter than we give him credit for, all that nonsense about getting seasick."

Wendigo warning

Their return journey through the Great Lakes passed in a blur of routine sameness, the boulder-strewn shoreline and snow-laced evergreens scrolling by endlessly on the horizon. Despite the serenity of their surroundings, a foreboding pall hung upon them and seemed to increase in weight with each passing hour. A gnawing pinch in the gut, knowing that, belowdecks, stuffed in a corner beneath a patchwork of canvas tarpaulins stained black with iron ore dust, behind stacks of canned pickled herring, sat the key to their future—or the instrument of their demise should they be discovered. Even the ship puttering into Duluth Harbor and the sight of Oscar waiting beside a pair of White delivery trucks on the shore didn't deliver the sense of assurance they craved.

Once the ship had been bound to the pier, tethered tightly with heavy, braided hawsers, Oscar boarded. He greeted the brothers with a hug, though he made a pinched face as he pulled away, waving a hand in front of his nose. "You two need to bathe. You smell like the north end of a southbound horse."

"We don't smell that bad. It's just that you've been enjoying the company of perfumed women all week," Niklas insisted.

"We all have our crosses to bear," Oscar sighed.

The crew set to work dragging the gun crates from their hiding place belowdecks onto a net of course manila rope sprawled limply across the deck.

"Tractor parts, eh?" one of the sailors scoffed as he dropped another crate into place. "Tractor parts my ass. Admit it: You've got booze in here, don't you? Something fancy from overseas, like Scotch or cognac." He pronounced it 'cog-knack.'

"Not booze," Kessler grunted, hefting a crate into place alongside the others.

"Then why the secrecy?"

"That's precisely the kind of question we paid you not to ask," Niklas replied, beating his gloved hands against his thighs to get the blood moving, but never slowing as he moved to grab another crate. The sooner they could get on the road, the better. Here, they were exposed. One curious port authority inspector could ruin them. "But don't worry, you can keep the pickled herring. Our gift to you."

Adjusting his watch cap to cover his ears, the first mate said, "Well if it's so important to keep this a secret, it only seems fair to pay us a little extra to stay quiet."

"Yeah, and throw in some of that high-brow hooch, too," added another sailor.

"We told you: It's not hooch. The least you can do is be a little more imaginative," Niklas said, not pausing in his work. "You know, maybe it's stolen German gold bullion from the war."

The first mate spat toward the side of the ship but didn't quite make it overboard. "Boxes aren't heavy enough."

"Maybe it's French underwear," Kessler added playfully, stacking another crate.

"Boxes are too heavy for that."

"Depends on the kind of underwear, doesn't it?" Oscar asked.

One of the sailors retrieved a pry bar from a tool chest nearby. "We can find out right now."

Intercepting him on his way toward the crates, Oscar planted a hand on the sailor's chest and shook his head. "Going back on your word is very bad. If you do not follow through with a deal you agreed on, there will be consequences."

"Are you threatening me?"

"Me? No. But if open those boxes, you will be damned to become a wendigo."

"What's this wagon-burner on about?" the sailor asked, looking at his crewmates as he slapped the pry bar against his open palm. "The hell is a wendigo?"

Oscar ignored the insult, no stranger to disparaging slurs. "In the Ojibwe tribe, when someone commits a grave sin, they are punished by the spirits. They become possessed by a terrible beast—the wendigo. It is a hideous thing. Tall as a telephone pole and gaunt, its bones pushing against skin the color of ash—the color of death. Smelling like death, too. Almost as bad as *they* smell," he said, pointing at Niklas and Kessler. They rolled their eyes and snorted. Oscar continued, face drawn in disgust, as though the telling of the story alone had put a bad taste in his mouth. "Its eye sockets are empty, like a months-old corpse picked at by the crows. Wandering the darkness of the woods alone for eternity, hungering for human flesh. Starving, never full, never satisfied. Preying on anyone alone in the woods at night. What's left of your humanity is frozen inside the monster's heart, and the only way you will ever be at peace again is if someone puts a knife through it."

The crew stood dumbfounded as he concluded his story.

"Is it really worth becoming a wendigo for a box of women's underwear?" Oscar asked plainly.

The sailor returned the pry bar to the toolbox and the rest of the men grumbled as they continued loading the crates atop the net.

A few minutes later, once they had moved away from the crew, Kessler whispered to Oscar, "Was any of that true?"

Oscar smirked and shook his head. "Given all the evil we saw in France, if the myths were true, there would be more wendigos than men walking the earth."

Roll the dice on the gallows

Niklas felt punch-drunk with exhaustion. He hadn't slept worth a damn the entire journey across the Great Lakes, constantly on the bridge, on the lookout for the slightest shimmer of moonlight on a ship's bow or the mutter of an approaching police boat's engine. The stress and anticipation of the trip, paired with the sudden wave of relief at finally having the guns back in his possession and being on the road to St. Paul, made for a powerful knockout cocktail. The Duesenberg's tires hummed a soothing bass note as they rolled atop the winding highway, frozen gravel pinging off the fender walls as the car led the small convoy of trucks driven by Kessler and Oscar.

Each blink became longer as Niklas resisted the siren call of sleep. A few times he flinched, suddenly alert as shadowy figures appeared at the periphery of his headlights only to vanish as his eyes sought them. His fatigued mind playing tricks. Oscar's story of the wendigo clung to his thoughts. The prudent move would be to pull over and nap for fifteen minutes, but he couldn't risk them being exposed for that long. They needed to get these guns back to St. Paul and hidden. He could sleep as long as he needed, then, he promised himself. Don't lose sight of the objective. Don't get careless in the final stretch.

He reached for the cup of lukewarm coffee he had bought before they left Duluth, sipping it sparingly, rationing it for the long drive ahead. It was mercifully strong, the amaroidal brew poorly strained of its grounds before being dumped in his cup.

As the car crested the next hill, more figures appeared, but these ones didn't vanish as he neared. A searchlight clicked on, illuminating the icy road and half a dozen policemen milling alongside their vehicles, parked sideways across the highway. Terror swelled inside his belly, crawling up his spine and embedding in his brainstem.

He glanced in his rearview mirror at the trucks behind him. Kessler was the first to follow, then Oscar. If only there was some way to signal them, to get them to stop and reroute before it was too late. But a hopeless realization dawned on him: They were already trapped in a funnel leading to their inevitable arrest.

Bribery. Maybe they could buy their way out of this. He felt for his wallet. How much money did he have left? Not much anymore, he realized. Bribing the laker's crew and that of the *Johanna-Rose* hadn't been cheap. The little bit he had left would never be enough to convince an entire crew of policemen to ignore an arsenal of heavy machine guns. They would have had better luck with booze—they could have offered that instead of money.

That didn't leave many choices, he realized. Swallowing hard, Niklas transferred the Steyr in his shoulder holster to the pocket of his coat, his thumb anxiously stroking the walnut grips as he counted the policemen, coldly weighing the mathematical probabilities of who would win a gunfight. He would have the element of surprise. He could take a couple of them with the Steyr before they could react. But he wouldn't be able to get them all, even if Kessler and Oscar joined in the fray. He wished he had taken the time to unpack and ready at least one of the light machine guns.

Are you really prepared to kill innocent men for this? he thought as he eased the car to a stop before the checkpoint. The uniforms leisurely approached, strolling alongside the convoy, wanding their electric torches up and down the trucks. *But are you really willing to give up everything you've worked for? Just go out with a whimper and let them haul you and your family away? Destroy the guns you've spent years and every dime you had to smuggle halfway around the world?* He forced himself to take a deep breath, a grim resolve taking shape. In for an inch, in for a mile. If a lifetime in prison awaited him already, he might as well roll the dice on the gallows.

A pair of heavy boots crunched the gravel and snow beside the car. One of the policemen, a portly fellow with a protuberant hammock of skin drooping from his chin to the collar of his coat, stopped beside Niklas and thumped the door with the heel of his mittened hand. Niklas slid open the window.

"Easy on the bodywork, pal," he said, trying to mask his panic with a disgruntled attitude.

The cop shot him a sour look. "Sorry to stop you." A hazy cloud of vapor escaped his lips as he spoke. "We're checking everyone who comes this way today. You wouldn't believe the number of bootleggers running trucks of Canadian hooch from Duluth to the cities lately. What are you boys hauling? Don't suppose you've got a couple of tons of 'kerosene' or 'castor oil' back there, do you?" He smirked.

"Just tractor parts for a steam shovel at one of my uncle's mines."

The policeman gestured for documentation. "Who is your uncle?"

"Ezra Abecassis." Niklas flipped open the license holder on the steering column and withdrew the bundle of documents, handing them to the officer. The policeman scanned the paperwork with his flashlight.

"Abecassis Steel?"

"That's the one."

"This his car?" he asked, scanning the vehicle with renewed interest.

"It's a beauty, isn't it? He's gonna be furious when he learns I'm driving it instead of one of those old beaters behind me."

The policeman chuckled. "I'm sure he could buy a whole fleet of these. Everyone knows the name Abecassis Steel around here. Big money. You're a lucky guy to have family with that kind of dough." He handed the documents back to Niklas.

He relaxed a little. "You might be surprised. He didn't get rich by being generous."

The policeman didn't seem to find that remark particularly funny. In fact, he suddenly appeared dubious. "Olson," he shouted to one of the policemen now examining the bed of Kessler's truck, "What do they have?"

The pressure in Niklas' chest grew again. Given the darkness, he couldn't see his brother's expression through the truck windshield, but he knew it was one of panic and desperation. Just like his.

"Buncha wooden crates that say 'tractor parts,'" Olson called back. "They're certainly heavy enough to be."

The officer standing beside Niklas turned to him with a grim expression. "Now, if you were delivering tractor parts to the mines, why are you heading back toward the cities with them?" he asked as though he already knew the answer.

Niklas's gut shriveled. He licked his lips and scrambled for a convincing lie, but his brain felt like it was swimming through a thick soup, each neuron paddling frantically but traveling at half speed. The safety came off the Steyr.

Then it came to him. He leaned out the window and said, "Uncle Ezra can't have any mine inoperative a minute longer than absolutely necessary, so he sent the three of us all the way up from St. Paul to fix that steam shovel. The morons at the mine couldn't figure out what was wrong with it—just stopped working all of a sudden—so we loaded up the trucks with every replacement part we could scrounge. I figured it was a cracked boiler. Turns out one of the new guys just opened the wrong valve. Five minutes after we got there we had it running again. Waste of two days of driving just because Uncle Ezra is too cheap to hire decent help."

The policeman considered that answer for a while before replying, "Not so bad in a ride like this, though, eh?" He patted the roof. "Safe travels." Whistling through his teeth, he twirled a finger in the air to signal his comrades to let them pass. Niklas leaned back in his seat and let out a breath that felt as stale as if he had held it in for an hour. Easing the car into gear, he pulled forward, eyes fixed on his rearview mirror. When the truck headlights began moving, too, he felt so relieved he could have cried.

No need for coffee now. He was wide awake.

Murderers they are not

Unlike the other detectives in the department, Stauss preferred not to go around shoving his badge in everyone's face or announcing his title like a prizefighter entering the ring. Doing so was polarizing. People either began cooperating once they learned he was a detective or they became even more recalcitrant. Besides, walking around as a civilian came with certain benefits: He got to see the most honest version of the people with whom he interacted. Who they were when they didn't care who he was. Honest. He liked honesty. Even when it was ugly.

The woman at the front desk of Ezra Abecassis' offices did not care who he was, and hers was the kind of ugly honesty that began by condescendingly telling him go fry a stale egg—no, Mister Abecassis would not be seeing him today—and finished with threats to have him forcibly removed from the premises. A crowd formed as office workers left their desks to get a better look at the spectacle. A rather large security guard with a hungry look about him stomped forward and grabbed Stauss' shoulder, spinning him around violently, away from the receptionist's desk. He quickly relaxed his grip as Stauss buried the barrel of his Smith & Wesson in the big man's groin. Slowly opening the lapel of his coat to reveal his buzzer, Stauss angled it so the others nearby could see it, too. A few grudging apologies were made and he was shown to a small antechamber outside Abecassis' office.

He took a seat and settled in. Powerful people, even those with an abundance of available time, made a habit of forcing guests—especially a police detective who hadn't made an appointment—to wait a good long while before they made an appearance. It was a subtle display of power. A way to showcase their own self-importance contrasted with the triviality of their guest's existence.

Stauss was nearly done reading a compelling argument in *Woman's Home Companion* about preventing mental fatigue in growing children with an ample breakfast of Cream of Wheat when Abecassis toed open his office door. Without looking up from the ledger in his hands, he ordered, "Come."

He was shorter than Stauss had expected, though he didn't really know why he was surprised. Where was it written that a man had to be a towering specimen to succeed in business?

Achingly rising from his seat, Stauss tipped his fedora and entered the office. Bookcases filled with matching red leather-bound tomes lined one side of the room. Opposite those, a row of sturdy-looking white oak filing cabinets stood behind a broad desk. The room's back wall featured two large radius windows painted with a magnificent view of the Mississippi River.

"Take a seat," Abecassis grumbled, pointing toward an uncomfortable-looking low-back wooden chair seated before his desk.

"Thanks, but I'll stand if you don't mind." He leaned against the chair with his hip, his hand resting on his lower back, fingers massaging the perpetually aggravated tissue. "My apologies for not making an appointment before calling on you. Your assistant made it abundantly clear that next time I should call ahead."

"Yeah, we're certainly busy. Tough to accommodate random guests. Even those with a reputation like yours."

"Oh? I had no idea I was so well known."

"I pride myself on knowing a great deal about the people in this city. Someday I'm going to run it. When I do, I'll need good people behind me. But more importantly, I'll need to know who might try to stand in my way."

"Am I to assume I'm among those in your way?" Stauss asked innocently.

Abecassis ran the tip of his tongue over his lips as they curled into something resembling a sneer. "You're one of those temperance types. Beating the Prohibition drum to save your countrymen from the evils of the devil's drink," he mocked. "It's naive. Childish, really. A sentiment born in sewing rooms and country church pews. Now, I don't generally imbibe—dulls the senses and robs a man of his initiative—but I'm no fool. I look around and see that everyone in this city—hell, this whole country—wants it. Will kill and die for it. Even the poorest are distilling and brewing by the gallon in their kitchen sinks. And here you are, running around poking fingers in a leaking dam holding back a sea of bathtub gin and raisin cake wine."

"Such is my lot in life, I'm afraid," Stauss said airily, not wanting to debate his position on Prohibition or inadvertently sabotage his opportunity to speak with Abecassis about the Kristofferson brothers. "But as much as I would love to discuss politics with you, I'm actually here to discuss your nephews."

He needed to navigate this carefully. The detective reasoned that the steel magnate stood to gain very little by participating in the Kristofferson brothers' gun smuggling. An operation such as theirs, concerning as it might be to Stauss, could hardly tempt a man with Abecassis' considerable wealth. But if he was in any way complicit in his nephew's activities, or simply protective of their wellbeing, he might go to great lengths to force Stauss off their trail. He was a man with limitless resources, one who could make a very powerful enemy.

"Oh joy," Abecassis said flatly. "What have those two imbeciles gotten themselves into now?"

His visceral disdain at the mere mention of his nephews made Stauss pause. Maybe he really didn't know what they had been up to.

"Quite some trouble if things don't change quickly, I'm afraid. I'll be direct with you, as you seem the sort who appreciates candor. I believe they have acquired machine guns from their time in the military and have smuggled them here with intent to sell them to mobsters."

Abecassis didn't blink, his expression stoic, but he did slowly close the ledger in his hands and dropped it gingerly atop his desk. "That so?"

"Their arrest a couple of weeks ago—the body they were carrying? Riddled with bullet holes."

"That could have been any mobster with a Tommy gun."

"Our coroner says they were caused by a high-powered rifle, not a submachine gun. Given their roles as gunsmiths during the war, I believe your nephews had the access and opportunity to acquire weapons capable of such damage."

"You don't mean to say you think they killed him, do you? I mean, they are a disappointment in many ways, but murderers they are not."

Shaking his head gently, Stauss said, "No, I don't believe they did. But the murdered man had ties to organized crime. The sort of criminal syndicate that might be interested in buying machine guns. You can see where the makings of a grander scheme begin to unfold."

Abecassis looked confused. "Why are you telling me all this?"

"I was hoping you could help convince them not to go ahead with the sale of these guns."

"Assuming they haven't already," Abecassis said.

"Yes, assuming that hasn't already happened."

The man was inscrutable. Clearly Abecassis was processing their conversation, but Stauss could not read any emotion at all. He must have been an incredible poker player. Perhaps a different approach, one focused on how this might affect him personally, would have better results. "Mister Abecassis, if they proceed with this, even if they don't get arrested, word will get out. Having a couple of criminals in the family could spoil your reputation as a venerated member of the community and may even threaten your legitimate business operations simply by way of your relation."

"Yes, I can imagine," he said. "Thanks for letting me know about this. As soon as they're back in the office, I'll speak to them and try to dissuade them from doing anything we would all regret."

"Back in the office?"

"They're taking personal time for a family matter, apparently."

His forehead wrinkling in doubt, Stauss drew a card from his pocket. Holding it between two fingers, he angled it toward Abecassis. "In case you need to reach me." He turned to leave, then paused. "If it's not too much trouble, can I ask you one final question simply to sate my curiosity?"

Accepting the card and tossing it on the desk before him, Abecassis gave a subtle tilt of his chin as if to say, "Go on."

"Why did you bail them out of prison if you dislike them so much? You strike me as the tough-love type who would leave them in there to learn a lesson."

The businessman smirked at that. "Detective, have you ever had a pet?"

"Sure. A few over the years."

"Ever had a really lousy one? The kind that makes you regret bringing it home? A dog that shits in your slippers or a horse that bites and keeps pulling up lame? Does it so often you start to think it's doing it on purpose. One of those?"

"Can't say I have."

"Well as much as they may try you, you can't just take them out back and shoot them. The neighbors would talk and your kids would never forgive you. So you suffer them out of some high-minded sense of loyalty or mercy. That's me and my nephews. They are the disappointing offspring of my dear departed sister, Anna— who was a fucking saint, by the way—and that Danish hayseed, Milas. They show up as useless teenagers, hands out, looking for a job and naturalization papers. I did what I could for them because my sister insisted. Then, fools as they were and still are, they run off and enlist as soon as the war kicks off. Right at the time I could have used them most. Had a business to build. Competitors to bring down. They could have been my right and left hands had they shown a little initiative. But off they go, marching straight back to Europe after trying so hard to get away from it." He shook his head with apparent disgust. "I'm convinced that's what killed her. Anna died from worrying they would catch a bullet over there or end up disfigured—come back missing pieces. Instead, the war ends and, lo and behold, once again, they show up at my doorstep like stray dogs looking for a meal. Once again, hands out, looking for work. And what do I do? Like a sentimental fool, I give it to them. They've been nothing but a burden to me from the beginning." He looked Stauss in the eye, his expression tired. "From everything you've told me today, it looks like that's not about to change."

There was nothing left to ask of him. If Abecassis was lying about his relationship with the Kristofferson brothers, he was damn good at it and would only continue to lie if asked more questions.

"Mind if I look around a bit before I head out? I assume your nephews have a workspace here."

"Downstairs. Feel free. Just leave everything where you found it."

Stauss touched his temple and gave an appreciative two-finger salute before heading out the door and down the stairs.

He made his way through seemingly endless rows of desks and closed-door offices. Typewriters clacked and papers shuffled, but not a single conversation could be heard. Singling out a young man hunched over a desk, muttering to himself as he read through a stack of documents, Stauss asked if he knew where to find Niklas' workspace. The man never looked up from his paperwork, but pointed toward a far corner.

The desk was pin-neat, everything tidily organized and in its proper place. No surprise given what he had learned of Niklas' attention to detail. Sliding open a drawer, he withdrew a stack of papers—copies of sailing schedules and ship manifests. Thumbing through them, he settled on one that caught his attention. It had been handled more than the others, the edges of the paper rolled and softened with repeated use. The text appeared more meticulously written than on the other documents, each pen stroke deliberate and clean. The page indicated that one of Abecassis Steel's lake freighters was scheduled for repair at the Superior Shipbuilding Company across the bay in Superior, Wisconsin. One of the laker's two steam turbines had begun behaving erratically. The ship would be taken out of service for several weeks. He scrutinized every detail of the page but found it unremarkable in any respect. No doubt such work occurred frequently when maintaining a fleet of cargo ships.

Stauss spread the other documents across the desktop and evaluated them closely until he found one detailing the maintenance history of several ships in the fleet, including the one Niklas had scheduled for the turbine repair. The laker had been in for the same repair only six months before. Hardly definitive proof of anything, but suspicious nonetheless. He puzzled on that for a moment, weighing the likelihood of an identical repair being required so soon after the first.

Suddenly, it struck him with glaring patency: a scenario where all the pieces suddenly fit neatly together. An explanation for why Stauss hadn't found any guns at the Kristoffersons' apartment. Why the brothers had disappeared so suddenly and stayed missing for weeks.

They didn't have them yet. At least, not all of them.

The brothers had fabricated a maintenance order for one of their uncle's ships and contrived an excuse to leave work for a protracted time. They would use that ship to retrieve their guns, likely from somewhere closer to the battlefields from which they came. Perhaps they would meet another ship somewhere off the coast. He looked at the date the laker was to be taken offline.

Two weeks ago. He cursed under his breath; he was too late. By now the Kristoffersons were no doubt already back in St. Paul with the guns. Niklas was no fool: He would have identified discreet places to store them. They were one step closer to putting those weapons in Barbieri's hands.

Stauss groaned, sweeping the documents into a messy pile and dumping them back into the drawer where he had found them. Slowly, he trudged his way back through the maze of desks, into the lobby, past the angry receptionist and the hungry security guard, into the welcoming anonymity of the city.

A passing familiarity

O scar had done his homework. True to his word, he had found several locations throughout St. Paul at which they could discreetly stow the guns without fear of them being discovered. One was an awning shop owned by a kindly older couple who were always willing to stitch up Oscar's greatcoat for free whenever it got a new tear or lost a button. Another was a dry cleaner with a particularly big basement, run by an elderly blind woman who was one of Oscar's best customers for gin. The third location was truly impressive: the Wabasha Street Speakeasy, the gateway to an elaborate cave network burrowed throughout the soft sandstone bluffs along the Mississippi. It had once been an old silica mine before becoming a mushroom farm, and finally, a blind tiger.

Inside, the walls that hadn't been covered in decorative tile bore old scars from pickaxes and chisels. Spilled drinks and muddy shoes had discolored the floors, while drunken shootouts and negligent discharges from intoxicated patrons had scarred the twenty-foot-high cave ceiling.

The house band began warming up in preparation for the evening crowd, an ebullient melange of scales and freeform solos, fingers flitting effortlessly over keys and tone holes. Oscar and Niklas crossed the empty hardwood dance floor—covered in a dusting of loose sand despite persistent efforts to sweep it clean—toward a bar that seemed to stretch on for fifty feet. They had left Kessler circling the block with the truck containing the last of their guns.

"Bartender's name is Bill Layman," Oscar said under his breath as they approached. "Owns this place with his wife, Josie. I had hoped she would be here. She likes me more than he does."

"I thought you had already gotten their approval to move the guns here," Niklas said, an edge of panic in his voice.

"Calm down, comrade. We talked about it. They seemed fine with it."

"Seemed? Oscar, where are we going to put the last load if they won't take them? Under our mattresses?"

"You worry too much, my friend. Bad for your heart."

Overhead, a fan spun lazily, nudging clouds of cigarette smoke around the caves. The air inside was cool and damp, but still a welcome reprieve from the wind and ice outside.

"Bill, we're here with that product I spoke to you about," Oscar shouted across the bar.

The bartender, lit cigarette bouncing beneath his black, toothbrush-style mustache, didn't look up from wiping dry the glasses he had lined up behind the bar. "We never did get around to the details of that, Oscar," he said. "Might I ask what this product is?"

"Afraid not," Niklas said.

Pausing his work to raise an eyebrow at the newcomer with the abrupt manners, the bartender snorted. "I figured you might say that. You fellows have a lot of faith that I won't just go take a gander as soon as you leave."

"Let's just say that you not knowing what we intend to store here may prove a great deal safer for you than if you did know."

Although Niklas didn't want to scare him out of accepting the guns, he also didn't want him to be careless with them, mistakenly thinking they were something harmless.

"You realize where you are? This ain't exactly a church." Bill pointed toward a distant corner of the cavern where a crowd jostled around the entrance to a small offshoot filled with roulette tables and slot machines. "We have more than a passing familiarity with illegal things."

"Trust me when I tell you that you do not have the slightest familiarity with what we intend to store here."

Bill took the hint. "How long do you need to keep…whatever it is…here?"

"A few weeks. Maybe more. Just depends on how hot the market is."

"If whatever you're selling is anything like booze, it will be sold faster than you can resupply it."

A young woman with a shingle haircut and a fur coat sashayed up to the bar, flipped open her coat, and unslung a flask the size of a snapping turtle she had concealed at her waist. "Fill her up, Billy Boy."

"What is your poison today?"

"Gimme some of that sweet gin, honey." She looked at Niklas and winked, bouncing her shoulder toward him playfully. "Hello, handsome. What are you up to later tonight?"

He kept his eyes on the mirror behind the bar. "You wouldn't believe me if I told you."

Licking her lips seductively, she said, "Come whisper it in my ear and I'll believe just about anything."

"I don't doubt that." Turning his back to her, Niklas leaned in so only Oscar could hear him. "I'm not sure I like this place for the guns. Too many people casually coming and going. All it would take is one amorous couple wandering off into the caves looking for some privacy"—a pair of children sprinted by, playing a game of tag—"or some kid to come across our gear. Word gets out, the rifles will be gone faster than we can move them somewhere new."

Patting his chest encouragingly, Oscar said, "These caves go on for miles through the bluffs. Bill will guide us to a spot where no one will find them, and even if they did, they couldn't get them out of here without him knowing about it."

Satisfied with Oscar's assurance, Niklas wrapped the bartop with his knuckles to get the attention of the proprietor again. "So do we have an arrangement?"

Bill waggled his cigarette at them as he moved down the bar to tap a fresh keg of Hamm's beer. "Not quite. We haven't talked about the most important part: What do we get in return?"

That was the part Niklas had been worried about. Until now, everyone had seemed satisfied with simply helping Oscar out. No payment necessary. At best, Niklas could only offer payment after Barbieri had paid them for the first load of guns, but Bill would have to trust Oscar enough to oblige. Niklas opened his mouth to speak but Oscar cut him off. "You get free whiskey and gin from me for as long as their stuff is kept here. A case of each every week."

With a surprised laugh, Bill shouted, "Well in that case, you can keep your stuff here as long as you like. In fact"—he swiped a bottle of whiskey off the wall and uncorked it, sloshing booze across a row of shot glasses—"let's have a drink to celebrate."

He whom the gods love

He found Uncle Ezra in a far corner of the St. Paul Athletic Club's gymnasium, sheathed in sweat, aggressively churning the oars of a crude rowing machine. He had a steady, resolved look in his eyes, forcefully inhaling in time with each heave.

Niklas tucked his coat in the crook of his arm and slipped his hat from his head. "Preparing for bathing suit season already?" he asked, waving his cap to fan away the heat and the musty stench of sweat.

"Beats what those fools are doing," he said between clenched teeth, nodding toward a row of portly men, their entire frames jiggling as they leaned against vibrating slimming belts.

"Not a believer in the miracle of modern technology?" Niklas asked sarcastically, resting a shoulder against a tall mirror on the wall.

Satisfied with his workout, Ezra released the oars on the machine and stood, wiping his face with a towel. "Nothing worth having ever came easy. Everyone these days is looking for rewards without hard work, but there is no substitute."

Typical Ezra. Always moralizing with the air of someone who could not believe the indolence of every other human being when contrasted with his own industriousness.

Sizing him up, Ezra said, "You know, you could become an athlete if you trained at it. Maybe boxing. You've got the right build. Well balanced. Good musculature—nice and lean."

"If I wanted to get paid for someone to hurt me, I would reenlist," Niklas deadpanned. "I could never afford a membership here, anyway."

"You don't need a gymnasium like this. Hell, I used to go for runs outside three times a week, all winter long. Just buy some barbells. A heavy bag. Do more manual labor."

That was rich coming from a man who had a full-time gardener and a staff of housekeepers.

He gestured for Niklas to follow him as he passed into a nearby locker room. Peeking into the shower stalls and alcoves to ensure they were alone, he returned to his locker and began peeling off his shirt and shorts.

Niklas turned his back to give him privacy and began husking the foil from a new pack of Clove gum.

"How's the family?" Niklas asked, if only to make small talk and fill the silence. His uncle had married a woman half his age and had a couple of young children at home he seldom saw or spoke about. Niklas had only met them once or twice and Ezra hadn't introduced them to him by name. Probably thought it better if they didn't know him.

"They're fine," Ezra said dismissively. "Healthy. Speaking of which, how's Milas? I understand you boys took a few weeks off to visit him. Must be in poor health to warrant a trip home."

"He's on the mend now. Thought we might lose him, but he pulled through," Niklas lied.

147

"He whom the gods love dies young, as the Greeks said. So your father's likely to live forever."

"He sends his regards," Niklas lied again. He found deceiving his uncle came remarkably easy considering he didn't make a habit of prevarication.

Ezra snorted. "No he doesn't. That man couldn't muster a kind word for me if you had a gun to his head."

"Can you blame him?"

"Not entirely." A shower hissed, a cloud of steam rising from the floor and filling the locker room. A long pause followed—long enough to make Niklas wonder if his uncle had invited him to follow him for a reason. "So you're selling guns now, eh?"

Bile rose in Niklas' throat and he felt his cheeks flush. "Where did you hear that?"

"I hear things. I have connections in this city who hear things, too." His voice softened. "The more I know of the truth, the more I can protect you."

That line betrayed him and instantly proved to Niklas his uncle's concern was an act. He wanted to know more about what they were up to for one of two reasons: so he could blackmail them into doing something for him, or so he could step in for a cut of the money.

"The less you know of the truth, the safer you'll be," Niklas replied. He was getting tired of having to tell people that.

"I just don't understand why you would waste your time importing old military hardware into the U.S. You can buy a gun from a Sears catalog, for Christ's sake. You should focus your attention on England and her colonies. Ireland, for instance. They have new gun laws and all manner of civil unrest. The Fenians are giving the Brits hell. It's the perfect market for even the most pedestrian firearms. Mucher higher returns, I'd bet."

He had probably read a newspaper article or two about the Irish rebellion and now believed he understood positively everything there was to know about the situation there and how best to exploit it. What he clearly didn't grasp was how hopelessly unfeasible trafficking guns into Ireland would be. They knew no one in the country's provisional government, the Irish Republican Army, or the Irish Republican Brotherhood. Even assuming they did, they would have to first identify a buyer, then smuggle the guns past the British Navy and port security, then hope the sale went to plan. It was difficult enough trying to sell the damn things in their own backyard. Niklas tried to conceal an insolent smirk. "How about you just worry about your business and leave us to ours?"

Ezra finished showering, wrapped a towel around his waist, and stepped out. "As long as you're working for me, your business *is* my business." Drying himself, he grabbed a bottle of cologne from his locker and applied a generous dab to his wrists and neck. "You should tread carefully. If you get caught, it'll be curtains for both of you. Nothing I'll be able to do to stop it. Not only are you empowering mobsters, you're doing so with goods stolen from Uncle Sam."

Empowering mobsters. Ezra had been chatting with Detective Stauss. The phrasing even belonged to the detective. He mustered a thin smile. "Well we would be far from the first to make money on the war. Wouldn't you agree, Uncle?"

That retort stung. Ezra pretended he hadn't heard him, but the glint in his eyes and the muscles writhing like embattled snakes on his jaw said otherwise. He had gone from a moderately successful local businessman who owned a small iron ore mining operation on the Mesabi range to one of the Midwest's most powerful magnates entirely because of the war. He had lobbied the War Industries Board and ended up serving on several influential war service committees whose job it was to direct each industry during wartime. With the government needing iron for everything from ship hulls to gun barrels, it didn't take much persuasion for them to buy every ounce his company could mine while paving the way for him to expand his operations. The sudden influx of capital, courtesy of the American taxpayer, enabled him to grow his business multifold. His mining, refining, and freight operations flourished. Within a few short years he had managed to drive out or buy up most of his competition.

"You do what you feel is best," he finally said. The towel dropped from his waist and piled around his ankles. Drawing out his suit from his locker and returning the hanger, he began dressing. "I didn't ask you here to talk about that, anyway. It's time for you and your brother to reciprocate the kindness I showed you when I bailed your asses out of prison."

"So soon?"

"I would have rather kept that ace in my hand a little longer, too. But needs must. I have found myself in need of a blunt instrument. And you two fit that profile nicely."

"You make me blush, Uncle."

"Listen closely: I'm hosting a gathering at my home tomorrow evening. Numerous members of the city council will be in attendance. Mayor Nelson himself is rumored to be stopping by. This is an excellent opportunity for me to ingratiate myself with them."

"Let me guess: You want Kessler and me to wear tuxedos and walk around with silver trays of hors d'oeuvres and champagne flutes? I'll need an advance for a haircut and shave."

"Not quite. One of the older gentlemen on the council has announced he will not seek reelection. He's leaving behind a very desirable position. One that belongs to me. Unfortunately, there's competition. My opposition is one Doctor Goldmann. He's very influential in the city. Pediatrician. Known for his philanthropy. Very wealthy."

"Sounds like a nice guy."

"He's a repugnant shitstain who has made most of his money writing 'prescriptions' for whiskey and gin. And that wouldn't bother me except that he's trying to wheedle his way onto the council and take the spot that belongs to me."

"You make it sound like the council decides its own members. Aren't these elected positions?"

Ezra shook his head benevolently, like a professor with a slow student. "Voting is a formality. We both have the money to easily influence the district to vote for us. There will be a gentleman's agreement in place before election season that only one of us will run. Who that will be is ultimately decided by the council."

"And how do Kessler and I factor into this?"

"Doctor Goldmann intends to join us at tomorrow night's event." Ezra seemed to recognize the confusion on Niklas' face at the notion of the doctor being invited to Ezra's home. "It's an obligatory invitation," he explained. "One he's sure to take advantage of, the bastard. But he is not to arrive. That's where you two come in."

"And how do you propose we keep him from arriving?"

"You seem to have developed a mind for criminality. Get creative."

"Just so I'm clear: You're asking me to assault an upstanding member of the community just so you can have alone time with the council members?"

Uncle Ezra buttoned his shirt and set to work on his cufflinks. "I'm not asking. Remember what I said at the jail? When the day comes when I need something—and today is that day—you two will deliver to me what is owed. No questions."

Niklas sighed through his nose and set his jaw. He knew he didn't have a choice. "We do this, we're square, right?"

"For the prison fiasco, yes."

"And we're back to our original salaries?" he probed.

"Not a chance." Wrapping his necktie into a neat knot and pulling it snug, Ezra paused and raised a finger warningly at Niklas. "Also, that will be the only time you go joyriding in one of my cars. Ever. Understand? It had better be washed and detailed before I see it again. And so help me if there's a single scratch."

The rarity of an honest man

Rivulets the color and viscosity of coffee meandered down the sidewalk, flowing along seams in the bricks and pooling in dirty little lakes hemmed in by dams of ice. The smell of yeasty fermentation and hops was strong enough to change a tire on. Ahead, a crowd had formed. Bystanders jostled with newspaper reporters and photographers while men in coarse wool coats and fedoras rolled wooden casks out of the back of a parked truck, down a ramp, and into a disorganized huddle on the sidewalk. The driver of the truck looked on with contempt as the barrels were pried or smashed open. The authorities joked with the crowd, grinning triumphantly as they waved around hatchets and pickaxes. They held them aloft with contrived expressions of determination on their faces, pausing mid-swing to make sure the photos turned out crisply. Niklas approached but hung back a few feet. The ground was at once wet and icy, sticky and slippery. Angling one of the barrels against the curb, one of the lawmen smashed it with a maul and the wood shattered, the crowd recoiling with a chorus of excited shouts as beer splattered their shoes.

"Quite the spectacle, isn't it?" A young Asian woman in a violet-colored, herringbone-pattern coat that draped to her shins sidestepped toward him, careful to avoid the growing puddle underfoot.

He glanced at her and for a moment struggled to place how he knew her. Then it clicked. "Maya." He smiled and snapped his fingers. "Something told me I would see you again."

"St. Paul isn't such a big place."

"Getting smaller every day." Niklas nodded toward the men with the axes. "U.S. Marshals, right? You and your colleague, Detective Stauss, must have known they would be here."

She shook her head and sighed. "For a detective, Eugene's no good at keeping secrets."

"I've grown to appreciate how rare an honest man has become in this city."

"You seem like an honest man yourself."

"Only because lies require too much effort to remember."

She smiled. It was a sad sort of a smile without any teeth showing, like recollecting a bittersweet memory. "It's funny, really: Eugene—Detective Stauss to you—would hate this more than anyone. Not because he's against Prohibition, but because he knows this little display is just theater to make the government look like it's actually doing something. Meanwhile he has to fight his own department to get anything done. The prison has a revolving door and we're helpless to stop it."

"We? So where's your badge?"

"I'm more useful than a police officer. I'm a woman who doesn't know when to quit."

"An informant, then?"

"When one is needed, sure. Or a mole. Or a lookout. Sometimes just a concerned citizen who is active in the community."

"How did you two meet? Seems lucky that Stauss was able to find someone like you to help him."

"He and my brother were very close."

"Romantically close?"

She hesitated, a distrustful glimmer in her eyes, then nodded. "They loved each other."

"You said 'were'—past tense. What happened?"

"Minneapolis happened. A dark alley and a man desperate for a drink. Desperate enough to shoot my brother in the heart for a two-dollar bill and a ten-dollar pocket watch that always ran fast."

"I'm sorry to hear that," Niklas said mechanically. He barely knew her or Stauss, let alone her brother. News of his untimely death meant nothing to him and he found it hard to conceal that. It was moments like this that made him realize the war had indeed changed him, left him with an enduring apathy to the pain of others. In France, he had borne witness to such human suffering as the world had never known. His soul had been inundated with it. By his estimation, most soldiers had dealt with it in one of three ways: they either went raving mad, swaddled themselves in religion, or became so numb to the pain they could never feel it again. Like a cauterized nerve. He must have been among the latter.

One of the reporters shouted out above the crowd, "Down with the profiteering Jews! Down with the Jewish cabal!"

"What's that fellow bellowing about?" Niklas asked. "What does German beer have to do with Jewish people?"

She sighed and shook her head contemptuously. "He's with the *Twin City Reporter*. It's an anti-semitic scandal sheet and he's as much a journalist as I am." For a moment she seemed to deliberate something before suddenly lunging forward into the crowd. She emerged a moment later, eyes downcast, and slipped her arm around Niklas' elbow, steering him away from the scene.

"What did you just do?" Niklas asked under his breath.

"Let's just say honesty is even more rare in this town than you originally thought."

A shout rose above the crowd. "Someone stop that woman! She stole my wallet!"

The reporter whose billfold she had pilfered pointed directly at them. A couple of the marshals, seeing an opportunity to make this a public relations boon, abandoned their beer smashing and gave chase.

"Run," Maya said. They sprinted down the street, tearing past a rowdy dice game at a cigar stand, plunging through a muddle of adolescent boys playing Kick The Can with an empty canister of Veedol motor oil. She was impressively fast and avoided onlookers and obstacles deftly.

"Left!" Niklas shouted, steering his shoulder into Maya and driving them into a narrow alley behind an apartment building. "You know," he said, pulling down a stack of pallets behind them to block the way, "it occurs to me that there's really no reason I should be running. You're the one who stole the wallet."

"Try explaining that to them now!" she laughed as she dexterously leapt over a tipped-over trash bin, the tail of her violet coat whipping through the air like that of a fox with dogs nipping at its ankles.

They turned a corner and stopped abruptly. From the shadows lunged a Doberman pinscher, all teeth and sinewy muscle writhing beneath its short black coat. The guard dog, probably protecting a moonshiner's still, strained to break the heavy logging chain fastened to its collar. It barked and snarled, soapy froth dripping from its lips. They flattened themselves against the opposing alley wall and passed just outside its reach. Reaching the end of the alley, Niklas cupped his hands and boosted Maya over a wooden fence. He could hear the pounding footsteps and shouts of the marshals as they neared.

The Doberman turned its attention toward the newcomers. Glancing back, Niklas evaluated the chain restraining the dog. It was anchored to the wall with a single steel bolt pushed through a link in the chain, then passed through a steel eyelet driven into the mortar between the bricks. Careful to avoid attracting the dog's attention, Niklas hastened toward the base of the chain. Just as the marshals turned the corner, Niklas gripped the bolt head and tugged it free. The chain went slack, dropping to the ground with a heavy metallic *clank*.

The dog paused for a moment, confused by its sudden freedom. The marshals stopped abruptly upon seeing the Doberman, making soothing sounds as they backed up. The growling grew to a ferocious barking, followed by the skittering of chain, feet, and paws as the dog pursued them back down the alleyway and into the street.

Niklas heaved himself over the fence. Maya met him on the other side, smiling as she tried to catch her breath. She patted his shoulder. "Well done. That could have ended badly."

"It could have. And for what? You think stealing that guy's wallet taught him a lesson somehow?" Not waiting for her, he set out walking down the sidewalk, looking over his shoulder for any sign of the marshals.

She hastened to catch up to him. "It's mostly for me to feel better. I don't expect someone like that to ever change."

"It was needless. And we nearly got caught."

"That wasn't even close. Besides, like you said, *you* didn't steal the wallet." She stopped mid-step and planted her hands on her hips. He turned to look at her. "They've got nothing on *you*. Not as though *you've* done anything unlawful, right?"

"I don't know what you're getting at."

"Selling Barbieri machine guns is a mistake. Reconsider."

He motioned with his hands for her to keep her voice down while looking around to see if anyone stood within earshot. A lone policeman hovered in the middle of the nearby intersection directing traffic, but he appeared wholly unconcerned with their conversation.

When Niklas spoke, his voice was low but firm. "You're entitled to that opinion. But I have no plans to reconsider." In fact, before leaving the apartment that morning, he had called Barbieri and informed him of the arrival of his guns. With any luck, the deal would be over and done within a day or two at most. Barbieri would be on his way back to Chicago and he and Kessler would be a great deal richer.

"This will have severe consequences. You'll hurt a lot of people."

"I'm not going to hurt anyone. What a mobster does with the guns once he's purchased them is his own moral quandary to work out. I'm looking out for me and my family, because I've learned the hard way no one else will."

"You have other options. You're young, healthy, smart. You don't have to do this."

Leaning in close so she could hear him clearly over the swelling grumble of traffic, Niklas looked over her shoulder at the passing vehicles. "Have you read about the Roman gladiators, Maya?" he asked rhetorically. "Most of them were slaves. Prisoners, ordered to fight and die for the entertainment of the emperor and the masses. Shoved into a hole together and given an ultimatum: You want to live to see another day? Kill the man across from you. But that doesn't mean they hated each other. They actually had more in common than anyone else in the Coliseum."

A man in an oil-stained boiler suit and a faded plaid coat passed by them on the shoulder of the road, leading a donkey and a cart piled high with hulks of rusted scrap metal. He tipped his hat to them as he traipsed along, in no particular hurry to get anywhere.

Niklas continued, "I thought about that a lot when I was in the trenches: How the man on the other side didn't want to be there, either. How we shared more in common with each other than with our countrymen back home. We all hung from the same fragile cliff edge. All of us praying the next artillery shell flew wide, or the marksman's bullet found someone else. But we also knew the truth: Some of us would survive, some would not. I was forced to accept that. Men more powerful, more influential than me—than everyone on that battlefield—had decided our fates. After that, it wasn't ideological anymore. It was just mathematics. I couldn't change the rules of the game, so all I could do was play like hell in hopes of surviving. Things weren't so different when we got home, either.

The poor are still fighting for the rich man's entertainment. We just keep slugging it out, hoping we're not the first to die."

"And this—the guns—is your solution to that?" Maya asked.

He sighed and shrugged. "Whatever it takes to get out of the arena."

She gestured for him to follow her. They strolled a short distance before stopping beside a brick building with a hand-painted sign bolted above the display window. *Hoffman Kosher Meats.*

"This store is owned by a very nice Jewish family. Seven kids." She lifted the lid on the brass mailbox fastened to the door and withdrew the reporter's wallet from her pocket. Plucking out a slim stack of bills, she stuffed them inside the mailbox. Glancing at the wallet, she smiled and flicked it into the street where it was promptly run over by a milk truck. "See? Doing the right thing is easy." She patted his chest. "Don't complicate it." She looked him over intently, then grabbed the lapels of his leather coat, rocked forward on the balls of her feet, and kissed him gently on the cheek. Her lips were pillow soft, and he caught just a faint hint of rose petal perfume. As she pulled away, she stared him in the eyes with the stern intensity of one reiterating a dire warning before walking away without another word.

Dethroning the king

S trands of electric lights curtsied above a scatter of large bonfires, the night sky glowing like smoldering embers atop the state capitol grounds. Jostled and driven along by the crowd, Niklas, Kessler, and Kosena passed through a gallery of whimsical ice and snow sculptures on their way toward the epicenter of the St. Paul Winter Carnival. It was a revelrous fete abuzz with activity. Playful music filled the air, accompanied by the ambient murmur of the bustling throng and the inviting aroma of roasted peanuts and hot chocolate.

Kosena slipped an arm through each of theirs and tugged them toward a tall, otherworldly structure in the distance constructed of thousands of blocks of translucent lake ice. "The ice castle! Oh, it's magnificent," she gasped, pointing. "Like something from a storybook."

How ridiculous, Niklas thought. Here they were, enjoying a carefree night out at a carnival like children, when in a matter of hours they would be committing a senseless crime against a local doctor just so their uncle could realize his political ambitions. He could tell that Kessler felt it, too, though he did his best to mask it. Although he smiled and seemed to encourage Kosena's enthusiasm, he would occasionally cast a discouraged glance toward Niklas.

Leaning over and shouting above the noise of the crowd, Kessler asked, "Did you know they only decided to start holding the winter carnival because some newspaper journalist out east called St. Paul as uninhabitable as Siberia?"

"Were they wrong?" Niklas grumbled, blowing warm air into the cuffs of his gloves before tugging the collar of his coat up a little higher on his neck.

"Come on, big brother! Lighten up a bit, huh?" He slapped his gloved hands together excitedly. "Wait here—I'm going to buy you both a hot cider. Warm you right up." Shouldering into the crowd, he forged his way toward a vendor's booth, digging in his pocket for his wallet.

Kosena snuggled against Niklas' arm and shivered. He stood rigidly without looking at her, instead watching as a crude toboggan flew by on a nearby ice slide. The children aboard screamed with delight as they slid by at breakneck speed, faces red and snot-covered, tails of their scarves whipping in the wind.

"Elizabeth, one of my friends in our troupe—a very talented ventriloquist—explained the lore behind the carnival to me yesterday," Kosena said, pointing toward several costumed figures waving from a nearby rostrum. "King Boreas and the Queen of the Snows—who represent winter—are being ousted by Vulcan—the one in the red cape—who represents springtime. At the end of the carnival, we celebrate the dethroning of the king and the coming of spring by storming the ice castle with fireworks. Doesn't that sound like fun?"

"Fascinating," he said quietly. Recalling the way Kosena had walked arm in arm with Julian when he had spied them together at the Astor Theater a few weeks before, he suddenly felt the need to push her away. As though she could sense his thoughts, she seemed to tighten her grip on his arm.

"You should meet her—Elizabeth. Recently single, very pretty. Your intellectual equal, too: very sharp and witty. I bet she would really go for a guy like you. You could use a woman in your life. You always act so gruff, but I bet you have a lot of love to give."

"So much love, all pent up inside," he said irritably.

She nudged his ribs with her shoulder. "I meant to ask you: How's your father? I was sorry to hear you and Kessler had to travel all the way to Denmark to be with him."

"He's doing better." He tried to fill his voice with notes of optimism, but it came out synthetic and flat.

She made a skeptical hum in her throat as though he had given the wrong answer. "You two didn't go to Denmark, did you?"

"Why would you say that?"

"I don't doubt you traveled somewhere. But it was something to do with whatever got you and Kessler beat up a few weeks ago. Why are you being so secretive about it?"

He began scanning the crowd in search of Kessler, hoping he would return and displace her attention.

"Not going to say? Let me guess: It's nothing to concern myself with, right?"

He jerked his arm free of her grasp. "I don't owe you an explanation for anything. You're dating my brother, not me. And I have good reason to question your loyalty to him, even. So no, I'm not going to tell you where I was or where I'm going, because—just like before—it remains none of your concern."

Reappearing from the crowd holding a steaming cup of cider in each of his gloved hands, Kessler said cheerily, "Here we are." He offered a cup to each of them. Recognizing the look of bewilderment on Kosena's face and Niklas' glower, he asked, "Everything all right?"

Niklas held Kosena's stare, jaw clenched. "Everything is fine."

An hour later, after observing a curling competition and a horse-drawn sled race, the storming of the palace began. The crowd cheered loudly as fireworks shrieked and whistled through the darkness, detonating above the ice castle and bathing it in kaleidoscopic hues. Niklas held his palms to his ears to block out the cacophony. Although he wasn't among those who had left the service with shell shock or a vulnerability to sudden loud reports, he didn't relish the noise. He had heard enough explosions for one lifetime.

Finally, the fireworks subsided, with only the occasional latecomer popping off in the distance.

"Thank you both for the lovely evening," Kosena said with a pleased sigh, giving Kessler a kiss on the cheek and turning to Niklas to do the same. She neared him but hesitated, seeing the look of contempt on his face. She patted his arm gently, instead.

"I'm going to walk Kosena home," Kessler said. "See you back at the apartment?"

"Don't take too long," Niklas reminded him quietly.

Kessler gave a knowing nod. They turned and disappeared into the crowd.

Within minutes, the hordes of onlookers had thinned to just a few stragglers like himself. Niklas glanced back at the ice palace. Shrouded in a curtain of pewter-gray smoke from the fireworks, it now looked more akin to a derelict fortress or abandoned chateau swept up in a haunting fog. He felt a flood of foreboding wash over him. Shaking it off, he set out for the apartment.

The good doctor

B rumal air crept inside pockets and under collars, through the leather of their boots and the seams of their coats like an insidious cloud. It penetrated deep and held on stubbornly.

Without a word, the three men steadily increased the pace of their walk, taking longer strides, shoulders shrugged against the night's bitter chill.

Summit Avenue was empty of traffic at this hour. Only a feeble light came from above, the stars and moon cloaked in a veil of clouds. The good people inside the luxurious homes on either side of the street were likely seated at opposing ends of long mahogany tables, evaluating the silverware as they leisurely poked at the meal the household chef had prepared. The few vehicles around were parked against the curb, snow covering their windshields and mounded atop the cabs.

They approached Doctor Goldmann's home, a colonial monstrosity set well back from the street, surrounded by a waist-high black wrought-iron fence that disappeared against the murk of the night. Two gas lamps had been mounted atop brick pillars at the base of the driveway, their blue-orange flames flickering invitingly. The men loitered at the edge of the pool of light in a semi-circle facing the road, as though merely stopping to have a smoke.

Niklas considered the final words Maya had said to him that afternoon: "Doing the right thing is easy." Clearly she didn't know him very well, because here he was, again, preparing to do something objectionable due to little more than a simplistic sense of self-preservation.

"Here, put these on," Oscar whispered, his breath hot and smelling like it could sterilize dentistry equipment. From the pockets of his heavy wool greatcoat he withdrew gas masks and shoved them against their chests.

"I'm never wearing one of those again," Kessler said, making a face as he pushed it away. "Besides, why would we?"

"Hide our faces while we're beating him up," Oscar said, sounding surprised an explanation was needed. "Otherwise he might identify us later. It's not such a big city. You would be surprised how often I run into the same people."

"That's because you visit the same places every day," Kessler said.

"We're not assaulting the good doctor," Niklas added. "We're going to sabotage his car and leave."

"What if he calls a taxi?" Kessler asked.

"A man of such repute as Doctor Goldmann arriving at a fancy council meeting by taxi? The shame of it," Niklas joked. "Look, we pour a little water in his gas tank and the car will run just long enough to get him away from the house before it stalls. By the time he has dealt with the car, found a phone, and called for someone to come get him, the party will be long over. Uncle Ezra gets what he wants and no one has to get hurt."

Kessler whispered, "Oscar, keep a lookout. We're going around back to the garage."

"What would you like me to do if I see someone coming? Kill 'em?" Oscar asked, feigning sincerity.

"I'm sure a simple maiming will do." Niklas winked and slapped his friend's arm.

Bent at the waist, the brothers scrambled into the yard and followed the perimeter of the fence, giving the house as wide a berth as possible. They kept an eye on the windows casting amber light into the darkness, expecting to see silhouettes moving within. Fortunately, given the enormity of the house, it would have required dozens of inhabitants to monitor any goings-on outside.

They slipped inside the garage. Kessler reached into a pocket and flicked on a small electric torch, sweeping the interior. The beam played along snow shovels, disused garden tools, and buckets of sand meant to prevent slipping on the icy pavement. The doctor's car was an unremarkable Ford Model T coupe with an enclosed cab and clods of dirty ice built up beneath the fenders and running boards.

"I think the gas tank is in the trunk," Kessler whispered. Stepping toward the rear of the car, his fingers sought the latch.

Drawing a canteen of water from beneath his coat, Niklas unscrewed the cap. Kessler had only just managed to get the trunk open before a firm voice challenged, "Who is in here?" The flashlight was extinguished.

The man standing between them and their freedom was tall—tall enough to spend much of his life stooping through doorways and ducking beneath light fixtures—but with a willowy, raw-boned build. The sort of physique that guaranteed a perpetually sore lower back. His gray mustache smothered most of his mouth and seemed to sag like the corners of his drooping eyes. In his hand he wielded a cane, gripping it like a bludgeon. Receiving no answer, he took a step forward and began drawing the bottom of the cane away to reveal a cruel-looking blade that protruded from the ornate handle like a shimmering icicle. "Just because I'm a doctor doesn't mean I won't defend my life and property from hooligans!"

Niklas and Kessler remained concealed behind the open trunk. "What do we do?" Kessler whispered.

Although there was no question the two could overpower the doctor and make their escape without him seeing much of their features in the dim light, doing so might very well come at the cost of several painful gashes and, perhaps more critically, Goldmann would still make his appointment at Uncle Ezra's. Although Niklas didn't care whatsoever about his uncle's political aspirations, he knew that failure of this one simple assignment would guarantee he and Kessler would never be free of their debt—or of Uncle Ezra's ire.

That didn't leave them much choice. They would have to hold him at gunpoint and tie him up.

This was not how he had wanted the evening to go. Niklas sighed and drew his Steyr from its holster.

Just as they prepared to step out, something blocked the light from the outside. Goldmann turned to find himself face to face with a fearsome sight: a thickset man with long black hair, wearing a wool greatcoat, his face concealed by a bug-like gas mask with two large, empty eyes staring back at him. Before the doctor could raise the blade in his hand, Oscar swung a gloved fist and connected solidly with the man's chin. Goldmann staggered backward into the fender of his car, gave a sad sort of groan, and collapsed in an unconscious heap on the garage floor. Kneeling over him, Oscar immediately began rummaging through his pockets.

"What are you doing? Let's get out of here!" Kessler hissed, grabbing a fistful of Oscar's coat and tugging him toward the door.

"Making it look legitimate," he replied, casually batting away his friend's hand before plunging his fingers into the doctor's pants pocket and fishing around. "What kind of criminal knocks out a rich guy without stealing his billfold?"

"Why didn't you warn us he was coming?" Niklas asked, holstering his pistol. He poured the contents of his canteen into the Model T's gas tank for insurance, then slammed the trunk. "You were supposed to be the lookout!"

Snaking a hand under the chin of his gas mask, Oscar took a desperate breath and attempted to wipe the condensation from the lenses with the pad of his pointer finger. He grumbled, "Honestly, I can't see shit with this on."

Whiz-bang

Saint-Mihiel, France
September, 1918

*T*heir truck heaved to a stop, buried up to the axles in clinging mud,
steam slithering from the seams in the hood like cigarette smoke from
a grimace. For the third day in a row the rain fell. Not intensely, but
endlessly, with droning persistence and upon already sodden fields. It
rendered all but the highest ground impassable.

*They spotted a mule nearby. The animal stomped about aimlessly, tugging a
limber but missing the artillery piece and rider. She seemed untroubled by the ear-
splitting concussions of the artillery nearby, like a bass drum in a closed room,
beaten quickly and out of rhythm. Strapping as many of their gunsmithing tools
as they could upon the limber and across the molly's back, Niklas and Kessler set
out on foot for the lines, leaving the other men from their team behind to see to the
truck. They led the mule around flooded shell holes deep as ponds, through sparse
thickets of what once were trees, their char-blackened trunks jabbing at the dismal
sky like the shafts of broken arrows. The mud sucked at their boots and spattered*

atop their leather puttees. Rain dripped from the brims of their helmets like endless strings of glass beads.

And still the artillery rumbled and boomed.

"You boys look lost," shouted a soldier as he sheltered beneath a crude lean-to made from an overturned caisson and sheets of corrugated iron. The badge on his collar—a twin-towered fortress—and the stack of chevrons on his sleeve indicated he was a sergeant with the engineering corps. "Where you heading?"

"Somewhere a bit drier, hopefully," Kessler shouted back.

The sergeant grinned and waved them over to join him under the lean-to.

"We're armorers with the Mobile Ordnance Repair Shop," Niklas explained as they stepped out of the rain. The mule gave them a doleful look as she waited nearby, too large to fit inside. "Truck broke down. The rest of the crew will be along shortly, but we thought we had better come on foot to start work if you have any machine guns that need repair."

The sergeant looked relieved. "We've been waiting on you boys. Everything's stopped working worth a damn since this rain started. Come with me and I'll get you set up in a bunker. We've got a stack of automatic rifles and machine guns that have given up the ghost and could use some attention. A few of the boys are manning the lines with nothing but entrenching tools and anger at this point. We haven't been resupplied in ages."

"The roads are shit," Kessler said, reaching into the rain and stroking the mule's nose tenderly as raindrops beaded on the tips of her long eyelashes like dew on grass. "Might be a while yet before it dries out enough for you to get that resupply."

The sergeant flagged down a couple of privates to carry their tools. The brothers said goodbye to the mule, wishing her luck and rubbing her ears once more before cutting her loose from the limber. They followed the sergeant through a warren of earthworks, across mud-slick duckboards, along the zigzagging communication trench leading toward the front. As they walked, clusters of weary faces looked out from dugouts carved in the trench walls, their vacant gazes following them wordlessly as they passed by. Eventually, they arrived at the support trenches. The bulk of the fighting occurred farther ahead, though on a day like this, neither side would be doing much more than waiting out the rain.

The sergeant led them inside a large dugout supported by stacks of sandbags and creosote-smeared beams, warmly lit by a flickering oil lamp. A few officers huddled over a makeshift table cloaked in a patchwork of ragged maps. They flashed the brothers a look of annoyance as they passed by, the low-ranking enlisted men interrupting what they no doubt believed to be a key strategic meeting of minds sure to turn the tide of the war, and certainly not result in the needless deaths of thousands of men.

They proceeded deeper inside the complex until it felt as though they must have been thirty feet underground and a quarter mile into No Man's Land. The sergeant finally stopped inside a large room piled high with guns of all sorts, cases of straw-packed grenades, and a table constructed of empty ammo boxes and one blood-encrusted stretcher. The atmosphere inside was frowsty, thick with lantern smoke and damp, as though the air inside had already been breathed. The privates stacked their tools in a corner and promptly departed.

"Here you go, boys," the sergeant said, waving a hand around like a real estate agent at an open house. "It's not much to work with, I know. But at least it's out of the rain. I'll have the men start rounding up any other faulty guns and bringing them to you." With that, he gave them a nod and departed, leaving them alone.

"Well, no use sitting around complaining about it." Dropping his haversack, Niklas grabbed an armful of Chauchat automatic rifles and laid them out atop the stretcher.

"You start. I'll spell you in an hour," Kessler said with a yawn. He had already discarded his soaking-wet wool overcoat and began kicking loose the more persistent clumps of mud from his hobnailed trench boots as he took a seat in the corner. "I haven't slept indoors in ages."

"One hour," Niklas said, holding up a finger. "I'm going to hold you to it." They both knew Niklas would let him sleep longer. There was no real rush on repairing the guns. Both sides were deadlocked while the rain held. Trying to traverse the mud while launching an attack on enemy trenches would be suicide.

Hours passed. Kessler snored softly, mouth open, head against the wood slats of the bunker wall. Niklas had repaired half a dozen rifles and begun tinkering with a Madsen light machine gun—a captured German automatic rifle with a thirty-round magazine curving out from the top of its receiver like a menacing horn. Most of the guns he encountered weren't really broken, they were just dirty, rusty, or jammed. *Guns were like clocks: They could work reliably for years if well maintained, or they could stop working entirely if the smallest spring, pin, or catch broke or became stuck. A horsehair-bristled toothbrush often proved the most effective tool in his toolbox.*

Disassembling the machine gun and drawing out the barreled action, he scrubbed away the filth and applied a few drops of oil. Checking the barrel for impediments, he discovered a brass ring where a spent cartridge had been ejected with such force as to rip the heel off, leaving the remaining case lodged inside the chamber. Not uncommon. The quality of the brass cartridges during wartime could be erratic—especially for the fatigued German war machine. He selected a shell-extractor tool from his toolbox and screwed it into the soft brass, then tugged the broken piece free. Satisfied with his work, Niklas reassembled the rifle, racked the charging handle a few times to check the action, and leaned it against the corner beside a stack of full magazines. Like new. That would give Fritz some heartburn, getting shot at with his own gun.

Out of the corner of his eye, Niklas noticed movement. Must have been a rat darting between stanchions. He reached for another disabled rifle. Glancing toward the corner, he spotted the movement again. Dirt sifting downward, like water in a whirlpool. My mind's playing tricks, *he thought, rubbing his eyes with his sleeve.* I'm just tired. *Probably time to wake Kessler up for his shift. He rocked his brother's shoulder gently to wake him. By now the entire corner seemed to swirl and fall into itself, the hole widening as though a demon would erupt forth any second from the bowels of Hell.*

It wasn't just in Niklas' mind.

Kessler saw it too. He scrambled to his feet, fumbling for a working rifle. Niklas grabbed the Madsen he had just repaired and slammed a fresh magazine into it, racking the charging handle.

A face materialized in the dim light. A young man clambered out of the hole, wiping dirt from his eyes, his nascent mustache flecked with soil. He wore no uniform, only a pair of wool trousers, his hairless torso bare and shimmering with sweat. In his left hand he gripped a Broomhandle Mauser.

A German pistol.

The man locked eyes with Niklas, his expression one of fear and bewilderment. Niklas shook his head as if begging him to withdraw, willing him to disappear.

The pistol wavered in the man's hand, then swung toward them. The shot went wide, shattering the glass lens on a nearby lantern, a dazzling cascade of flaming fuel showering the floor. Niklas' finger instinctively tugged the Madsen's trigger. Everything became silent and slow. His vision narrowed. All he could see was that face, stupefied and incredulous, shrouded in a mist of crimson. A line of ragged red holes burst from his bare chest. He tumbled backward into the hole and Niklas followed him down, shoving the muzzle of the machine gun inside the tunnel and firing until the magazine had been spent. Approaching with a Mills bomb, Kessler primed it and pitched it downward. The brothers turned away from the hole just as a cough of dirt and smoke cascaded into the room.

Ringing. Choking dust clouded the still air. Seconds ticked ponderously by. A few of their comrades, including the officers they had passed on their way in, rushed into the room to investigate the noise.

One of them gestured toward the hole. "Well? Get in there, Corporal. See if there are any others." Drawing a Webley revolver from his hip holster, he offered it to Niklas by the barrel, along with an electric torch.

Hands shaking from the adrenaline of the gunfight, he reluctantly accepted the handgun and light. He cast a worried glance at his brother. Both men knew they couldn't disobey a direct order from an officer, no matter how suicidal it might be. Moving to the edge of the tunnel, he cautiously peered down as though daring a look from the rooftop of a tall building. From where he stood, the feeble beam of the electric torch illuminated only a vague mound of bodies. He sat at the edge of the hole, fully expecting that the second he entered, he would be met by dozens of Germans, guns raised, expressions grim, and would be summarily cut down. Taking a deep breath and forcing those thoughts from his head, he slipped inside.

A noxious blend of spent cordite and TNT, upturned soil, and blood assailed him. The torch revealed a dozen bodies at his feet, mangled and contorted like broken marionettes, their strings tangled and limbs crossed at ridiculous angles. The tunnel had partially collapsed from the grenade's explosion, but it still reached impossibly far into the darkness, beyond the reach of the light's beam. The thought of that empty conduit leading directly to the enemy lines filled him with dread. As though waves of enemy troops were mere seconds from materializing before him out of the darkness.

"Check the bodies for intelligence," someone shouted down.

Taking as deep a breath as he dared without vomiting from the smell, he stepped gingerly between the corpses, sliding his boots through the few gaps between bodies, blood smearing his pant legs. He made a quick search of uniform pockets and satchels, which seemed to have only been filled with grenades and hand-to-hand weapons the German tunnelers never got the chance to use. A wheeze sounded in the darkness. Nearly falling over in his urgency, he raised the Webley and aimed blindly into the inky black. Nothing. He swept the cave with the light. The beam fell upon a wounded man stirring amidst the rubble. An officer, half buried by the cave-in, still feebly drawing breath. Blood leaked from shrapnel wounds in his chest and neck, bubbling around his lips and staining his teeth as he panted and gasped. Locking eyes with Niklas, the soldier feebly tapped the holster at his belt. Niklas approached him slowly, unsure of whether he should try to comfort him as his instincts would have him do, or remain distrustful should it be a trap. The wounded man tapped the holster again. Tucking the Webley into his belt, Niklas knelt down and unbuttoned the holster flap, withdrawing the officer's sidearm—a Steyr-Hahn pistol. Press-checking the chamber for a live round, he glimpsed a flash of brass and knew it was loaded. The wounded man gave a small nod and closed his eyes, a wordless request to mercifully end his misery.

Whetting his lips and blinking away tears, Niklas thumbed back the hammer and placed the pistol in the officer's palm. His hand quivered as he helped the man raise his arm, the muzzle of the handgun an inch from his temple. For a moment, nothing happened. Niklas silently prayed the wounded man had expired. His chest no longer rose and fell, the pain-filled whisper of air no longer forced from his lips.

He jumped at the loud report and sharp recoil of the pistol.

Staring at the dead man before him, memorizing his features and trying not to focus on the hole in his temple, Niklas suddenly felt overcome by grief. He buried his face in his hands and wept.

When he clambered out of the hole, he was greeted by a dozen soldiers slapping him cheerily on the back. The engineering corps sergeant from before had arrived. He bellowed, "Sounds like you boys got yourselves into a real scrap. Too bad I couldn't get here in time. Looks like you had it well handled, though. Gave them a rude surprise, eh?" He elbowed Kessler playfully. "I'll be sure to put you in for an award." He gave them a sly wink.

Returning the revolver and electric torch to the officer who had loaned them to him, Niklas said solemnly, "Please don't."

"Why not? You deserve it. Must be a dozen Huns down there." He grinned and gave Niklas a stiff slap on the shoulder. "You're just being modest. You boys saved our necks tonight."

An hour later, the tunnel had been collapsed with the help of a sapper with an explosive charge. Niklas and Kessler sat amidst the piles of guns, staring at the hole in the corner. They had been given a ration of warm rum to help calm their nerves. Kessler drank his within minutes. Niklas just cradled the mug in his hand and stared.

"Why did you tell the sergeant not to put us in for an award?" Kessler finally asked, his voice low. "Isn't that why we enlisted? To prove our allegiance to our country? When we go back home after the war, I want to be able to wag those medals in the faces of anyone who makes fun of our accents. We fought and killed for our country. What have they done for it? Sure, I may not speak perfect English, may not have been born in America, but I've earned my place all the same."

"A dozen men." Niklas' voice cracked and he felt hot tears forming in his eyes as he stared at the Steyr in his hand. "We killed a dozen men. You and I did. There's no ambiguity about it. No shooting over the top of the trench into the darkness and wondering if we hit someone. We looked them square in their faces and we killed them. Why would we want a medal for that? It's an atrocity, not an accomplishment."

Outside, the shelling grew in intensity, the earth around them quivering and throbbing like a subterranean beast preparing to swallow them whole.

It took him a moment to respond to the sounds of splintering wood and the slam of a door colliding with the wall. In his dream, the thumping sounds had been the whiz-bang reports of German 77mm field guns. Awake now, Niklas realized someone had been kicking in their apartment door. He leapt from his bed and scrambled for the Steyr on his nightstand. Light flooded the bedroom and blinded him. As his fingertips brushed the grips of his pistol, he heard something swish through the air before colliding with his head. A dazzling fireworks display shut out what remained of his vision, followed by an electric jolt that raced angrily down his spine. He collapsed and collided with his nightstand, splitting his brow. Warm blood, thick as molasses, coursed down the bridge of his nose and into the corner of his mouth. It tasted like sucking on a penny. He tried to react, to swing a fist or kick out, but everything felt sluggish and distant, like he had fallen into neck-deep mud. Strong hands grabbed his ankles and dragged him into the living room, the rough wood floor driving splinters into the bare skin of his shoulders and back. He found himself lying alongside Kessler, also blinking against the light and holding his hands protectively before his face. Half a dozen figures hovered above them in a loose semi-circle, clutching electric torches and leather saps in their hands. A heavy boot—cold and snow-covered—struck Niklas in the ribs. He gasped for air.

"Hello again, friends," Barbieri said jovially. He leaned against the fireplace mantel examining his fingernails. "Nice joint you've got here. Quaint. Very…rustic." With the heel of his shoe, he tipped over a wicker basket filled with coal. It spilled across the floor, leaving behind streaks of black carbon.

"At first your lovely lady friend—what's her name…starts with a K, kinda Russian-sounding—anyway, she wasn't too cooperative when I asked where you live. But we Sicilians are great at getting people to open up. It's our sociable nature."

"Where is she?" Kessler pleaded, only to be dealt a kick in the jaw that rolled his entire body over.

"I wouldn't worry about her. She's with me now. At least until I get bored with her. Then, who knows? I may just slit her throat and dump her in the river. Or, you know what?"—he snapped his fingers—"I could dump her off at the new can house I just opened up in town. We're looking for more grade-A girls like her to keep the customers coming back." He paced around the room, glancing at photos in frames before tipping them over, the glass shattering as they struck the floor. "But really, I would be more worried about yourselves at the moment." He nodded toward the bedroom and a couple of his thugs went inside. They could hear the jangle of bed frames being overturned and the hollow thud of drawers being yanked out and dropped to the floor. Barbieri lit a cigarette and smiled as he drew on it, like he had just remembered a good joke. "I know you're wondering: Why is he doing this? We had a deal, after all. Well, it's simple, really. See, my *famiglia* entrusted me with all this money. Thousands of dollars to pay for your guns. I may have even told them they cost quite a bit more than what you are charging." An impish grin crept across his lips and he shrugged. "A little extra for my trouble, you know? It's not cheap looking this good." He swiped a hand along the pomade-soaked hair at his temple. "So here I was, carrying around all that money, waiting for your guns to arrive, and I got to thinking: What if I were to just *take* the guns from you and keep all that money for myself? What could stop me from doing that? There's only the two of you, after all."

"Please don't do this," Niklas pleaded. "We can negotiate the price. Sweeten the deal. It doesn't have to be ugly."

"It doesn't look so ugly from where I'm standing," Barbieri said coldly. "In fact, it has a certain beauty to it. Real pretty. Now, tell me where I can find my guns."

Neither brother spoke. Barbieri had the upper hand. They knew they were cornered. But the second they gave up the guns, any chance of their payday would evaporate. There was also the strong possibility he would kill them as soon as they revealed the location. He would do it as quickly and carelessly as he had killed Vicenzo.

Reaching into a pocket of his coat, Barbieri withdrew a device that looked like a round pitch pipe with a stubby barrel on one end and a flour sifter handle on the other. It was chrome and fit neatly in the palm of his hand. The barrel protruded from between his knuckles and hovered over Kessler's face. It didn't take a gunsmith to recognize what the device was. "I only need one of you alive to tell me."

"Wait!" Niklas shouted, hot tears forming and clouding his sight. "I'll tell you. Please, don't hurt him. Let him leave and I'll tell you where the guns are. I'll take you to them myself."

"If you don't tell me right now, he'll leave all right—in a rolled-up carpet." Barbieri's men chuckled at that.

Niklas' voice broke, his desperation evident. "I'm begging you. I'll hand over every gun we've got. Just don't hurt him, please."

"Write it down," Barbieri said, his fingers tapping an impatient rhythm on the pistol in his palm.

One of his men tossed a pencil on the floor before Niklas and followed it with a newspaper from the kitchen table.

"My men will go there now. If they come up empty handed, your brother dies. I'll shoot him right in the middle of his handsome face, here in front of you. And you? You'll spend the next few days tied to a chair in the same warehouse where we met, begging me to be so merciful."

Struggling to grasp the pencil, his hand shaking, Niklas dragged a corner of the newspaper toward him and began scribbling an address. It was hard to see his handwriting through the tears and the blood trickling into his eyes. His throbbing ear felt double its normal size. "They're all right there. Basement of Royal Shade and Awning off of Fairview. The crates say 'tractor parts.'"

As Barbieri reached down to grab the newspaper, he noticed the trench watch on Niklas' wrist. "Hey, nice watch." He raised a leg and smashed the heel of his boot down atop the crystal guard. A scream tore from his lungs as fire raced down his arm and up his neck, as though his blood had turned to acid.

"You Minnesotans don't understand Chicago rules. Consider this a free lesson. The strongest take what they want."

From the hallway came a voice. A meek voice with an Irish lilt. "Is everything all right here, boys? Sounded like something fell."

It was their neighbor, Cillian. The priest-in-training. He stood in the doorway in his pajamas, hands clasped before him, taking in the scene with childlike puzzlement.

Kessler shouted, "Cillian, run!"

Before he could take a step, Barbieri raised his palm pistol and squeezed. A loud clap, then a haze of gray smoke filled the room. Cillian clutched his abdomen and staggered backward against the door frame, his expression one of absolute surprise.

"Goddamn nosy neighbors," Barbieri said, shaking his head. "The same in every town, I swear. Drag him in here and let's dust out before anyone else shows up." His men complied, hurling the wounded Irishman down alongside the Kristofferson brothers. As Barbieri turned to leave, he said, "You two get any wise ideas to come after us, you'll end up just like Paddy here. And so help me, if those guns ain't where you said they'd be, I'll hunt you down. And next time I won't be so kind."

Niklas pressed a palm tightly against Cillian's wound while Kessler cradled his head. The blood spurted between his fingers like water through a burst dam. The young priest scratched frantically at his neckline, tugging at the scapular beneath his shirt. Placing the wool square to his lips, he mumbled a desperate prayer. "Go forth, Christian soul, from this world in the name of God the Almighty Father, who created you—"

Niklas didn't recognize the creed even from his distant past, but he still fumbled for some word of comfort he could share with the dying man as he struggled through administering his own last rites. Cillian's voice grew softer and softer until only his lips moved. The color faded from his cheeks, the lucidity of his gaze softening. Choking on a sob, Kessler buried his face against the dying man's shoulder. Cillian stared up at the water-stained ceiling as if hoping to see a glowing path to Heaven. Finding none, he turned his tear-filled eyes toward Niklas and wheezed his dying breath.

Folded hand

During the war, while waiting around for orders or passing the time during a lull in the fighting, Niklas and Kessler would occasionally join a game of poker, blackjack, or, if the Brits were nearby, Crown and Anchor. The men would bet cigarettes and chocolates when they had them, rolling paper and matches when they didn't. Poker proved the most costly, especially when two men had particularly good hands and the betting escalated, each man raising and re-raising, emptying pockets and scribbling IOUs on scraps of paper. On one such hand, Niklas had raised a pack of chewing gum—one of his last—and tossed it into the upturned steel helmet that served as the game's pot.

That was when the uncertainty crept in. He began to doubt if his hand would win. Surely the other man wouldn't bluff to such an extent if he didn't have an excellent hand, too.

Still, he laid down progressively bigger wagers, unwilling to fold. Cutting his losses and backing down wasn't an option. He was in too deep. Better to bet more on a fair chance than lose with certainty what was already in the pot. And so he grudgingly continued, gritting his teeth and doubling down until at last—surrounded by an entire platoon of curious onlookers—the hands were revealed.

He went without gum for a while.

That was how he felt now. Staring at Cillian's lifeless body through swollen eyes, Niklas wondered how much more he could bet against Barbieri before it bankrupted him. And he wasn't so sure of his hand anymore.

After serving the brothers whiskey like an attentive nurse handing out medicine to patients, Oscar began peeling away sheets of newspaper, laying them reverently atop the Irishman's body like a funeral pall. He happened to be delivering a load of hooch to the Wabasha Street Speakeasy down the street when Niklas called, asking if they had seen him. He made good time getting to the apartment, especially considering Niklas had never seen Oscar run unless he was being shot at.

"If you're feeling strong enough to lift him, we can get rid of the body tonight." Oscar stood over Cillian's corpse, looking down at it with the impassivity of a gothic statue. With as many dead bodies as he had seen—and made—in his lifetime, the sight of one more did little to elicit a visible response from the grizzled veteran. "I know a place."

"No, leave him." Niklas nudged his shattered wristwatch around the table, the hands flopping uselessly atop the face like dead flies trapped behind the crystal. "I'll call Stauss in the morning and tell him we had a break-in, we got roughed up, and that Cillian came to investigate. No point in covering this up. Besides, Cillian deserves a proper funeral."

Kessler held a slab of refrigerated beef to his eye and cheek, which helped disguise the fact he had been weeping for half an hour before Oscar arrived. And Niklas couldn't blame him. In a span of mere minutes, he had been beaten up, learned his girlfriend had been abducted, their guns would be stolen, and watched helplessly as a young man—a friend—bled out in his arms. He slid the steak from his face and looked at his brother with bloodshot eyes. "Do we tell him Barbieri did it?"

Niklas contemplated that for a moment. "No. We should take care of Barbieri ourselves. If the cops get him—assuming they would even make the effort—a murder rap will never stick. The Gennas will have him out in days and the guns will already be long gone."

Shaking his head as he looked at Cillian's lifeless form, Kessler whimpered, "He was just a kid, too." The tears came again. He buried his face in his steak.

Seeing his brother injured and vulnerable renewed Niklas' anger, but it was an impotent rage. Nothing he could do about it at this moment except brood, allowing himself a moment of despondency before gathering himself and coldly, analytically, determining what to do next.

"We'll avenge him." Although he said it with certainty, he had no idea how and no confidence they actually would.

Examining the deep laceration on Niklas' eyebrow still trickling blood down the side of his face, Oscar asked, "Did he get all of the guns?"

"No. I only gave him the address of one of our warehouses," he replied glumly.

"Which one?"

"Royal Shade and Awning."

"So that's—"

"Everything we prepared for Barbieri: half a dozen Madsens, same of the Hotchkisses, and three Vickers. Plus a few Chauchats that were still on the truck when we unloaded."

Kessler sniffed, wiped his eyes with the bloody sleeve of his pajamas, and mustered a scoff. "The Chauchats are hardly a loss. Worst machine gun ever made."

"Just because they were shit in the trenches doesn't mean they wouldn't work here. They could have brought us a decent payday." Niklas heard the sullenness in his own voice.

"You think he's stupid enough to believe that's all the guns we had?" Kessler asked hopefully.

Shaking his head, Niklas exhaled through his nose, which was so swollen it made an audible whine as the air passed through. "I don't think he's stupid at all. Here's another good word to know, little brother: hubris. Excessive pride. Barbieri has too much hubris to think for a second he didn't scare us into giving up everything." He swiveled gingerly in his chair and looked at Oscar. "I need a favor."

"Sure, I'll stitch up your eyebrow." Oscar pinched the laceration closed with his thumb and forefinger. "Can't promise it won't leave an ugly scar, though. My hand's not as steady as it used to be." He leaned close and whispered loudly, "I think it might be the drinking."

Wincing and slapping his hand away, Niklas said, "No, I need you to get me a meeting with Danny Hogan. As soon as possible."

"What makes you think I know him?"

"Who is he?" Kessler asked.

"Dapper Dan Hogan. Head of the city's criminal underworld," Niklas explained. "Owns the Green Lantern. The man has his fingers in every kind of criminal enterprise you can think of. Gambling, bootlegging, money laundering, fencing stolen goods…if it's illegal, he's making money at it. He's the guy who out-of-town criminals have to check in with and pay a bribe to every time they visit St. Paul."

"In other words, someone who would never know or care that I exist," Oscar said, scratching absently at his scalp.

"Come on, Oscar. You know everyone in this town. Can you ask around and get us an audience?"

"Demons and devils," Oscar scolded. "You're just trading one for another if you ask him to help you with Barbieri."

"Hogan is more pragmatic than Barbieri. Runs things like a businessman, not a petulant teenager. And if he learns that the Sicilians in Chicago are doing business in his town without his permission, we might be able to get his help."

Kessler's forehead wrinkled in doubt. "Even if we were the ones doing business with Barbieri without his permission?"

Shifting in his seat, Niklas tried to get comfortable, but the throb in his wrist, ribs, and head made comfort a thing of the past. "Probably best if we downplay that part."

"And we're assuming Hogan hasn't already given Barbieri approval to operate here."

"Fingers crossed that he hasn't."

"But even if Hogan agrees to help us and is willing to mobilize every man he's got, it won't be enough. The Sicilians have the machine guns now. And we sure as hell don't want to equip Hogan's men with the guns we have left. Pretty soon everyone in the city will have machine guns but us."

Standing, a swell of nausea threatening to make him vomit, Niklas limped to the kitchen—slowly, each step agony—where he retrieved a large glass jar from the back of a cabinet. He gave it a shake, the metal parts inside clinking. "I removed the firing pins from the guns before we repacked them in Denmark. Just a little added insurance." Placing the glass on the table before his brother, Niklas squeezed his shoulder encouragingly. "Our advantage, for now, is that they believe they have superior firepower. We need to move on them before they realize that, right now, those guns are a liability, not an asset."

Like a lame bloodhound

S tamping the snow from his shoes at the base of the stairs, Detective Stauss began his painstaking trudge toward the second floor of the apartment building, fingers gripping the tarnished brass handrail. A uniformed officer walked behind him with the patience of a caregiver at a retirement home, awaiting the detective's slow ascent so he could take another step.

Niklas met them in the hallway, making no effort to disguise his physical discomfort as he leaned against the doorframe. "Welcome back, Detective. I assumed you knew the way given your previous visit."

Lingering near the apartment's shattered door, Stauss poked it with a finger and watched observantly as it swung freely, bumping the stops and rebounding. The doorknob lay on the floor amidst a confetti of wood splinters. "Indeed. Looks as though not much has changed since my last visit. Besides the redecorating and the dead body, of course." He hung his fedora on a hook above Niklas' coat.

Glancing at the telephone on the entry table, he said, "I bet you're the only one in the neighborhood with one of those."

"An unsolicited gift."

"Quite the cost and effort for such a casual gift."

"On that we agree."

The detective shrugged and moved on. "Any point in us dusting for fingerprints?"

"You can try, but they wore gloves."

Skepticism flickered across the detective's features, but his expression quickly returned to his usual insouciance. "Of course they did. Go ahead and repeat your tale of woe to the good sergeant here so he can catch up."

The sergeant was young, clean-shaven, with an earnest face. He drew a notepad and pencil from his breast pocket, eager to take notes.

"I woke up to the sound of our door getting kicked open," Niklas said. "It was dark. They grabbed me and my brother from our beds and worked us over." He waved a finger at the laceration on his brow to reinforce the point. "There were five or six of them. Cillian"—the sergeant pointed his pencil at the corpse questioningly and Niklas nodded—"came to investigate the noise. He must have surprised them. There was a shot from a pistol. Cillian went down and they ran."

Leisurely pacing around the room while Niklas recounted the attack, Stauss stopped and knelt to look at the photos Barbieri had swept from the mantel, picking free the broken glass from the frames. Looking them over as if to memorize the faces, he returned them to where he estimated they belonged. "Speaking of your brother, where is he?" He glanced around the apartment as though Kessler was simply hiding behind the furniture.

"Getting medical attention. They roughed him up pretty badly. Needed stitches." That was a lie. He had gone with Oscar. He insisted that sitting at home, waiting to make a move on Barbieri and rescue Kosena, would drive him mad.

185

"Now, once again, so I'm certain I heard you correctly when you first called me, you didn't recognize any of them and you have no idea why they would choose your apartment to break into." Stauss said it like a school principal gently probing to get a delinquent student to admit they had cheated on a test.

Niklas gingerly pressed a hand against his bruised ribs and winced. "I have no idea. Bad luck, probably."

The detective made a skeptical hum in the back of his throat. "Naturally. Bad luck. But worse luck for your neighbor, it seems."

"Yes. It would seem so."

The detective approached Cillian's body and swept away the newspapers Oscar had used to cover it. Hooking a gloved finger under the dead man's blood-stained sleep shirt, he assessed the wound. "One small-caliber bullet wound to the liver, looks like. Judging by the radius of the blood spatter, I'm guessing he must have bled out quickly."

"He only lasted a couple of minutes. Bullet must have hit an artery," Niklas mumbled.

"Bright red blood?" the detective asked, looking up at him. Niklas nodded.

"I'm sure you're right, then." He didn't bother putting the newspapers back in place before standing. Glancing around the floor, he said, "No shell casings?"

"It was a palm pistol. Doesn't eject brass."

"You certainly have an observant eye. Surprising to me that you can't recall any distinguishing characteristics of your assailants." He gave Niklas a knowing look but didn't press the point. "Sergeant, be a dear and have the medical examiner send a car around for the body." He pointed toward the phone.

While the sergeant made the call, Stauss stepped closer to Niklas and spoke under his breath. "The body count is getting rather high around you Kristoffersons, isn't it? How many more will it be, do you think? Are you going to call me when it's your brother, next?"

"There won't be a next time," Niklas said firmly. And he meant it. Despite his earlier doubts and misgivings, he had galvanized his resolve and reminded himself of how far they had come to reach this moment. What was at stake. Barbieri had declared war on the wrong people. Niklas wouldn't quit until he had gotten the money owed to them or Barbieri took his last breath. Preferably both.

The detective chewed his lip and raised his eyebrows. "I wish I believed that."

The sergeant concluded his call. "Car is on the way. I can stay with the body, sir."

"Marvelous. I'll be on my way, then." Stauss retrieved his fedora and laid it gently atop his head. Pausing at the door, he said, "Niklas, every bad turn, every cruelty you dispense, comes with a consequence. Sometimes immediate"—he pointed toward Cillian's body—"sometimes in a slow, tireless trudge that follows you inexorably through life, trailing your scent like a lame bloodhound—with plodding, deliberate obsession. One day, when you're old and worn out like me, you'll stop to rest your weary bones and your tired muscles. That's when it will catch up to you. By then, the rage it has nurtured in its bitter, miserable heart will be nothing short of biblical."

Niklas looked down at Cillian's ashen face, the young man's scapular now plastered to the floor with dried blood. "By then, I may welcome it."

A discrepancy

The medical examiner had only just removed the body from the apartment when the phone rang. Uncle Ezra's administrative assistant, very formally, very cryptically, informed Niklas he was to meet his uncle at the home of one of his friends in Anoka. She gave him the address and promptly hung up. As he flagged down a taxi, he considered why Ezra hadn't called himself. Perhaps Barbieri had learned of his relationship to the Kristoffersons and had threatened him, too, forcing him to flee to the safety of one of his friends' homes. Niklas had never known his uncle to back down from anyone, but there was a first time for everything. Perhaps now Uncle Ezra would realize he wanted nothing to do with selling guns.

Half an hour later, the taxi driver cast an impressed glance in the rearview mirror as he turned off of Ferry Street and pulled through an elegant stone archway. The car coasted along a private drive, lined on either side by a fence built of smooth river rock—stacked and mortared, three feet high. Below, visible through the winter-bare trees, the Rum River meandered past the property, ferrying floes of snow and fallen branches. In the center of the horseshoe driveway sat a weathered, three-tiered concrete fountain, covered in dunes of snow like a carelessly frosted wedding cake.

The car eased to a stop beside the tall Grecian columns of a pearl-white, two-story house. Niklas paid the driver and disembarked. The weather was favorable for a change, unseasonably warm for February. White-breasted nuthatches and black-capped chickadees flitted and hopped among the tree branches overhead. Icicles dripped steadily from the eaves as the sun beat down upon the building's rooftop. Everything would freeze again overnight and turn the ground to a skating rink, he knew.

He approached the entrance to the house. Even from the outside, the residence appeared to be of the variety furnished with sweeping oak banisters and thick ornamental rugs, bedecked with portraits of dead ancestors in scarlet red fox-hunting liveries or military dress uniforms. Such a place would come with its own retinue, of course. A vast one made up of chefs and butlers, valets and maids, all devoted to accommodating every passing whim of the owners in between compulsory brunches and garden parties. House wasn't a fitting word, really. Estate seemed more suitable. If it had been located somewhere more exotic, it might have even qualified for villa.

His hand had almost reached the ornate brass handle on the front door when a shotgun blast erupted from behind the building. His heart thundered in his chest. Barbieri had beaten him there. He envisioned Uncle Ezra staggering and dropping to his knees, glasses askew, mouth open in shock, clutching at his guts as they poured forth like ground meat from a tear in butcher paper. For the first time in his life, he realized he actually cared whether the man lived or died.

Leaping off the porch and racing around the house toward the sound, Steyr in hand, he arrived to find a line of men dressed in tweed shooting jackets and breeks.

189

"Pull!" A domed terracotta disc the size of a tea saucer soared through the air. Another shotgun blast reduced it to a fine powder that peppered the snow-covered lawn. The thrower—Ezra's chauffeur—heaved back the spring-loaded thrower and placed another clay pigeon atop it.

Niklas holstered his pistol and seethed. All that apprehension about his uncle's wellbeing—undeserved to begin with—only to find that he was simply enjoying a day of target shooting with friends.

Shouldering his shotgun, Ezra called "Bird!" around a thick cigar. The clay leapt into the air. He fired, but the disc continued on its path unmolested, descending on its arc until it vanished into a drift of snow. "Damn." He cursed, violently levering open his shotgun and plucking out the smoking hull.

Impatiently observing the rest of the round, Niklas watched as the final shooter finished and the men slung their shotguns over the crooks of their arms, meandering toward the scorekeeper.

"Niklas!" Ezra shouted with insincere joviality. "Welcome. Grab a cigar from the table if you're so inclined." He knew Niklas didn't smoke. "Too bad you just got here. Could have shown these boys a thing or two." Turning toward the others, he said, "My nephew here is a skilled hand with guns. In fact, he was a gunsmith during the war. Kept up the tools so our boys could stay in the fight."

The other men muttered a chorus of trite acknowledgments.

"Well done."

"Thank you for your service, young man."

Head down and hands in his pockets, Niklas struggled to meet their eyes. Their appreciation was aggravatingly superficial. These men—these noble captains of industry—chewing their expensive cigars, wallets and bellies fat with excess, were just profiteers who had stood on the sidelines during the war, growing their fortunes at the cost of millions of young men like Niklas and Kessler. Men who had been piled up like refuse and rolled into unmarked graves, buried in flooded shell craters or used as makeshift sandbags. And for that sacrifice their families received a pension so meager that the men before him now wouldn't deem it worth picking up off the sidewalk. "Uncle, you needed me for something? I'm in a bit of a hurry."

"Yeah, I do. This lousy shotgun is inaccurate as hell. And I paid a premium for it. Must be something you can do to fix it." He shoved the double into Niklas' hands. It was a lovely Greener sidelock, festooned in ornate scrollwork and fine checkering—worth a fair sight more than his life on the best of days.

There was nothing wrong with it. He had watched Ezra's technique closely in the previous round. His uncle didn't seat the shotgun properly against his shoulder before firing, began pulling his cheek off the stock to see the results the instant he fired, and didn't follow through on passing shots.

"Maybe the sights got bumped," Niklas mumbled, wondering if the taxi driver was still in the driveway and could take him back to St. Paul straightaway. There was no telling when Oscar and Kessler would return to the apartment and there was no time to waste if they were to stop Barbieri before he skipped town.

"Yeah, I'm sure that's it." Ezra lit a match and wanded it across the tip of his cigar.

"I'll take it back to the apartment and work on it." He would keep the shotgun for a few days and return it without doing a damn thing. And his uncle would be none the wiser.

"Great. Great. Now, gentlemen, if you'll excuse us for a moment," Ezra said graciously, gripping Niklas' shoulder and steering him away from the others.

"What happened to you?" he whispered harshly. "You look like you went sledding down a flight of stairs—on your face."

"Sidewalks are slick this time of year."

"Spare me. There's no way Goldmann did that to you, is there?"

"No, he didn't. I take it he didn't make it to your little dinner party?"

"He did not, but now he's ranting about having been accosted, insisting I'm responsible."

"You are."

"That's not the point. The point is he's linked your assault to me. That's you and that halfwit brother of yours making a complete mess of things. The simplest task, and you've botched it." He leaned in close, threateningly, breath warm and stinking of tobacco. "I have a reputation to maintain and people talk. These people talk." He nodded over his shoulder. "And that might impact my livelihood. If there's one thing I've taught you over the years, it's that you don't fuck with a man's livelihood."

"You know I would hate to endanger your livelihood. That said, don't ever insult my brother in front of me again. You can look down your nose at anyone, including me if you're so inclined. But leave his name out of your mouth."

"You think the word halfwit is too harsh?"

"You wouldn't know. You've spoken, what, three words to him in your lifetime? We didn't even know you existed until we moved here. You couldn't even be bothered to mail a letter during our entire childhood."

"You weren't worth knowing until you came here."

"That's the problem with you, Uncle. You only see value in terms of dollars or utility. Think you can buy a family when they suit you, but it doesn't work that way."

"I bought you and your brother cheaply enough."

Niklas breathed out through his nose. He bit down so hard he thought his teeth might shatter. The pragmatic side of his brain screamed for him to bite his tongue and move on. Don't take the bait. He needed to get back to the apartment before Kessler got impatient and attempted a rescue of Kosena by himself. But he felt an embittered rage building in his chest, threatening to combust if he didn't say anything. The words came out as though they were spoken by someone else. "We won't be bought anymore."

His uncle grinned wickedly. "Does that mean you're resigning?"

"I suppose it does. Effective immediately."

"You speak for your brother, too? That's sure to be a shock when you tell him. No more fancy clothes. No more wining and dining floozies."

"I speak for my brother, just as he speaks for me. And he would have done the same in my stead. Something you couldn't possibly understand."

"You know, without me, you two never would have made it here. I gave you a job when no one else would, as a favor to your mother."

"A job?" Niklas asked incredulously. "You shoved us in your back offices and paid us half what you paid everyone else despite doing twice the work. While you sit on your mountain of money, smoking fine cigars and collecting fast cars, we've scraped by on pennies, living in the slums. You'll forgive me if I'm less grateful than you had hoped."

"That's your problem, Niklas: You think you're owed something. You don't think I pay you enough? Go ask 3M for a job. They'll take anyone. Go burden them with your incessant whining."

Niklas leaned the shotgun in his hands against a nearby tree and headed for the driveway.

"One of my foremen found a discrepancy in the logbooks," Ezra shouted after him, staring at Niklas' back.

He stopped walking.

"You filed an order to take one of my lakers out of service for repairs on one of her steam turbines. Curiously, the same issue that had been fixed on that same ship six months ago."

"Same issue, different turbine," Niklas said flatly. "The turbines are the same age, from the same manufacturer, subjected to the same conditions. Stands to reason if one fails, the other will follow soon after."

"Even assuming that's true, when the crew was asked about it, none of them could seem to recall where they were during said maintenance. Stranger still, the Superior Shipbuilding Company has no record of the ship ever arriving at their yards. Yet it was gone for two weeks." Arrogance glittered in his uncle's eyes. He clearly relished this moment, having cornered Niklas, cajoling him into a position of weakness. "Come to think of it, you were gone during those same two weeks. Any explanation for that?"

Niklas said nothing. Instead, he stepped toward Ezra, picking up the shotgun leaning against the tree, and shouldered past him. Approaching the table where the rest of the group had congregated around a crystal decanter of cognac, he shook a pair of shells from a box and thumbed them into the open action of the shotgun. "Miller, put two birds on the thrower for me, please."

Glancing first at Ezra, the man complied, hustling back toward the thrower and prepping two clay pigeons.

Closing the action and shouldering the shotgun, Niklas shouted, "Pull!"

Two clays soared through the air. Two shots followed in rapid succession, both birds exploding into a dark cloud of molecular pieces. Extracting the wax-paper hulls with his fingertips and letting them tumble into the snow, he returned to his uncle's side, shoving the gun into his hands. "There's nothing wrong with this gun. It must be you."

A friable foundation

Returning to the apartment, Niklas nearly collided with Kessler as he leapt down the stairway, taking three stairs at a time on his way toward the door. He had a wild look in his eyes tinged with a cruel excitement that Niklas had never seen before. It was unsettling, a look of righteous anger that had found an outlet. "We got one of Barbieri's men. We were at the Green Lantern to ask MooMoo about setting up a meeting with Danny Hogan, right? We look over, and this guy's at the bar, three sheets to the wind, bragging about last night and how Barbieri's got our guns."

"What did you do with him?" Niklas asked, his voice tense. "You didn't bring him here, did you?" His eyes darted up the stairs toward their apartment.

"No, no. Oscar's got him tied up at the warehouse now—the same one we met Barbieri in. I came here hoping to find you."

"You left him alone with Oscar?"

"Well, yeah. Once Oscar starts working on him, he'll fold like an origami swan," Kessler said, rubbing his palms together eagerly. "He'll tell us where the guns are and where Kosena is being held, then we'll go kill that sonofabitch Barbieri."

"You left Oscar alone with him?" Niklas repeated gravely. "You told him not to touch the guy until we're all there, though, right?"

"Well, no. I figured we don't have any time to waste. I asked him to get anything he could from him."

Niklas groaned and ran out of the apartment, Kessler following on his heels, calling after him. Ignoring his shouts, Niklas sprinted across the street, the soles of his shoes slipping and sliding on the ice. A dairy truck swerved, narrowly avoiding flattening him. Cheeks flush, feeling his heartbeat in his ears, he quickened his pace— running as fast as he trusted on the icy sidewalk.

Oscar knew numerous people throughout the Twin Cities and was generally well liked, strolling between different factions and social classes with ease. But he didn't consider many of them friends. It took a lot for him to trust anyone, but once he did, the loyalty he showed them was absolute. Niklas and Kessler were among those few he trusted completely. They had fought and bled together, experienced cold and deprivation, victory and horrors. As such he would willfully commit any assortment of crimes of both a legal and moral nature if they asked him to—or if he mistakenly thought they had asked him to. If Kessler instructed Oscar to get information from Barbieri's man, he would do it without protest, without reservation, without pity.

Even if it struck another blow to the already friable foundation supporting what remained of his sanity.

Niklas drove his shoulder into the warehouse door and stumbled inside, Kessler following close behind. Silence greeted them. The smell of blood and urine hung in the air.

As he walked further inside, Niklas heard a soft weeping. Like a stifled laugh from a church loft. He knew what had happened before he even laid eyes on the scene. His stomach lurched dangerously as his fears were realized.

Oscar stood before the prisoner, the man bound wrist and ankle to a steel beam with coarse rope, head twisted at an unnatural angle, hair matted, gone black with coagulated blood, eyes staring emptily into the distance like those of a taxidermied deer. A gallon of blood stained the man's shirtfront and pant legs. Small, fleshy pieces lay scattered at his feet like peanut shells on a bar floor.

Fingertips.

A pair of rusty tin snips, dripping red, hung from Oscar's right hand.

Approaching slowly, Niklas swallowed back the bile threatening to scale his throat and placed a hand on his friend's shoulder. Oscar jumped as though he had been shocked. Clearing his throat and wiping at his eyes with his sleeve, he grunted, "Soo Line Freight Yard. They'll load the guns on the train tonight at eight o'clock. He's still got Kosena. She's alive—for now."

"Thanks, Oscar."

"I didn't want to..." he trailed off. His lip quivered and his eyes filled with tears again. "But he wouldn't...."

"It's all right." Niklas said comfortingly. "You did what needed to be done. I'm sorry you had to do it alone." He glared at his brother as Kessler looked on in horror. "You can stand down now, comrade."

Hand automatically reaching inside his coat pocket, Oscar retrieved his flask, fumbling with the cap, smearing the tarnished copper with bloody fingerprints. After a long drink, his eyes pinched shut, he said softly, "I'm gonna take a walk. Clean myself up. Get drunk. I'll meet you at the apartment later." The tin snips clattered sharply upon the concrete floor. He turned and slowly made his way toward a far wall like a listless child being led away by his mother.

Grabbing his brother's shoulder, Niklas steered him toward the exit.

"Jesus, I had no idea—" Kessler whispered, still breathing heavily from the run from the apartment. "I mean, dear God. That..."—he shook his head, pointing a finger in Oscar's direction—"...that was not our Oscar. How could he—"

Niklas didn't stop walking or turn to look at him.

"How could I have known?" Kessler added, clearly seeking to console himself rather than expecting an actual answer.

Jaw set, his face contorted in barely suppressed fury, Niklas halted mid-stride and grabbed Kessler by the epaulets of his coat. "We don't have time for this. Our future hangs in the balance. Everything we have planned for, everything we have risked since before we left France is tipping on a razor's edge. One more mistake, one more careless misstep, and we lose the guns and Kosena forever."

"You don't think I know that?" Kessler shot back, grabbing his brother's wrists and breaking his grip with a sharp tug. "I'm not stupid. I know what's at stake. I just...didn't know Oscar would take it this far."

The two men stood quietly a few feet apart, anger ebbing, grim resignation taking its place.

"He took it as far as he needed to," Niklas muttered. "Now it's our turn."

Toothpick

The yips and whines of dozens of greyhounds straining impatiently at their leashes punctuated the grumble of the crowd milling along the periphery of the makeshift racetrack. Unlike summertime horse races at the St. Paul Fairgrounds, where men sipped mint julips in their expensive suits, their wives and mistresses parading new dresses and large floral hats, Dapper Dan Hogan's dog races were entertainment for the masses. Here, the city's working class congregated to make a bet or grab a cheap drink and while away the dreary winter months. Today's race was held in an abandoned brewery—one of those that hadn't outwardly transitioned to making soft drinks or cereal beverages when Prohibition first began, and so had gone out of business. Sunlight bled through the dust- and mildew-covered windows, slicing through panes missing shards in blinding white spears.

Niklas and Kessler pushed and writhed their way through the mass of bodies, sliding against coats censed with woodsmoke and stale sweat.

A bell clattered and a gate opened. The crowd erupted in cheers as the greyhounds zipped by, a vague blur of legs glimpsed between onlookers. Begrimed hands held wrinkled wads of cash overhead, then began stripping off notes and exchanging them, the incoming and outgoing bets lively and constant. Voices hollered odds, bookies holding their hands up and signaling across the crowd, whistles and shouts ringing out like the New York Stock Exchange—if the Stock Exchange had been relocated to a root cellar.

They made their way to the front of the crowd. Niklas identified one of Hogan's lackeys, overseeing the betting while chewing on a toothpick and rolling a coin across the tops of his knuckles. A quick scan revealed at least half a dozen more such men, none of them participating in the betting, instead chatting idly among themselves, hands crossed at their fronts, chests out, eyes watchful, scanning for foul play or the makings of a fight.

Nearing the man with the toothpick, Niklas shouted above the din, "Excuse me, I'm looking for Dan Hogan. You know where I might find him?"

Toothpick laughed derisively. "Might as well have come in here looking for Jesus Christ. He's everywhere and nowhere. He lives in our hearts and minds." He tapped the auburn hair at his temple playfully. "And someday, if you're not careful, you'll meet him face to face." He said that last bit with a menacing smirk, looking straight into Niklas' eyes as if daring him to respond. He was a young man, early twenties, well built, with a few telltale white scars on his cheekbones and knuckles proving he was no stranger to a fight.

Niklas only nodded. He wasn't going to make this easy. "It's a simple question. Where can we find him today? It's urgent."

"Oh, ye hear that, boys?" he said to no one in particular, his voice a mocking singsong. "Urgent, he says. Well, in that case." He slipped a hand into his pocket and casually withdrew a set of brass knuckles that looked as though they had been exercised on more than one occasion. "Let me explain something to ya, ya dense fucker." He poked Niklas' chest with his index finger. "You don't go around looking for a man like Mister Hogan. He finds you, but only if'n he wants te. You keep on askin' questions like dat, you're gonna end up missing teeth."

From behind him, Kessler materialized from the crowd. His arm wrapped dexterously around Toothpick's neck and pulled tight like a snare trap. At the same time, he punched his other arm upward beneath the man's armpit, planting his palm against the back of his head. The toothpick fell from his lips and tumbled to the floor, his face blossoming purple, tumescent veins rising across his forehead and neck as he squirmed helplessly.

"We're done asking nicely," Kessler muttered into Toothpick's ear as he tightened his hold. A pained grunt emerged from between the man's lips as his feet skittered a desperate tattoo atop the floor.

Hogan's other security guards began shoving their way through the crowd, moving toward them quickly. One brandished a leather sap, another a nickel-plated revolver.

Reaching into his pocket, Niklas pulled forth an American Mk II grenade. He tugged the pin and placed it between his teeth, mockingly rolling it around and bouncing it on his lip like a toothpick. Holding the explosive over his head so the approaching guards could see it, he looked around defiantly. A series of gasps followed from the nearby crowd. "Let's try this one last time, because I'm getting the sense you don't believe we're serious."

A space opened up around them as people fled. Hogan's men froze mid-step.

Easing off the pressure, Kessler allowed Toothpick to take a breath. "The hell is wrong with ye?" he wheezed. "You could kill dozens in here with that. Put it away, all right? We can talk."

Nodding to Kessler to let him go, Niklas moved the grenade into his coat pocket but didn't return the pin, keeping it between his lips where it could remind Hogan's men of the risk of starting trouble.

Once Toothpick had recovered and was breathing normally again, he gestured for them to follow him. "Stay and keep an eye on the last race," he ordered the other guards. "This will only take a minute."

They followed Toothpick through the crowd. Reaching a far door, he led them inside an adjacent room. The sound of the crowd faded behind them. Around them stood derelict boilers, silos, and tuns, orange rust nibbling away at the steel.

"All right, then. You now have my undivided attention," Toothpick said, crossing his arms and attempting to sound gruff despite clearly being unsettled by his rough handling, something he was no doubt used to giving, not receiving. His neck remained bright red from Kessler's attack, the makings of a bruise already forming near his throat. "Why do ya need t'see Mister Hogan so badly?"

"I can't disclose the details to you in full," Niklas said.

Toothpick looked at him incredulously. "Then take your goon and your grenade and fuck off," he spat. "Quit wasting my time. It's a race day, in case you hadn't noticed."

"What I mean is, the situation is as delicate as it is urgent. If I tell you all the critical details and you start running your mouth around the city, it could derail everything and get us killed. I can't take that chance."

"I can keep quiet. You have my word."

"Your word means nothing to me. I don't know you. Hell, a minute ago you were threatening to cave in my face if I didn't leave." Plucking the pin from his mouth, Niklas slid it back through the handle of the grenade before returning it to his pocket. "Here's what I am willing to tell you: Mister Hogan is in the business of things that men will kill for. We're in the business of things that men use to do the killing. Some…commodities of ours were stolen last night. If your boss helps us recover them, we will reward him handsomely and we can do business together in the future. And trust me when I say he *will* want to do business with us."

Toothpick seemed to contemplate that before nodding. "I'll make a phone call. But fair warning: If you're acting the maggot, Mister Hogan will kill ya faster than you can blink."

"Noted."

"Monkeys!" Kessler exclaimed, a broad smile erupting across his face as he pointed at the window, toward the track beyond. Handlers had begun saddling the greyhounds with capuchin monkeys, the primates dressed in colorful jockey outfits.

"Aye, it's the last heat of the day," Toothpick said with a subtle grin. "You fellas should get out there and throw a bet at it." He sighted down his finger, pointing at a specific monkey. "That jammy bastard with his hand fastened to his langer wins most often."

This isn't goodbye

Rudkøbing, Island of Langeland, Denmark
September 1920

*T*he battlefield opened up like a seismic rift, drawing into the void everything near it. Soldiers, dogs, livestock, beasts of burden, all plunging and tumbling downward, falling until they were so deep they could no longer see the sky. Bathed in a red glow, Niklas could make out thousands of writhing bodies as they funneled toward rows of enormous steel gears. As the teeth of the gears meshed together, they pestled the sliding bodies into a bloody paste. The screams and the grinding of the steel pulverizing bone swept a chill through him. He scrambled madly to climb away from the gears, every muscle in his body straining, but each inch he advanced was promptly lost as another flood of limbs swept at his feet, desperate hands tugging at his wrists and ankles, pulling him down with them, pleading to no one in particular to be saved, to show mercy. Just as the gears began to chew at the soles of his feet, his eyes snapped open and he sat bolt upright. For a few moments he sat at the edge of his bed, head in his hands, running fingers through his sweat-slicked hair and willing his heartbeat to slow. He tried to match his brother's slow, rhythmic breathing coming through the darkness from the adjacent bed. Feeling desperately thirsty, he left the room for a drink of water.

Stepping lightly toward the kitchen, toes curling against the ice-cold oak flooring, he stopped mid-step. Sitting in a chair by the woodstove, his father stared intently at the flames, chin in hand, cheeks glistening with tears. Niklas hung back, concealed in the shadows. He willed himself to step into the room, to sit beside him, rest a sympathetic hand on his shoulder, and assure him everything would turn out fine. But he knew they were at an impasse. Milas would never support their plan to sell the guns, and Niklas would never yield to his father's wishes for them to stay in Denmark. There was no room for discussion or compromise, only sadness and regret from both of them. Niklas returned to bed and lay awake amidst the tangled, sweat-soaked sheets until morning.

The day of their departure dawned. The horses, harnessed and tethered to the wagon, stomped expectantly at the dirt. The boys hefted their luggage into place, fastening it down with a length of dirty rope worn glass-smooth with handling. Last to go on the pile was a leather trombone case. It weighed more than the others. Kessler had vowed to keep that one close until they reached the States.

Milas wore his Sunday best to take his sons to their ship. Such was the occasion that he had even dusted off his tarnished gold pocket watch—a modest inheritance from his father—the delicate fob chain draped across his midsection. Niklas had only ever seen him wear it for weddings. And funerals.

Milas didn't look at either of them or speak for the duration of the ride.

Closing his eyes, Niklas focused on the early morning sunshine warming his face, the smell of dew on the grass and the oaky musk of the horses' sweat-stained leather bridles, the rhythmic clop of their hooves, and the steady grumble of the wagon wheels as they churned atop the gravel road. These were familiar sensations from his childhood, enduring relics from a past life to which he could never return. He fought to hold onto the faint glow of nostalgia, like shielding a dying ember from a heavy rain.

As the wagon crested the top of a large hill, the harbor appeared below. A coastal steamship bobbed beside the wharf. Despite being a modestly sized ship compared to an ocean-going vessel or the warships they had seen during the war, it seemed to tower over the hive of fishing trawlers and shallow-draft barges at anchor beside it. She would take them to Aarhus, where their passenger liner—the *Oscar II*—would deliver them to New York via a third-class stateroom.

Tugging on the reins, Milas coaxed the horses to a stop beside the wharf. They disembarked.

Milas hugged Kessler tightly and held on until Kessler finally eased him away with a melancholy smile.

"I'll get a dolly for our things." Nodding knowingly at Niklas, Kessler turned and entered the crowd milling along the wharf.

Milas and Niklas stood shoulder to shoulder beside the horses and stared at the ship docked before them. Streaks of rust, caused by water dribbling through the hawseholes, had discolored the massive panels of steel that made up the hull. Passengers had already boarded and now hung over the bulwark, shouting to their loved ones standing on the quay, fluttering handkerchiefs and waving.

"You'll write to me, won't you?" Milas asked, stroking one of the horse's ears. His voice was so quiet Niklas could barely hear it over the murmur of the crowd nearby. "I set aside some money…." He rummaged through the pocket of his trousers and withdrew an envelope filled with bills and a few coins. With a quaking hand, he tried to forcefully stuff the envelope into Niklas' pocket. "Should pay for postage for a while."

"Dad, no." Niklas wrapped his hand around his father's wrist and resisted. The Danish krone had lost much of its value after the war. Milas needed that money now more than ever. All it would take was one bad crop, one protracted drought, and he would lose the farm. For a moment the two men pressed and strained against one another, the coins sliding out from the creases in the envelope, clinking on the stone quay and disappearing into its cracks and crevices. Tears streamed down Milas' face. Niklas felt his cheeks flush and his eyes burn and swell with tears of his own. "I don't need the money," Niklas assured, finally succeeding and pushing the envelope back into his father's hands. "I'll write to you. I promise. And when this is done, I'll send for you. Or we'll come home. You won't live out your days alone."

"Promise me you'll be safe?" Milas choked out. "I don't care what happens to me, but look out for your brother and keep yourself safe, too. If anything were to happen to you, I…." His voice faded, his eyes pinched together as his chin dropped to his chest, his sobs lost to the sound of the surrounding crowd and the crash of waves breaking against the stone pilings of the pier.

Gently clasping his hands, his skin like sun-warmed leather, Niklas rested his forehead against his father's. Niklas whispered, "I promise. You will see us again. I swear it. This isn't goodbye."

Even as he said it, he knew it was a lie.

Unproductive negotiations

The air in the cavernous abattoir carried upon it a metallic sharpness, a pervasive malodor of blood and death. The floor held a permanent claret-colored stain, the surface clutching at the soles of their shoes with each step. Heavy chains equipped with fearsome hooks as big as boat anchors dangled through dark apertures in the ceiling. Niklas and Kessler passed through a long corridor lined with cow carcasses split lengthwise, suspended by the legs from steel hooks and crossbars. White ribs lay sandwiched between carmine flesh like piano keys.

The drone of livestock trucks and the shouts of laborers came from nearby Concord Street.

Motioning for a piece of gum, Kessler leaned toward his brother as they walked, his gait uneven from the limp in his step. "I thought you said Hogan was a businessman. I was expecting to meet in a nice warm office or a club somewhere."

Patting his pockets for a pack of gum and coming up empty, Niklas instead tore half of the gum he had been chewing with his teeth and fingers, then offered the oddment to his brother. "We're just lucky to have found him as quickly as we did."

Waving the gum under his nose for a moment to purge the smell of their surroundings, Kessler then flicked it into his mouth with an appreciative nod.

They turned the corner to find Hogan and a few other men butchering cows, the animals suspended from the floor by their hind legs.

"Go on, then. Hands outta yer pockets." Hogan didn't look up as he cut free a gobbet of tissue from a hindquarter and tossed it into a porcelain bowl. "Grab a knife and start cuttin'. Make yerselves useful." His shirt sleeves were rolled to the elbows. A white apron, covered in blood and errant lumps of flesh, hung from his neck— thick as a chimney. Hogan was a heavyset man, stout and barrel-chested, in his late fifties. White hair had overtaken the red in his beard, a lattice of deep wrinkles spanning his forehead and the corners of his eyes. He sported a wide nose upon a wide face parked atop wide shoulders.

The brothers complied without protest, shedding their coats, rolling their sleeves, and selecting knives from a bin nearby.

Drawing a broad circle around the front shoulder of the carcass using the tip of his knife, Hogan said, "You two work on the brisket and foreshanks. Can't hardly do that wrong. It'll all get ground up anyway."

They set to work, carving away fist-sized pieces.

"Quite the operation you have here," Kessler observed.

"Eh, we're small potatoes compared to Swift and Armour down the street. Their factories are like wee cities. Make everything from soup to soap to fertilizer over there. Not us, though. We still do things the old way. Can't afford what it would take to compete. And why would we want to? What we do takes skill. Not just some assembly line of southern negroes and fresh-off-the-boat communists doing one simple thing over and over, not a single man knowing how to do it all himself. These boys here are of good Irish stock. The best butchers in the Midwest."

"You help out here often?"

"Naw, I've got a business to run. But I grew up workin' in a shop like this back in Wicklow. I still like to come down here to carve up a few choice pieces for supper and remind the boys that I'm not above getting my hands dirty. Speaking of which...." He turned to the other butchers and shouted, "Oy. Break time, gents. Take a walk." All the butchers immediately stopped their work and exited the room without hesitation or a word of protest. Waiting until the last one had departed, Hogan turned to them and spoke with a different voice. One stripped of any conviviality, filled instead with the sort of what-do-you-want-already impatience of a man who'd had his supper interrupted by a door-to-door salesman. "Most of them are good, honest men with families. Don't need to burden them with overhearing our conversation, which I can only assume involves things of an illegal nature given the way you introduced yerself to my man at the races. Now, I'm told you have a proposition fer me."

"We do," Niklas confirmed. "We need fighting men. I expect you have a few on your payroll. In exchange, we have some...commodities I believe you may find of interest. I think we can work together."

"You need men fer what, exactly?" Hogan asked, casually inspecting the brothers' technique as they continued to carve away at the carcass.

"That requires a little background. We've been negotiating with a Chicago mobster named Nunzio Barbieri."

Hogan gave a sort of knowing growl. "Aye, I know him. One of those guinea dagos from Chicago. With the Genna family."

"A nephew or cousin, I think," Niklas added. "He's close with the brothers, I know that much."

"So I take it by the state of yer bakes your negotiations haven't been productive."

"Barbieri doesn't subscribe to any notions of honor or integrity." Using the knuckle of his pointer finger, Niklas rubbed the bruise on his jaw, now the kaleidoscopic hues of an oil slick.

"What were you negotiating with?"

Kessler plunged his knife into the flank of the carcass and looked for a place other than his nice slacks to wipe his hands. A pregnant silence filled the air as the brothers first looked at each other, then at Hogan, reluctance obvious on their faces. "Guns," Niklas finally said.

The word seemed to resonate and hang in the air, like a wrong note played loudly at the end of a song. Hogan stopped cutting and looked at them with what appeared to be a frown, though his lips disappeared into his beard, and the permanent creases above his eyes revealed no more insight into his mood. With surprising speed for a man of his age and girth, he launched himself at Niklas, shoving him backward against a butcher block table. He batted the knife in Niklas' hand away as though swatting at an obnoxious fly, the blade clattering and sliding atop the floor into some distant corner of the room. Amidst the screeching of the sliding table and the grunting of the embattled men, Kessler shouted in surprise and went for his Bergmann.

Like a charging water buffalo, Hogan continued to force Niklas backward. The soles of Niklas' shoes slipped on the concrete as his hands tried to find something to push against, to gain purchase and resist. The searing chill of Hogan's knife blade raced up his neck, surgically sharp despite being covered in shavings of red flesh. Hogan held it against him with just enough pressure to ensure he wouldn't move, the Irishman's hands stinking of blood and cigar smoke.

Hogan leaned in close, ignoring the pistol trained on his back and Kessler's shouted orders to release his brother. His voice was low and firm. "I cannae abide those running criminal enterprises in my city without my knowledge. It's a rule that goes beyond me, you understand? It's my job to enforce that rule. If I don't, everything this city is built on falls apart faster than a lace handkerchief in a toilet bowl. You and Barbieri have broken dat rule, so I should kill you both."

Niklas didn't dare a word. His body, already weakened from the beating he had received the night before, began to falter, his muscles trembling as he tried to hold himself away from the knife. But Hogan knew how to use his size and weight to his advantage and kept him pinned in place, one hand wrapped in his shirtfront, the other pressing the knife tightly against his skin, shoving him backward and off balance until only Niklas' heels touched the floor.

Staring unblinkingly at his attacker, Niklas muttered, "We've realized our mistake. And we want to make it up to you."

The big man stared him in the eyes as if searching for a sign of deception, a glimmer of duplicity. Finding none, Hogan released him with an accepting grunt. Turning back toward the cow carcass, he resumed cutting, apparently satisfied with Niklas' admission.

Kessler lowered his pistol but kept the muzzle trained on Hogan, still distrustful of his radical change in temperament.

"What sort of guns were you selling to Barbieri?" Hogan asked over his shoulder.

"Madsens, Vickers, and Chauchats."

The knife fell from Hogan's hand and clattered on the floor, ringing like a railroad conductor's handbell. "Jesus, Mary, and Joseph. Those aren't just guns, lads, you're talking feckin' artillery! Where in God's name did you come up with those? And you want me to send my boys up against them now? Are you mad?"

"They're all missing their firing pins."

"Do the Sicilians know that?"

"I doubt it."

A caterpillar brow rose slowly into an intrigued arch above Hogan's eye. "So we'd be going up against a bunch of banjaxed machine guns and not much else?"

"That about capturses it."

A subtle grin crept onto Hogan's face as he picked up his knife from the floor and wiped the blade on his apron. "That's an entirely different story, then. And you have more guns like those for us?" he probed.

"As payment for helping us take down Barbieri, you can keep the guns you take off of Barbieri's crew. We'll give you the parts to make them functional again," Niklas said. "All we ask in return is for your protection. We plan to continue selling guns to out-of-staters from Chicago and out east. We want you to provide the muscle and the influence to make sure they don't upset future deals with any more of this kind of funny business."

Hogan scratched contemplatively at his beard with the spine of his knife blade. "I'm still not sure about going to war with a gang from Chicago. Strikes me as a daft plan. See, I'm a diplomat at heart. Don't like unnecessary bloodshed when it can be avoided."

The boys exchanged skeptical glances as Niklas swept a hand across his neck where, just seconds before, Hogan's blade had rested. "I would look at it less like starting a war and more like delivering a cautionary shot across their bow. Barbieri is operating on your territory without your permission. If the Gennas learn that Barbieri ripped off gun sellers who were under your auspices, they will realize he delivered the opening salvo."

"This could be an opportunity to flex your muscles a bit, let everyone know you, and you alone, run St. Paul," Kessler added.

Niklas nodded. "And in return, we will equip you with the tools to become the head of the most indisputably powerful organization in the upper Midwest."

Hogan tossed another chunk of meat into a bowl and wiped his hands on his apron. They became no cleaner.

"Ye make a convincing argument, boys." He offered a hand—big as a baseball glove—to them both to shake. "Besides, how much trouble could a little pissant like Barbieri be?"

"He's dangerous. A former soldier. I wouldn't dismiss him," Kessler cautioned.

"You think Barbieri is a veteran?" Hogan asked.

"He kept going on about his fighting the Germans at the Marne Front."

The Irishman laughed, a deep, hacking, ugly roar. "He wasn't in the war. His da bought out his service. Called in a favor from the governor and promised him thousands in campaign funds for reelection."

"He seemed pretty ruthless for such a coward," Kessler said.

"Never said he was a coward. Just said he didn't fight in the war. If anything, that probably made him worse for it. While his childhood friends and classmates were in the trenches, he sat at home, trying to avoid being seen and publicly shamed. Now he feels like he's got something to prove. Instead of fighting his war in France, he's fighting it on the streets of Chicago. And, now it seems, St. Paul."

Too late for a plan

It was clear no one casually visited the St. Paul Medical Examiner's Office. There had been no effort to make any part of it, even the entryway, in any way welcoming. Every surface had been painted a muted brown or gray. The acrid fumes of vinegar, Borax, and embalming fluid seemed to force their way up the nostrils and nest behind the eyes. A single wooden bench adorned the waiting area. It looked about as comfortable as a medieval rack.

Rumor had it that the doxies from Nina Clifford's brothel a few doors down frequently came here for inexpensive venereal disease tests.

Niklas approached the front desk. The clerk, a skeletal harridan in tortoiseshell glasses, her skin the same shade of gray as the walls, looked up from her newspaper. She stared at him with the intensity and cruelty of a magnifying glass hovering above an anthill.

"Is Detective Stauss available?" he asked quietly, as if anything louder than a whisper might wake the dead.

"Young man, this is the coroner's office. It's not open to the public."

"I understand. But he asked me to meet him here. Said it was a matter of some urgency. If you could just get him for me, I would be most appreciative."

Her defenses were not to be overcome with mere pleading from a stranger, no matter how charming or polite. "You should leave," she snarled, her voice laced with venomous undertones. She looked like the type who kept a few baneful curses, hexes, or spells close at hand, so Niklas resolved to retreat to the front steps and try not to freeze to death while he waited for Stauss to come out of the morgue.

"Send him in, Mildred." Stauss' familiar, nasally voice echoed along a concrete hallway leading into the depths of the building.

Mildred huffed at him before returning to her newspaper.

The hallway seemed to get colder with each stride. He eased down a few steps before passing through a set of double doors propped open with scarred wood wedges. He found Stauss alone, standing before the body of a young man. The two were bathed in dim light, motionless. The scene looked like a baroque painting—stark and tense, awash in darkness and sorrow. The dead man's expression was one of forlorn acceptance. His bare torso was the color of chalk, nearly as white as the sheet draped from the top of his hips to the end of the autopsy table. But there was no outline of legs beneath the thin fabric, nor the rise of toes pressing upward where feet should have been.

"This kid came to me a few days ago," the detective said solemnly, his voice a hollow echo in the bare room. "Said that he and a friend of his got an invitation to try out some new can house that had just opened on St. Peter Street. Claimed they had the cleanest and cheapest women. They got there and half of the women were underage girls—kids his little sister's age. So I did a little digging. Turns out the owner of this new joy house is a mutual acquaintance of ours: a man named Nunzio Barbieri." He let that hang in the air for a moment before continuing. "He's been taking orphan girls from Chicago—most of them immigrants who can't speak a word of English—and bussing them up here, forcing them into prostitution." He glanced at Niklas coldly, with a look of condemnation and disgust. Stauss aimed a finger at the corpse like a dog owner pointing out a mess to a disobedient pup. "He said he would testify against anyone I arrested for this. I told him to be careful. If anyone saw him with me or learned he had gone to the cops, I would end up finding him in a ditch. Well I was wrong." His eyes glistened and his voice wavered. "It wasn't a ditch. I found him half submerged in Phalen Lake, his legs taken off at the knees with an ice saw. They stuffed the rest of him through a hole in the ice. All he could do was cling to the edge and hope someone would hear his screams. The frigidity of the water slowed his blood flow, so he survived much longer than he otherwise would have. His suffering must have been…immeasurable. Now his friend is missing, too. I don't have high hopes for him."

Niklas stared at the floor and said nothing.

"The station's coroner is overworked with all the killings in the city and he was an imbecile to begin with." Glancing down at a notepad near the table, Stauss ran a finger in line below the text as if to underline it. "He listed the cause of death as hypothermia." His lips curled up as though to smile. Tears forged a shimmering path down his cheek. "Hypothermia."

After a long, silent moment, Niklas said, "Was this what you wanted to meet about? To make sure I knew Barbieri was a bad man? Color me surprised."

The detective shook his head and wiped his eyes with his sleeve, his expression pained. "Those guns…I warned you."

"I take it you already know."

"I know a great deal more than you give me credit for. I have ears all over the city. A pair of those ears happened to be across the street from Royal Shade and Awning when a truckload of Sicilian gangsters kicked in the door and hauled out a number of crates curiously labeled *tractor parts*. Somehow, the owners—a very sweet older couple—seemed to have no recollection of those crates being there or have any idea what they might need with tractor parts given the nature of their business."

Niklas bit his lip and winced.

"So now the same man who did this"—Stauss nodded at the dead man before him—"has an arsenal that would be the envy of the Irish Republican Army, the Italian fascists, and every other fledgling insurgency on the planet. Due entirely to your recklessness and greed. In spite of my pleading with you not to do it."

"I'm trying to make it right. I have a plan."

"It's too late for that," the detective said dismissively. "Here's the deal, Niklas: If we can't find Barbieri before he skips town—assuming he hasn't already—someone is still going to prison for those guns. At this point, it looks like that will be you and your brother. You are certainly the most obvious and accessible suspects. And I'm afraid this time you won't be getting out with only a donation from your wealthy uncle." He sighed sadly and rubbed his protuberant nose with the back of his wrist. "Embezzlement of government property, aiding and abetting criminals…there's a manslaughter charge or two wrapped up in there, too. And when those guns make their first appearance—and I can't imagine it will take Barbieri long to put them to use—it will get the full, undivided attention of the Bureau of Investigation. And you know what the feds love more than anything? A quick win. They will find you and your brother rotting in Stillwater, follow the little red line of yarn back to Barbieri and his guns, and make an example of you."

He weighed the detective's words carefully. He knew what Stauss was implying: If he could find a way to hand him Barbieri and the guns—or even just the guns—he could save himself and Kessler from a life behind bars. The problem was, if the police made a move to capture Barbieri before he left town, they would end up clashing with Dan Hogan's men, too. That was bound to be messy for the Kristoffersons and Detective Stauss. The former because Hogan would believe they had set him up and would seek revenge. The latter because Hogan all but owned the city's police department and had most of St. Paul's politicians in his pocket, too. But he didn't have many options at this point. The most pressing threat was imprisonment. Stay out of prison, stay alive. That would give him enough latitude to figure out how to get their money. He could salvage this.

"I can get you the guns," Niklas said quietly. "They're being loaded up tonight. Soo Line Freight Yard. Barbieri won't be expecting trouble. He thinks he's scared us off and he's home free."

The detective nodded his head subtly, as though he knew the confession of Barbieri's whereabouts had been forthcoming all along.

"There is one complication," Niklas added.

"There always is," Stauss sighed.

"We've already convinced Dan Hogan to move on Barbieri in exchange for the guns." He felt his pulse quicken and the words came faster now. "You could arrest the lot of them in one place tonight."

Stauss looked at him with the revulsion of someone who had been served a decadent dessert covered in rancid onion. "Hogan has deep connections in the department. It would be career suicide to arrest his men."

"I understand. But if you want the guns, I don't see how else you can get them."

"Just call him off," the detective said plainly. "I'll get a squad together and we'll take down Barbieri ourselves."

"I tell him the cops are getting involved, he'll make a call to the chief of police and you'll find yourself working security at the local skating rink for the rest of your career. He wants those guns for himself. That was our arrangement: He takes out Barbieri's men, he gets the guns."

Like a general formulating a strategic plan of attack, Stauss began pacing slowly before the wall of steel doors where the bodies were stored, his chin in hand, tongue playing across his teeth. "That is problematic."

Niklas continued. "Here's the thing: Barbieri violated the O'Connor Layover Agreement. He never checked in with Hogan or the police before he began negotiating with us for the guns and setting up his prostitution racket here in the city. That should be all the explanation you need to move on him. You can arrest Hogan's men to maintain a veneer of neutrality, but let them go before you get to the station. You'll just have to manage the messaging afterward to make sure Hogan knows this was critical to taking Barbieri down and preserving his authority."

"He won't like that."

Sighing deeply, Niklas turned to leave. "Well, that makes three of us."

"One more thing, before you go," Stauss said, turning his back to him and staring at the ceiling, as though doing so would anonymize his words. "Barbieri's can house: It's called 'Little Italy.' St. Peter Street. Seems to me, if the police will be preoccupied with preparing to move on Barbieri tonight, someone should free those girls."

Inside the magician's hat

Despite not being included in the conversation that led to his termination from Uncle Ezra's employment, Kessler took the news of his sudden joblessness surprisingly well.

"I just couldn't bear to work for that pompous ass anymore," Niklas explained as he paced back and forth in their small bedroom, passing between the two beds, brushing Kessler's knees as he passed by and returned to the doorway. "I shouldn't have told him you were resigning, too. That wasn't my decision to make."

"I don't care about that, brother." The panic in his eyes suggested he cared more than he was letting on. "Where you go, I go. I hated being under his thumb, too."

"Yeah, tell him I quit, too," Oscar added, his eyes closed as he leaned against Kessler's headboard, feet crossed at the ankles atop the thin mattress. A nearly empty flask lay on his chest. He seemed in much better spirits after consuming a liter of them.

"You don't work for him, Oscar," Kessler reminded him.

Eyes opening drowsily, Oscar took on a contemplative air. "Well you remind him of that, then."

"If this goes to plan, and we can get the money from Barbieri, we'll have enough to be independent," Niklas said. "Start our own gun shop. Go legitimate while we discreetly move the rest of the machine guns. We won't need Uncle Ezra for anything ever again."

"Right now, all I care about is getting Kosena back safely." Kessler spoke it softly, a quiet reminder to his brother that it wasn't just their money that hung in the balance.

"And revenge," Niklas added.

"Absolutely. I intend to make Barbieri pay for everything he's done."

"Do you want to make an impression with the Madsen?" Niklas toed the empty trombone case toward his younger brother, the rifle still safely hidden beneath the floorboards.

"No, I'll stick with my Bergmann. The Irish are going to do the fighting. We're just there to get Kosena and get out."

"You're gonna take down Barbieri with a meager six shots? Might as well be a revolver."

"Six shots has always been plenty. I expect to need no more than one. Two at most if he happens to have a friend willing to die for him. And a man like Barbieri having a friend like that seems unlikely."

"How about thirty shots, instead? Just to be sure." Flipping open the lid of the steamer trunk at the foot of his bed, Niklas began digging toward the bottom and retrieved a long stick magazine, slapping the blued steel against his palm like a baton. "As luck would have it, Bergmann used the same dimensions for their submachine gun magazines as their pistols."

He handed it to Kessler, who dropped the flush-fit six-shot magazine from his Bergmann and inserted the submachine gun magazine in its place. It stuck out a foot and a half. "It's a touch unwieldy," he said, hefting the pistol in both hands.

"It will give you something to complain about while everyone but you is reloading."

"If we get to the point where we need that, we've made some big mistakes." Kessler shook his head and returned the magazine to his brother. "What do you intend to bring to the party?"

Niklas grinned. "Thought you'd never ask." He reached back inside the steamer trunk, pushing aside tools and keepsakes, and withdrew a small crate the size of a jewelry box, a wooden buttstock protruding from it. He opened it and withdrew a pair of Steyr-Hahn pistols welded together, the buttstock anchored between them, triggers bolted together, extended magazines protruding below. "Experimental design. The Huns called it the *Doppelpistole M.12*. Fully automatic. Nice and compact. Would have been great in the trenches if they had come up with it earlier in the war."

"How did you get that? And how long have you had it in there?" Kessler asked, peeking into the steamer trunk as though looking over a precipice into a bottomless chasm. "It's like a magician's hat. This apartment is barely big enough to sleep in. What other secrets have you squirreled away?"

"I can't tell you or you'll know where I've been hiding your Christmas presents."

"You're not actually going to bring that, are you?"

Niklas rocked his head ambivalently. "A little much?"

Holding his pointer finger an inch above the pad of his thumb, Kessler said, "A bit." Turning to Oscar, he asked, "What about you? Need to borrow a gun?"

"You know I'm a lover, not a fighter," Oscar replied airily. Tugging his pant leg up, he slid free a tarnished, bronze-handled trench knife from his boot—the violent lovechild of a combat knife and brass knuckles. First buffing it against his shirt sleeve, he began using the tip of the blade as a toothpick. "When do we leave?"

"You're not coming," Niklas said firmly. "You've earned a break."

Oscar's eyes narrowed, forehead wrinkling. "I don't need a break. I'm fine. Rest is for those too weak to march, and my legs are still strong."

"We could use his help—" Kessler began before Niklas shut him up with a finger aimed at his nose.

"You and I can handle Barbieri alone. Oscar has done enough for us these past few weeks. He deserves some rest and more payment than we can ever give him."

Sitting up from the bed, Oscar roughed his raven-black hair as though he had just awakened from a nap. "I know what you're doing. You are my comrades and you're looking out for me, just like in France. But you don't have to worry. I'm OK." He poked his temple. "All the baggage is tied down nice and secure now. Besides, what are my brothers going to do without me to look after them? You would probably go and—"

"Slip off the duckboards," they all said in unison.

"Well, if you're coming with us, I have one additional thing to ask you both before we meet Barbieri tonight," Niklas said, a hint of reluctance in his voice.

The other men looked at him expectantly.

"Turns out Barbieri wasn't just in St. Paul to buy our guns. He came to set up a brothel."

They looked at him with confused expressions. "So?"

"He's filled it with adolescent girls kidnapped from the streets of Chicago."

"Christ."

"We need to shut it down."

"Do we have time? They're loading the guns in just a few hours."

"It will be worth the time," Niklas explained. "Not only on principle, but because Barbieri will hear about it and send some of his men to investigate. That means fewer guards we'll have to deal with at the depot."

Oscar stood from the bed, a determined sharpness returning to his eyes despite his inebriated state. "When do we leave?"

"As soon as you're ready."

"Just like the old days, eh boys?" The smile faded from Kessler's face as if recalling a somber memory. "Only, it wasn't personal, then, was it? The Boche did what they were ordered to do, just like us. But this feels different."

Niklas knew exactly what he meant. This time, it was very different. A swell of contempt and animus bloomed inside him unlike any he had felt before. He would use that. Channel that hatred and wield it like a weapon.

He would do whatever was necessary to see things made right.

Violence of action

The air felt heavy with the promise of snow. Niklas and Kessler watched from across the busy street as Oscar entered the front door of Barbieri's brothel. Their friend had volunteered to impersonate a patron in order to get inside. That would provide them with a layout of the building's interior. Once Barbieri's guards discovered Oscar didn't have the money to pay for any services, he would undoubtedly be invited to leave. He would refuse. Loudly. That would inevitably result in his being forcibly thrown out, which would then reveal how many security guards Barbieri had inside.

Although none of them had been officers responsible for elaborate battlefield strategies during the war, all three men had seen enough combat to know what worked and what did not. The first priority, long before a single shot had been fired, was gathering intelligence. Learning their enemy's habits and rhythms. Assessing their resources. Identifying their weaknesses. Any insight they could gather now would provide them with the edge they needed to overcome superior numbers with precision and violence of action. Their attack would be sudden and brutal, shocking the guards into paralysis long enough to eliminate them. Niklas suspected that some of Barbieri's men inside were veterans themselves. Such men would be well-versed in the art of violence and would respond more quickly to a surprise attack than those without battlefield experience. All the more reason they would have to be quick and decisive, with every detail of the plan going precisely as arranged.

As anticipated, five minutes after entering, Oscar appeared at the doorway again, loudly remonstrating the two large men gripping him under each arm. They hurled him through the door and onto the icy sidewalk, where he slumped dramatically into a pile, his long hair a mess, a quavering hand outstretched as though desperately reaching for aid.

"Built for theater, that one," Niklas mumbled. Kessler chuckled around his pipe.

Once convinced he had sold the act and the guards had returned inside, Oscar clambered to his feet and hustled down the sidewalk away from the brothel.

He made a full circle of the block before materializing behind Niklas and Kessler. "Saw three of them inside. Two working the door, one working inside on the lower level. Sounded like a couple more upstairs, but those might have been customers. The bartender could get a wild hair to join in the fighting, too, but he doesn't seem like the type."

"That puts us at a minimum of three and as many as six," Kessler said. "I like those odds, as long as they don't see us coming."

"Were any of them armed?" Niklas asked.

"I didn't see any guns, but I would bet on it," Oscar said. Lowering himself to a knee, he began drawing the building's floor plan in a drift of dirty snow with his pointer finger. "Stairs are on the far wall, past the bar. We could take the two at the door, but that will alarm everyone inside and they'll dig in, probably using the girls for cover. We can't slug it out with them for long. We have to attack quickly and get away before backup or the cops show up."

"We also can't leave any survivors," Kessler said coldly. "If one of the guards escapes and gets to Barbieri before our raid tonight, he might just move the timeline up and escape before we can get to him."

"We need a man inside," Niklas said decisively as he scrutinized Oscar's illustration. "Get upstairs. Create a scene, draw them in, away from the front door. That will free up the entrance for the other two to get inside and take them out while they're preoccupied."

"They've seen Oscar. They'll recognize him, now," Kessler said. He looked at Niklas expectantly. Both men waited for the other to volunteer for the task of going in first.

After a long pause, Niklas said, "Swords it is. Odds or evens?"

"Evens, naturally."

"On three."

The two men pumped their fists toward each other three times before extending a single finger.

Smug in his victory, Kessler grinned. "Good luck in there, brother."

"Fine. Lucky bastard." Drawing his Steyr, Niklas press-checked the action for a live round.

"They check everyone at the door for weapons." Oscar held out a hand toward Niklas, palm up.

Handing his pistol to Oscar along with a pair of loaded stripper clips from his pocket, he asked, "You remember how to use this?"

Oscar shrugged and slipped the pistol into a pocket of his watchcoat. "Like riding a bicycle. Or so I'm told. Never ridden one."

Glancing over his shoulder at the brothel, Niklas said, "You two had better be right on time when this kicks off. Listen for the first gunshot. Hopefully it won't be the only one."

"We'll be right on time," Kessler assured. "And remember: No hesitation, no mercy. These bastards deserve it."

The sting of competing perfumes assailed his nose as Niklas entered the brothel. The two guards at the door gave him a cursory pat down, taking his pocketknife and tossing it in a box at the foot of the doorway. "You can get it on your way out."

He walked inside and entered the parlor. Young women by the dozen loitered within, resting on settees, chatting with one another, and brushing their hair. Despite their makeup, it was obvious many were underage.

A Victrola crackled and hissed a Paul Whiteman song from a distant corner. Behind an ornate bar, the bartender poured cheap champagne into flutes and nodded at him with a welcoming grin.

An older woman approached him. "Hello, sweetheart. My name's Alma. Is there a particular girl you would like to see tonight?"

"No one in particular," Niklas said. His voice sounded alien, distant, as though spoken by a stranger. He fought to disguise strong feelings of agitation and anxiety—he alone knew what was about to happen here—and make it appear as though he was merely new to this experience and unsure of himself.

"How long do you anticipate needing?" Alma asked.

"However much this will buy," he said, offering up a few wrinkled bills.

She accepted the money, looked it over, then waved at one of the young women to approach. "Arabella here will take good care of you."

"Right. Sure."

Without a word of greeting, Arabella took his hand and led him up the stairs, steering him toward a vacant bedroom.

During the war, many of the French villages they fought in or near still had civilian inhabitants. Women, young and old, desperate to feed their families after months spent enduring starvation and gunfire, would offer the troops the only thing they had—their bodies—in exchange for rations and money. He remembered thinking how unspeakably tragic that was. He couldn't help but to imagine if the war had been in his country, instead—if his own mother was forced to sell herself for a loaf of bread or a tin of corned beef. How helpless that made him feel. How disgusted he became at the men who took advantage of such desperation.

Arabella guided him to the foot of the bed and sat beside him. Niklas swiveled to face her. "Arabella, how old are you?"

"Eighteen," she said. Her voice had a strong rural English accent.

"Tell me the truth."

She hesitated, blushing and turning away.

"You're not in trouble," he assured. "But you don't belong here."

"I don't understand, sir."

"You were taken here against your will, weren't you?"

Tears welled in her eyes. "My name isn't even Arabella," she whispered. "It's Grace. They just thought Arabella sounded more exotic."

Nodding compassionately, he leaned toward her, keeping his voice low to ensure no one overheard. "I'm going to hurt the men who brought you here. Tonight. Very soon." He stood and approached a nearby floor lamp. Unplugging it from the wall, he hastily disassembled it, ripping out the cord and separating a two-foot length of the cast iron tube with a heavy decorative column on the end. Hefting it in his hand as if to weigh it, he gave it a few practice swings. "I don't want you to see what comes next, but I will need your help."

"What do you want me to do?" she asked, wiping away the tears with her wrists and giving a firm, resolved nod.

He glanced at the door and breathed out slowly, anticipating what came next and welcoming the adrenaline beginning to boil in his gut. "I need you to scream."

It took only a few seconds for the first of the guards to arrive once Grace let out the first shriek. Niklas instructed her to stay low, sheltering behind the headboard of the bed, and to not look out no matter what she heard. Positioning himself beside the door frame, he waited until the guard had flung open the door and stepped inside before swinging the makeshift weapon in his hand. He drove it home hard and met the man's temple. Collapsing to the floor, the guard's hands and legs went limp, save for his fingers twitching and gripping the rug, carrying on the fight alone with no more oversight from their owner.

The next guard in line approached more cautiously, a revolver drawn and held out before his chest. Grace emitted another piercing scream, making him jump, the gun going off in his hand and leaving a dime-sized hole in the plaster wall. Niklas launched himself at the gunman, slamming into him with his shoulder. The pistol thudded to the floor as the two men scrambled and fought to claim it.

More footfalls from the stairway. Niklas hoped the gunshot had been loud enough to signal Oscar and Kessler, and that they would make their move quickly. He had about ten seconds before the room would be filled with every remaining guard in the building. No clemency would be shown to him once they saw what he had done to their colleague.

A muted drumbeat of gunshots rang from below. The feet on the staircase stopped their ascent, turning to address the new threat. More thumps, louder now. A clamorous din of upset furniture and scrambling feet. Women screaming. The feral bellow of a wounded man followed by the heavy thud of a body pitching lifelessly to the floor. Amidst the chaos, Niklas and the remaining guard continued their desperate skirmish, sliding around the floor, neither man strong enough to break free nor incapacitate the other. Suddenly, Niklas felt a blinding heat and noise above him, followed by the spatter of warm blood. His opponent's body went limp instantly. He looked up to see Grace hovering nearby, the dead man's revolver quivering in her hands, looking far too heavy for her to hold.

Niklas leapt to his feet. Gingerly taking the gun from her, he gave it a cursory wipe down using the comforter on the bed to remove fingerprints. "If anyone asks, I shot him. The police will be here soon. I'll see to it that you and the other girls are taken care of when the dust settles."

She nodded absently, her eyes locked on the dead men on the floor. Niklas checked the hallway to make sure there were no more guards waiting outside, then descended the stairs, hollering for Kessler and Oscar not to shoot him.

They met in the parlor. Most of the girls had fled the building. Those who remained did their best to hide behind overturned furniture, whimpering softly as they held hands over their eyes and ears. Bodies of Barbieri's guards littered the floor, blood saturating the ornate carpet.

"Alma," Niklas called out, scanning the room.

The madam appeared from behind the phonograph, the device somehow unmolested by the gunfire and now insensitively belting out a joyous rendition of "Ain't We Got Fun." Her entire body trembled as she reluctantly approached.

"It's all right. We're leaving. I'm sorry you had to see this. Will you look after the girls until we can get someone to help them?"

She nodded slowly, her eyes fixed on the pistol in Oscar's hand.

Niklas motioned for Oscar and Kessler to follow him outside. They would have to hurry to get to the freight yard in time to stop Barbieri.

He paused on his way out as he spotted the bartender slumped over the bar, a sawed-off shotgun still clenched in his hand, a weeping bullet hole in his head and champagne soaking into his shirt sleeves.

Oscar followed his stare and shrugged. "Turns out I was wrong about the bartender."

Onerous lethality

S now fell thick and fast, in blinding, milk-white sheets. Small drifts had already accumulated on their shoulders and hats, their hands forming fists inside gloves, inside pockets, as if one's fingers—of their own volition—sought to escape the cold. Niklas, Kessler, and Oscar stood before Hogan's men, most of whom smoked anxiously or took furtive sips from flasks, their eyes darting across the empty Soo Line Freight Yard. If one looked too long into the darkness, ghostly apparitions seemed to take shape—the construct of a nervous mind.

"Give us a ten-minute head start before you go in. Keep the gunplay to a minimum unless you want to invite the cops." Niklas said it grimly, his jaw set as he looked them in the eyes and lied. If Stauss had followed through on his end, the police were already there, just waiting in the shadows for the right moment to make their move.

On one hand, Niklas recognized how needlessly complicated this entire operation had become and resented that it hadn't been as simple as Barbieri buying their guns and returning to Chicago. On the other hand, he would be lying if he said he didn't enjoy the challenge of engineering this plan—the strategy of it, carefully positioning the many disparate pieces, persuading them to act while only giving them limited information. Steering them toward working harmoniously together, unknowingly doing precisely what he wanted while thinking it was all their own idea, to their own benefit.

"We figure he has at least a dozen men with him," Kessler added, checking the action of his Bergmann and blowing the snow off the slide. "Maybe a few more. They'll probably have some of the light machine guns out of their crates, but none of them will work."

"You had best not be wrong," grumbled one of Hogan's crew, a towering Irishman with a thick red beard and bald head covered by a watchman's cap. He hefted a two-foot-long cast iron wrench in one hand, a sawn-off double-barrel shotgun in the other. "I've seen what those guns can do. Lost a dozen of my mates in Ypres before I could blink."

"We're not wrong," Kessler said confidently. "You'll have the advantage of surprise and firepower. They'll be falling over themselves trying to make those guns fire or find a working weapon."

"Ten minutes," Niklas reminded them, tapping the bare spot between his gloves and coat where his trench watch once sat. "No sooner."

The three men turned and entered the train depot. They moved silently in the dim light, gliding through the snowfall like deadly wraiths. They followed the few wandering lines of faint bootprints, already washed over by fresh snow. In the distance they could hear the Sicilians chatting and cursing as they hefted the crated machine guns onto a railcar, preparing them for the journey back to Chicago.

The repair shop and roundhouse were dark, but the windows of the dispatcher's office glowed dimly, amber light spilling onto the snow.

Niklas angled his head toward the building. Kessler and Oscar nodded, following on his heels as they approached. They swept around the perimeter, checking for guards. A pair of Barbieri's men hovered outside, Madsens slung over their shoulders on leather straps, the cherry glow of their cigarettes bobbing in the darkness.

Oscar slipped the trench knife from his boot, sliding his fingers through the bronze knuckle guard. Looking back at the Kristofferson brothers, he placed a finger to his lips, then pointed at the guards. Like a mountain lion stalking prey, he slinked across the snow, crouching as he went, silently rolling his feet from heel to toe upon the icy ground. When he had closed to within ten feet, he pounced. The knife blade slid across the first guard's throat. A cascade of blood arced through the air and stained the snow, accompanied by a desperate gurgle as he collapsed, cigarette hissing as it struck the snow. Before the other guard could bring the machine gun to bear, the bronze knuckles of Oscar's knife connected with his throat, crushing his windpipe. Oscar followed with three quick, decisive thrusts of the blade into the man's chest.

After the dead man's body struck the snow, everything fell silent. Sliding the steel across one of the fallen men's pant legs to clean off the blood, Oscar replaced it inside his boot. He set upon extricating the two Madsens from the fallen guards, slung them over his shoulders, and returned to the brothers.

"I'm going to go find a place to stow these," he whispered. "Unless you need me here for this next part."

Kessler shook his head. "We've got it from here." He patted Oscar's shoulder. Their friend nodded, then turned and vanished into the darkness.

The brothers, now alone, stood shoulder to shoulder before the dispatcher's office door, pistols drawn. Niklas glanced at Kessler. The younger man's expression was the same as the one he had worn in the trenches when things looked the bleakest. Defiance bordering on anger, brow furrowed with intent, eyes narrowed, jaw set. Accepting the inevitability of death but unwilling to meet it timidly.

"Ready?" Niklas whispered.

"Ready, brother. Let's get this bastard."

Placing a hand on the doorknob and finding it unlocked, Niklas shoved the door open. They rushed inside, guns up, scanning the room.

A large clock click-clacked rhythmically in the faint light. Dog-eared calendars, pencil-smudged track schematics, and bloated clipboards packed with hastily scribbled-on forms draped the walls. In the far corner sat a large L-shaped desk. Upon it rested a telephone. Beside that, a microphone on a scissor extension. A switchboard above. And before it all, reclining in a swivel chair, sat one Sicilian mobster with perfectly coiffed hair. Seated rigidly upon his lap was one bedraggled blonde woman with tear stains on her cheeks, makeup smudged at the corners of her eyes.

"I had no idea Kosena here was a contortionist," Barbieri said, his voice rounded and sloppy. An amber bottle, mostly empty, sat at the edge of the desk. He didn't seem surprised to see them. "Lots of fun to be had there, I must say. She can put on quite the show when properly incentivized, can't you sweetheart?"

"You're going to die tonight. Right here. By my hand," Kessler growled. Niklas trained the Steyr's front sight on Barbieri's forehead, but he wasn't confident he could hit him without endangering Kosena. Barbieri knew it. He kept his left arm wrapped tightly around her waist, pinned to his lap.

"You won't do shit," Barbieri snarled. "You lay a finger on me, all three of you die before you reach the door." Regaining his composure, he smoothed his hair back at his temples with his fingertips. "You forget who you're dealing with. I have an army at my beck and call. I belong to one of the most powerful criminal organizations in all of Chicago. My name's known in New York. And what are you? A couple of nobodies. Foreigners with German names who most people wouldn't trust to handle their garbage. And you think you're gonna go to war with me? How fucking arrogant." He drew a small knife from his pocket and gave it a theatrical flick, a thin blade flashing forth from the abalone pearl handle. Waggling it in the air where they could see it plainly, he angled it against Kosena's ribs. She jumped at the touch. "Cigarette, baby."

Swiveling on his lap, she reached into his pocket and withdrew his cigarette case and lighter. She lit one for him, took a ragged draw, and held it up for him.

"You were the ones who knocked off my cat house," he said matter-of-factly as he leaned forward and pinched the cigarette in the corner of his mouth. "That's irritating. Gonna take me a while to round up those girls again. An inconvenience, that's all."

"More like a harbinger of the end of your time in St. Paul," Niklas said.

"Hardly." Puffing thoughtfully on his cigarette, Barbieri glanced down at the knife in his hand. "You know, there's an intimacy about killing with knives." Gathering a handful of Kosena's long blonde hair, he held it to his nose and smiled cruelly. He gave it a firm tug and her head followed, exposing the alabaster skin of her neck. The knife hovered half an inch above her throat. The cigarette bounced on his lips like an orchestra conductor's baton as he spoke. "Killing with a gun is too businesslike. Too impersonal. Frankly, it makes it too easy. Even a little kid can squeeze a trigger—nothing special about that. But using a knife? Now that takes dedication." He took the dull spine of the blade and drew it slowly across her throat. "You can actually feel it severing the muscle. Sliding against the bone. Heaving through to the vitals. The squeamish and irresolute can't do it. It takes dedication. Decisiveness." He wanded the knife down the front of her dress, sliding it below the fabric. "You fools and your machine guns don't realize it takes so very little to end a life. For instance, a few meager pounds of pressure applied...right...here—"

Kosena yelped and fresh tears started down her face as Barbieri pushed lightly against the knife handle, the tip of the blade slipping into the skin above her left breast.

"Stop, damn you. You cruel bastard." Kessler gripped his pistol so tightly it shook, his knuckles white.

Ignoring him, Barbieri moved the knife to the inside of her thigh. "Or a quick slice here." He drew a thin, shallow cut across her leg. She screamed in anguish but didn't move.

Holstering his Steyr, Niklas held up his hands. "Enough of the perverted theatrics, Barbieri. You're going to let her go. You're going to give us the money you owe us for the guns. And we're going to walk out of here free and easy—casual as a stroll in Como Park. You take the guns back to Chicago and you stay there. The deal can still happen like you planned."

Barbieri looked at him incredulously. "The deal? The deal is, you lost. I took your guns. They're mine now. I'm not paying you a fuckin' dime for anything. In fact, you're not walking out of here alive. Are you really so stupid? I have dozens of men—with your machine guns—surrounding us. I have a knife to your woman's throat. You're powerless. You should be on your fuckin' knees begging me to spare your pathetic lives, not demanding money." He shook his head. "You know, it's my fault, really. I should have piled you up with that kid at your apartment. Would have been easier for everyone, wouldn't it, baby?" He kissed Kosena's cheek roughly.

Outside, men began shouting in surprise. The Irish had commenced their attack—right on time. A pair of shotgun blasts were followed by an anguished howl. Barbieri stood hastily, dragging Kosena toward the nearest window where one of his men bellowed something unintelligible through the glass. The knife wavered a few inches from her neck. She leaned forward and sank her teeth into the tendons of his wrist. Barbieri cried out and dropped the knife, striking her in the back of the head with his other hand. As she fell to the floor, the pistol in Kessler's hand barked and Barbieri collapsed, his kneecap shattered. Blood trickled between his fingers as he clutched the wound and groaned.

Kosena scrambled away, but seeing Barbieri disarmed and disabled by pain, returned and planted a hard right hook against his cheek. One of his teeth skittered across the floorboards and disappeared into the dusty shadows. "Bastard."

Running to her and hugging her tightly to his chest, Kessler rested his chin on her head and pinched his eyes closed gratefully.

Niklas slowly approached Barbieri as he writhed on the floor. "Where's the cash?"

"I'm not giving you shit," he whimpered, but his eyes flicked toward a corner of the room where several leather suitcases had been dropped in the shadow of a tall cabinet. Niklas began opening them. One was filled with women's clothes. Another contained suits and Barbieri's palm pistol. The last was packed with banknotes. Stacks of them, like bloated green bricks. His heart raced. This was far more than the cost they had agreed on for the guns. He reclosed that one and moved it toward the door.

The gunfire outside subsided, replaced by authoritative shouts and whistles. The police had arrived. Kessler looked at Niklas with alarm and confusion.

"Time to go." Niklas urged them toward the door.

"But what about Barbieri?" Kessler asked, his eyes still filled with boiling rage as he looked at the wounded man.

"We got what we came for."

"That's not what we—"

Niklas put his hand on his brother's chest and pushed him back gently. "I'll take care of it."

Compelled by another shrill blast from a policeman's whistle outside, Kessler grudgingly accepted. Grabbing Kosena's hand, he poked his head outside to see if their path was clear. Satisfied it was, he tugged her wrist and the two hastened across the switching yards, toward the road.

"My boys are gonna get you before you leave the railyard, you Boche fuck," Barbieri growled. "You're gonna eat a dozen bullets from your own guns and I'm gonna piss on the holes."

Letting out a long sigh through his nose, Niklas turned to look at him. Blood dripped from the gangster's hands, his hair a disheveled mess cascading down his brow, sweat-plastered to his skin in errant strands. His jaw muscles writhed as he gnawed against the pain like an animal chewing its own leg to free itself from a steel trap.

Niklas returned to his side. "That's a nice ring." He nodded at the ornate gold cigarette holder on Barbieri's hand. Raising a leg, he smashed his heel upon it, flattening it and breaking fingers. Barbieri howled.

"That one was for Cillian." Looking down at the gangster with contempt, Niklas said, "Consider our business concluded." He flung open the door and strolled outside.

Cradling his injured hand while still trying to stem the bleeding from his knee, Barbieri managed to raise himself on his good leg, hopping and staggering toward a window. He heaved it open and pitched himself outside, into the snow, hollering for his men. "Help me! Eligio! Filberto! Alfieri! You worthless *bastardi*. Come protect me, damn you."

Spitting his gum into the snow, Niklas paused as his eyes followed Kessler's and Kosena's footsteps away from the dispatcher's office. If he left Barbieri alive, there was a chance the Irish wouldn't reach him in time to dispatch him before the police got to him. If he ended up in prison, the Gennas would undoubtedly buy his way out. There would be no stopping him, then. He would see to it—with fanatical resolve—that Niklas, Kessler, Kosena, even Oscar, would die horribly at his hand. Niklas couldn't allow that. With grim resolution, he turned toward the distant sound of Barbieri's hollering.

Blood stained the snow like an ink spill on crisp white paper, Barbieri's body packing down the drifts in a clumsy meander. A few yards away, the wounded man crawled on his elbows in the snow beside a train car. His injured leg dragged behind him, the toe of his shoe digging in and slowing his movement like a stuck brake. He breathed heavily, an audible rasping pant, his skin glistening with sweat, steaming in the cold.

Hearing Niklas approach, he rolled to his back and faced him. "You can't run from me, you know." He mustered a wry grin. "I will find you. No matter where you go, I'll find you. And when I do…." he clicked his tongue and chuckled cruelly. "I'm gonna rip your eyes from their sockets and force feed them to you. I'll slice you from balls to belly button and hang you from my hotel balcony by your guts. And I'll make your brother and lady friend watch. Then, I'll do the same to them. I'm gonna bring the full might of the Gennas, the Unione Siciliana, every ally we've got, down upon you like a divine fucking retribution."

Sighing resignedly, Niklas set down the briefcase, leaning it against his leg. Reaching beneath his coat, he slid the Steyr from its holster. His grip tightened around the familiar checkering of the walnut grips. Squeezing and releasing. Feeling the stinging frigidity of the steel against the warmth of his fingers, contemplating the weight of it. The mass of it pushing against his palm, onerous with its lethality.

Engorged veins rose upon Barbieri's neck and forehead, his face red and contorted in wrath. "You hear me? I'm gonna lay waste to everything and everybody you've ever known or cared for, then toss your miserable corpses in the fuckin' lake."

Slowly, deliberately, Niklas thumbed down the pistol's safety. "I hear you," he whispered.

The arrogant defiance in Barbieri's eyes drained away, trepidation taking hold as he realized his fate had been decided. He had misjudged Niklas' resolve. Instead of backing down in fear as so many others had when Barbieri made threats over the years, he had coldly accepted the inevitability of his situation. The wounded man's lips quivered as if fumbling for the words to make his executioner pause, to buy him a few more seconds to negotiate. Maybe suggest he walk away with the money and they could forget the whole thing.

Niklas didn't wait for the words.

He raised the pistol, the front sight hovering over the wounded man's face. Barbieri managed to raise a hand to shield himself, turning away as Niklas squeezed the trigger. The nine-millimeter slug tore through his palm and met Barbieri's lower jaw, the skin and bone rupturing. Before he could utter a scream, the second shot dispatched him, painting the boxcar behind him in brain matter and skull fragments.

Atop the sacrificial altar

A whistle hung from Detective Stauss' neck by a thin, braided chain. A child's toy, really. Three little pieces of flimsy stamped steel and one cork ball the size of a pea.

Such a simple thing. But with it, Detective Stauss could call down a small army of thirty heavily armed policemen eager for a decent scrap. He could instantly and irrevocably change the outcome of lives with a meager breath.

He let the toy rest beneath his coat for the moment.

Through the veil of falling snow came the dim glow of a red lantern placed high atop a gantry crane overlooking the railyard. That was the signal from Stauss' informant that the Irish had closed with the Sicilians. Not that a signal was really necessary. The cacophony of shouts, curses, and thudding blows disrupting the tranquil night air offered an obvious sign that the battle had commenced. He would give them a minute before intervening. Didn't want the police presence to appear too prearranged.

243

Chief of Police Crepeau had given him more than a little pushback when he told him his plan and requisitioned the officers for the operation. But as he explained it, the cost of inaction would be far higher. Crepeau instinctively groped for the phone on his desk with intent to call Danny Hogan directly and "sort it out right away." Stauss reminded him that Hogan would do everything in his power to make those guns his; it would be better to apologize later than involve him before the bust, unless he wanted to deal with those guns again down the road. Stauss could see the gears turning as Crepeau contemplated that, weighing the likelihood of the guns being used outside the city, effectively becoming someone else's problem. "These guns will bring down the federal authorities on the entire state if they're allowed to get out," Stauss added with poignancy. "But if we get them and hand them over to the Bureau of Investigation, perhaps they'll favor us with some…special dispensation the next time they visit."

A great deal of finger-wagging and threats of an ended career later, he had gotten what he needed—a grudging approval and a large contingent of mostly trustworthy, mostly sober cops. Now he desperately needed to deliver. If those guns weren't here, if they for any reason came up empty-handed, he was in trouble. Like an Aztec fertility ceremony, every failed police operation required a sacrifice. And there was no doubt who would be the one dragged atop the altar in this case.

A gunshot—a muted thump, as though the bullet had been fired through a down pillow—echoed across the barren freight yard.

Tugging the whistle free of his coat, he blew three shrill blasts. The men near him leapt from their hiding places behind stowage and unloaded freight, many blowing whistles of their own as they ran, nightsticks and lead-filled leather saps gripped firmly in hand, cocked back and ready to deliver. They filtered into the train yard in a vague pincer-like approach, two masses of dark blue uniforms converging on the melee already underway between the Irish and the Sicilians.

As they came upon the scene, they found a dozen men in various states of consciousness and vitality, felled by knives and blunt weapons. Those who remained standing seemed to have little fight remaining in them and quickly surrendered to the police. A few light machine guns lay in the snow, evidently unfired. Stauss made a quick check of the nearest train car, a swirl of boot prints near the open doors. Inside lay stacks of wooden cases bearing the words *tractor parts*. Stauss felt a wave of relief wash over him.

They had gotten them. The guns were theirs. Not only would this keep them from falling into the hands of a criminal syndicate, turning them over to the Bureau of Investigation would engender some goodwill from the agency and prove that the St. Paul police weren't entirely corrupt or useless.

The plaintive cries of a wounded man reached his ear over the din. Detective Stauss thumbed back the hammer on his revolver and ran toward the noise. As he distanced himself from the others, he strained to hear another howl over the crunch of his shoes on the snow and his own heavy breathing. Both sounded deafening to his ears. Checking his corners as he approached the dispatcher's office, pistol held close to his side, he slowed his pace. Instinct told him to move with caution; the dark freight yard could conceal an ambush easily.

He eased around a corner to find Niklas standing ten yards from Barbieri, the Sicilian lying wounded in the snow in a pool of blood. Niklas drew his pistol from the holster beneath his coat, stared at it for a second, then raised it toward the wounded man.

"Wait!" Stauss shouted, but his voice was lost to the pistol's report. He pinched his eyes shut. The *crack* of the second round nearly made his heart stop.

Reholstering his pistol, Niklas stood before Barbieri's corpse, his face as solemn as a gothic statue. Abruptly, he turned and walked toward Stauss, a briefcase swinging from his hand. "Good evening, detective," he said, his voice calm and businesslike. Stauss stared at him, mouth agape in horror.

Murder. That's what it was. Indisputable and obvious. And he had witnessed it himself. No need for piecing together evidence, determining how things had transpired using an autopsy report and unreliable witness accounts. He had every justification for putting Niklas in handcuffs and dragging him back to the station to face justice.

Justice.

In St. Paul? No matter what he did, justice wouldn't be realized. Ezra Abecassis could just buy Niklas out of prison again. Or perhaps Dan Hogan would intervene on his behalf and get him released, considering Barbieri had been operating outside the O'Connor Layover Agreement. Either way, it was unlikely the young man would ever see the inside of a courtroom.

And there was something else: Was Niklas wrong to have killed him? Barbieri's many crimes against both society and humanity undoubtedly warranted punishment of the severest magnitude. Although he personally didn't agree with it, some might even suggest death was the only appropriate punishment for a murderous brute like Barbieri. But capital punishment had been abolished in Minnesota a decade ago, and taking Barbieri alive would all but guarantee that, after a short time behind bars, he would bribe his way out and resume terrorizing the Midwest as he had been— emboldened and vicious. No telling how many lives would be spared by ending his, even if the execution Niklas had just conducted was outside the law.

And once again, as he had experienced so many times during his career, Stauss faced the familiar battle between maintaining the integrity of the law and honoring the greater good. The former was his obligation as a policeman. The judicial system, no matter how flawed, would decide a criminal's fate. Not him. His role was simply to maintain order and adhere to the rule of law as it was written, whether he agreed with it or not. As such, in the simplest terms, he had seen Niklas commit murder and should arrest him for it. But how was he to reconcile his duty with the knowledge that St. Paul's judicial system was a sham, and the world was ultimately a safer place without Barbieri in it? Which was more important: obeying the law or protecting innocent people from a monster?

Niklas paused beside Stauss, giving him an opportunity to react, eyes scanning his face, curious to see what action the detective would take. When he said and did nothing, Niklas continued silently on his path toward the street.

The detective stood frozen, the revolver quivering in his hand, a shout trapped in his throat as he watched Niklas' form vanish into the snowfall.

Little toy soldiers

A garish neon sign spilled a vibrant red glow upon the brick and asphalt, inviting passersby to enlist the services of the best undertakers and embalmers in the state. Kessler and Kosena stood beneath it, illuminated in crimson as they waited for a break in traffic to cross the street. Wearing Kessler's long coat, hem dragging in the snow, she looked almost childlike. She sagged against him, his arm wrapped around her waist as if to hold her upright.

Near-death experiences always invited a flood of adrenaline, and to the uninitiated, that was often followed by dizziness, trembling, and confusion as the body recalibrated. She clung to Kessler like a castaway clutching a life preserver.

"Got the money," Niklas said as he approached them, breathing heavily from the jog, features obscured by a haze of vapor gusting between his lips.

His brother looked at him as though he had just made an off-color joke during a funeral service.

As if suddenly coming to her senses, Kosena jerked away from Kessler, dumped his coat in the snow, and walked into the street.

"Where are you going?" Kessler shouted after her.

She flagged down a Blue and White taxi. "Away from you. Both of you."

"Wait!" He took a step to reach for her but Niklas grabbed his shoulder and pulled him back.

"Best to let her go."

"Since when do you know what's best?" he snarled, yanking himself free of Niklas' grip. He turned to watch as Kosena ducked into the back seat of an idling car. Her door slammed and the driver shoved his arm out the window to signal his merge into traffic. Within seconds the car had disappeared around the corner.

Watching the street longingly, Kessler stood frozen in place, unblinking. As if willing her to return. "This is all your fault," he said finally. His voice wasn't accusatory, but soft and sorrowful.

"My fault? Maybe you've forgotten the briefcase filled with money in my left hand. Here, you hold it." Niklas grabbed his brother's wrist and shoved the handle into his palm. "This was the mission from the beginning, little brother. This. Since before we even left France, long before Kosena, this was our plan. *Our plan.* And it succeeded. It may not have been clean or simple like we wanted, but it succeeded all the same. We've put things in motion now. Everything will be fine. This was all planned carefully."

A realization dawned on Kessler's face. "You made a deal with the cops, didn't you? That's why they showed up when they did."

A firm nod. "I did."

As though the handle was red hot, Kessler let the briefcase drop to the pavement. "Why? They're the weakest of the lot. You think this money will be enough to protect us from the Sicilians *and* the Irish? We had an out with Hogan. He could have protected us. Now he's an enemy, too. These are powerful people, Niklas, and we've fucked them all. You think they're just going to let us get away with it?" Kessler was in tears now, his voice straining with incredulity and exasperation. "You think your detective friend can protect us? We're dead men. Dead."

Holding his hands up as if trying to calm a spooked horse, Niklas said, "Hogan doesn't know we tipped off the cops. To him, it will just look like bad timing. Stauss is gonna let his boys walk anyway. We tell him the cops must have been watching Barbieri. Hogan's crew just happened to arrive right when they made their move. Stauss will make sure that's the story that gets passed around the department so the cops on Hogan's payroll bring that story back to him."

"The story doesn't matter, even if he believes it. We were the ones who convinced Hogan to move on Barbieri in the first place. They wouldn't have been there at all if not for us. He'll blame us."

"We can make it up to him. You'll see."

Sniffing back his tears, Kessler stared at him in disbelief. "Kosena was right about you. You can never be wrong. You always have an answer for everything, even when the hangman's noose is tightening around your neck. You, with your big words and your big plans. Always scheming. Playing general with his little toy soldiers." He kicked the suitcase toward Niklas, the leather sliding on the ice. "I'm sure all that money will make for a really lovely funeral for both of us."

Killer with a knish

At the foot of one of the Wabasha Street Bridge's three piers, planted atop a rubble of stones and sliver of snow-covered lawn in the middle of the Mississippi River, perched the Minnesota Boat Club Boathouse. Some architect's idea of what a Spanish mission might look like if it had been accidentally transported to the Arctic. Detective Stauss stood looking out at the river, chewing something idly. He appeared to take deliberate half bites, slow and methodical, as if profoundly contemplating each mouthful. As Niklas approached, the detective held up a newspaper wrapped in a cone shape, the bottom stained dark with grease, and tilted it toward him invitingly. "You ever tried one of these? Called a knish. I bought a handful from a nice little Jewish man with a food cart on West Third."

Not wanting any but trying to be polite, Niklas drew one from the wrapping and took a bite. The frigid wind had already chilled the small pastry, but the savory potatoes, onion, and eggs still had a wholesome, comforting taste. "Not bad. If you like these, though, you've gotta find Old Man Wexler in the Flats. Sells the best knish in the Midwest."

"That so?"

"That's what he says, anyway."

"I'll look him up the next time I'm over there. Hopefully next time it won't be because you called me to collect another dead body."

Leaning against a low galvanized guide rail separating them from the water, careful to avoid touching it with bare skin, Niklas said, "I'm hoping those days are behind me."

Wrapping the newspaper over the remaining knishes, Stauss raised his scarf to cover his mouth and nose, the wool garment wreathing his neck like a pet snake. "I would be delighted if that were true. But even if it's not, it appears, for the moment, we've both gotten what we wanted."

"Appears so," Niklas replied softly.

"The guns are in police control and will be destroyed."

Niklas winced at the mention of the guns' destruction. He and Kessler had spent months making them serviceable again, risking death and incarceration to smuggle them into the country, and the thought of them being melted down and turned into park benches or guide rails stung.

The detective looked at him with humor in his eyes. "You're lucky: I wanted to return them to the Bureau of Investigation to earn some points, but I was told we shouldn't involve the feds."

"They would have wanted to know where the guns came from and would have come sniffing around. I'm guessing your boss didn't want that kind of attention."

"Astute observation, as always." The detective sighed wistfully, then shrugged. "But at least the guns are off the streets and the Sicilians are in prison, though I doubt they'll be there for long. Barbieri is dead—body on ice and heading back to Chicago—his brothel shot up and dismantled, which I'm sure comes as news to you." He gave him a knowing look mixed with the subtlest hint of approval. "And you…well you got your money in the end, didn't you?" A pair of mallards swept by, cruising low on the pewter-tinted water, silent but for the flapping of their wings. "This feels like a Pyrrhic victory for me, though. You familiar with that expression?"

A nubilous stream of vapor poured from Niklas' nose as he exhaled. "Very."

"Yes, well, I can only believe a man like yourself won't be content with one big score. And assuming you managed to get your arms around weapons of war once, you'll undoubtedly be able to do it again."

"That could be," Niklas replied vaguely. "But you and I have an arrangement all the same, correct?"

"A tentative and very fragile one. Think eggshells. Ming vases. Your grandmother's fine china, fragile."

"But an arrangement nonetheless."

It looked like it pained him to do it, but the detective nodded. "You get a pass this time. And from here on you will be treated like every other racketeer in this town. So long as you obey the rules, take your troublemaking outside of St. Paul and give Hogan his cut, I can't do anything to stop you." The detective slipped his scarf down to his chin, stood as straight as his form would allow, and turned to face him. His gloved hand reached out and offered a handshake. There was a glint of challenge in his eye. "In the spirit of honor and respect between opponents on equal footing, I'll tell you this: If you step out of line, and if I happen to be there when you do, expect no clemency from me. I let you walk away this time because it was a net gain for humanity. Taking Barbieri down saved countless innocent lives. But if the scale tips the other way, I will not hesitate to lock you up or put you in the ground."

Niklas shook his hand firmly. "I believe you."

Despite the cold, a dense fog had settled over the water, veiling the city skyline in a shroud of gray. From upriver, a barge approached, chuffing languidly toward them, belching onyx-colored smoke from her stacks that swirled and vanished into the haze.

The detective turned to leave but stopped a few steps away, turning toward Niklas with a curious expression. "Before I go, would you answer something for me? This has been bothering me since the night we raided the freight yard."

"Oh?"

"I like to think of myself as a fair judge of character. Need to be in order to survive in my line of work. So it surprised me when you—someone who appears by all standards to be a man possessing reason, scruples, and at least a passing respect for morality—turned out to be so ruthless. I watched you murder a man in cold blood. He was a horrible man and certainly one who deserved his fate, but he was wounded, unarmed, and you executed him with the apathy of a seasoned hangman."

Eyes affixed to the passing barge, Niklas didn't blink. "Your mistake is in thinking that, because he was wounded, he was powerless. Only an amateur chess player fixates on the board as it is, ignoring the moves his opponent has yet to make. Say I had let him live. Shown mercy. You and I both know Barbieri would harbor a vendetta against me and seek vengeance. He would gleefully murder everyone I care for before coming for me. I would never be able to protect them from a man with his influence."

"But you don't think the Gennas will seek retribution for his death?"

Niklas shrugged nonchalantly. "They might. Or maybe I did them a favor. Maybe he was so sadistic and uncontrollable they would thank me for getting rid of a problem that would have inevitably brought the feds down on them."

"I wouldn't count on their charity," Stauss cautioned.

"I don't. But the possibility of vengeance is still preferable to a guarantee of the same."

They stood in silence for a moment, resuming their observance of the passing water. The rhythmic slosh of the waves cresting the smooth stone below joined the distant murmur of traffic and the huffing rasp of a departing train—like sandpaper on wood. Upriver, a mechanical crane dumped a bucketful of snow from the recently plowed streets into the river.

"I take it you've never killed," Niklas said.

"No, fortunately. I've come close a few times. Weighed a few men down with an extra ounce of lead they'll carry for the rest of their days or had plucked out by the prison doctor, but I've never stopped a heart."

Voice as low and quiet as if spoken in a confessional, Niklas said, "I hope you never have to." He hesitated, deliberating whether to swallow his words or allow himself a moment of frank honesty with the detective. After a long pause, he resolved to continue. "It leaves you cold, like a void has opened up deep inside you and drawn in all the color and beauty of the world into it. And it chafes, like an itch in a place you can't reach. You replay the moment again and again in your mind, wondering if you could have changed the outcome somehow. Eventually, like any wound, it hardens and becomes an ugly scar. An enduring part of you that still aches, especially on cold days." He sighed deeply, as if purging a contaminated breath from his lungs. Then, he turned and looked at the detective, his eyes as cold and gray as the river water below them. The tone of his voice changed, revealing a resolve inflexible as steel. "I've done things I'm not proud of in the defense of my life and my country. They will haunt me until my dying breath. But when it comes to choosing between the lives of my loved ones and human garbage like Barbieri, I will never hesitate, nor will my conscience carry a heavier burden for my actions."

The detective nodded subtly, not so much in agreement, but as someone considering what has been said with great solemnity.

Niklas turned to leave but stopped after a few steps, bouncing the heel of his fist upon the guide rail. He wanted to give Stauss the same kind of parting advice he always seemed insistent on doling out. Warn him that perpetually viewing the world as a humanitarian would only gut him, slow and ragged—as though it was being done with a dull knife. The detective could live out his days wringing his hands and shouting himself hoarse crying out to the heavens, beseeching an apathetic God to intervene, but it would change nothing. The evil ways of man were ceaseless, the timeline of mankind suffused with atrocities, from the savage dark ages to the cultured grandeur of the modern era. Civility was a pretense. Veneer thin. Humanity had been and would always be dominated by selfishness, lust, and greed—no different than the tiny organisms beneath their feet, writhing and seething, crawling over one another for a taste of sunlight. Stauss' efforts to change that would only drive him to madness.

Instead, Niklas smiled brusquely and said, "Thanks for the knish."

Time to move uptown

K nocking softly on the doorframe at the threshold to their bedroom, Niklas stepped inside. It smelled stale, of sheets repeatedly gone wet with sweat, then dried. Of trapped tobacco smoke. Of a trapped soul. In the three days that had passed since the shootout at the freight yard, his younger brother had left his place beneath the blankets only long enough to piss and smoke. The dunes of ashes on the nightstand and the scattered ribbons of unburned loose-leaf tobacco on the floor suggested he had given up rising for the latter.

"You seeing visitors?" Niklas pried open the bedroom window an inch to air the room out. A rush of cold air, clinically clean, surged inside and rustled the curtains.

"Not if it can be helped," Kessler muttered into his pillow, not turning to look at him. He stared hopelessly at the wall. The shadows under his eyes suggested he hadn't slept much.

"Oscar's been asking about you. Wanted me to give you a pint of his best hooch. Says there's no surer cure for a broken heart."

Glancing at his brother's hands expectantly, Kessler said, "I don't see it."

"And you won't. Liquor makes good things great and bad things worse." Moving to his own bed, Niklas sat on the mattress across from his brother, tucking a pillow behind his back. "Still thinking about her?"

Kessler snorted, the answer being too obvious to warrant a reply.

Niklas took a deep breath. It was time to come clean. "She was seeing Julian, you know. I saw them at the theater together. I didn't tell you because I didn't want to hurt you, but maybe that was a mistake. Would have saved both of you a lot of pain and heartache if you had separated before Barbieri showed up."

For a moment, Kessler didn't speak, and Niklas wondered how he was processing the news. He must have felt betrayed that his own brother had kept this from him. Or simply furious that Kosena had been seeing another man while they were together. Probably both. Finally he spoke, his voice barely audible and ragged with emotion. "I knew the whole time. She didn't do much to hide it. I just wanted to believe she would come around if I could prove I was the better man. I guess I secretly hoped once we had the money from Barbieri I could propose. You know, wave a big diamond ring under her nose and make her forget all about Julian and his stupid theater."

"I don't think that would have solved the problem, brother."

"Probably not. But I still didn't see it going this way. Her just walking away like that."

Niklas nodded. "She blames us for everything that happened. And she's not wrong for feeling that way. She wanted to know what we were doing with the guns and I refused to tell her. Made you swear to keep it from her, too. And she got dragged into it anyway, only she was completely blindsided." He laced his fingers together and worked his jaw. "I failed her. And I failed you, too. When Barbieri and his men were here, and they had a gun to your head—"

"—that wasn't your fault." Kessler interrupted, turning to face him. "We both knew that what we were doing was dangerous. I agreed to it every step of the way. We were...*are*...partners in this."

"I just don't ever want to feel that powerless again. Whatever the cost, whatever the sacrifices I need to make or the blood I need to spill, I will not allow us to be put in that situation again. I swear it."

"But what can we do?" Kessler asked hopelessly. "It's just a matter of time before Hogan sends a team to wipe us out. Or the Gennas decide to get revenge."

"I'll see to Hogan. He won't be a problem. I also suspect the Gennas knew Barbieri would meet an untimely end sooner or later, and they're just glad to be rid of him. Regardless, I think it's time we leave the apartment. Move into a bigger place."

"Oh yeah? Got a few kroner in your pocket and suddenly you're looking to move uptown?" Kessler chuckled, but his voice was humorless. "Maybe we can move in next to Uncle Ezra on Summit Avenue. Steal his newspapers. Get a dog and let it shit on his lawn."

"Something like that, yeah." Standing and slapping his knees, Niklas said, "Get up. Bathe. Get dressed. And for the love of God, eat something. I've seen corpses that look healthier than you."

Cast iron and Amatol

A simple fire in one of the garbage cans outside the Merchants National Bank & Trust building might have been enough to draw out Hogan's security guards, but Niklas wanted to make a big impression that could not be ignored. As he approached the corner of Wabasha and Fifth, he swept the pad of his thumb across the gridded surface of a British Mills bomb in his coat pocket. In his other hand swung a leather trombone case. He glanced up at the building's carved colonettes and Roman arches, carved from red Lake Superior sandstone. The structure loomed above the adjacent buildings like the keep of a medieval castle. He imagined King Hogan looking down from his penthouse upon the peasants scurrying below.

Entering an alleyway behind the building, Niklas stopped, glancing over his shoulder to check for anyone who may have gotten curious and followed him in. He palmed the grenade.

Seven seconds.

Seven seconds from when he pulled the pin and released the lever to when a pound and a half of cast iron and Amatol explosive would detonate and mangle anything within one hundred feet. He had seen what could happen to a man who didn't throw the grenade far enough. Hell, he had seen what could happen to a man who got careless when installing the detonator assembly. It was not a weapon to handle recklessly.

He wasn't out to hurt any passersby, so he tugged the pin from the Mills bomb and slipped it inside a garbage bin behind a stack of pallets where it would detonate harmlessly. At most, it might shatter a few windows. Maybe scar the brickwork a bit.

Hastening around the corner, he began walking with purpose toward the building entrance, trying not to look as though he was anticipating an ear-drum-shattering report any second.

The explosion, especially given that it occurred downtown during the lunch hour, achieved the desired effect. The thunderclap of the detonation, the cough of gray smoke, and the cascade of wood splinters and garbage fluttering through the air was followed by a sudden ringing silence as everyone stopped and stared. That was in turn followed by a frenzied rush of fleeing colporteurs and deliverymen, spooked horses and entangled traffic. A chorus of shouts and rapid footfalls rang out as a dozen of Hogan's guards flooded through the building's front doors and dashed into the street, pistols drawn.

With the guards distracted, Niklas slipped inside, brim of his hat down low to conceal his face, the trombone case swinging at his side. He took the stairs two at a time until he reached the top floor. In the empty stairwell, he dropped to a knee and opened the case, withdrawing the Madsen machine gun Barbieri had used to kill Vicenzo. Flipping the leather sling over his shoulder, he rocked a fresh magazine into place atop the receiver. Taking a deep breath to calm his heart rate following his brisk ascent up the stairs, he set his jaw and shouldered open the door leading into a carpeted vestibule. Across from him stood a frosted-glass-paned door bearing the title

"Dan Hogan, Ambassador" in gold-painted lettering. He flung it open and stepped inside.

The office was well lit by large windows and expensively furnished, with coffered ceilings and gold-plated sconces on the walls. The smell of neatsfoot oil, leather, and cigar smoke hung thick on the air.

Hogan's secretary, a middle-aged woman with a spinsterish haircut and billowing floral dress, was midway through arranging a vase of silk flowers at her desk when Niklas entered. She looked up, her mouth dropping open as she stared at the machine gun in his hands. Although her eyes sought to flee her skull, her hands continued automatically shuffling the stems. Niklas moved past her without a word.

He kicked open the door to Hogan's office, the heavy oak slow to swing but making a mighty thud when it collided with the stops on the wall. The big man sat behind his desk, in the middle of a phone call. A cold cigar stub teetered on the edge of a glass ashtray. An unused typewriter sat on the opposite corner of the desk.

"Oy, I'll need to call you back. Something's come up." Hogan returned the earpiece to its cradle and leaned back in his chair, the springs beneath it creaking loudly in protest. "Come to snuff me, eh, Danish?"

Niklas didn't say a word. He kept the muzzle of the machine gun trained on Hogan's broad chest. It was an immense target. He didn't shrink or shy away from the barrel.

Hogan shook his head and laughed. "Credit where it's due, boyo. You must be draggin' about balls of solid steel, coming in here waving that bean shooter around like that. But I haven't heard any gunshots yet today. So you must have tricked me boys to get up here without any new holes in ye. Clever fella, ain't ya? Maybe more clever than I thought. Now, you gonna use it or feckin' play with it?"

Niklas approached him slowly. The secretary wept quietly outside the office. Deep, hiccupping, ugly sobs. The Irishman raised his chin defiantly, staring his executioner unblinkingly in the eye. No supplications to God to intervene nor muttered prayers asking for a swift transition to the afterlife. Hogan knew the score. A man who had risen through the ranks of the criminal underworld to reach his position hadn't done so without developing more than a passing familiarity with death. Clearly he held no illusions about what possible fate awaited him around every corner. If it hadn't been Niklas with a machine gun, it would have been a rival with a poisoned bottle of whiskey, a desperate debtor with a two-dollar pistol, or some upstart looking to make a name for himself by leaving a bomb beneath the seat of Hogan's car.

Stopping at the edge of his desk, Niklas swung the Madsen onto the desktop with a thud that made the Irishman jump. "On the house. For the inconvenience at the freight yard."

The Irishman looked from the rifle to Niklas and back, his eyebrows knit in skepticism. "You certainly know how to make an entrance, Danish." He evaluated the gun from muzzle to buttstock and the makings of a smile formed on his lips. "I'll take the rifle with thanks, but Detective Stauss already explained the situation to me. You were up against it with that wop. Heard you put him in the ground, too. I appreciate you doing that fer me. If you hadn't done it, I'd a had to. To make a point. Can't have others like him coming into St. Paul tinkin' they can get away with just anythin'." He freed the magazine from the top of the Madsen and slapped it against his palm, then waved it at Niklas. "If you ever decide this gun-selling business isn't your speed, come talk to me and I'll find you a place on my crew." He chuckled and shook his head. "Balls of solid steel." As if suddenly hearing his secretary's bawling outside the room, Hogan's face contorted with annoyance. He shouted, "Maybel, quit yer bellowing, for Christ's sake. And get this man a drink."

Higher out of the mud

Niklas had only been to Kosena's apartment once, grudgingly dragged along by Kessler, for a party that had started too late in the evening for his tastes and included too many loud and melodramatic people. He had spent most of it enduring a drunken lecture on logical empiricism from a St. Thomas philosophy major with patches on the elbows of his tweed coat and an affected English accent he had likely contrived after spending a few months studying abroad. It wasn't even Kosena's place, really. It belonged to a few of her friends; she just stayed with them when not on the road with her vaudeville troupe.

He wasn't certain of the apartment number—the doors all looked about the same, banged up and dirty around the bottoms, the glass of their peepholes cracked and smudged—but still he boldly knocked on the first one that looked somewhat familiar.

A few seconds later, the door opened a crack, to the limit of the tarnished brass chain lock, revealing half of Kosena's face. She wore no makeup. He had never seen her without it. It made her appear diffident, timorous. Her eyes betrayed her caution and uncertainty, feelings still unfamiliar to her, no doubt.

She unlocked the door but didn't open it much further. "What do you want?"

"Coffee on?" He shouldered past her into the cramped entryway. It smelled overpoweringly of peppermint. He glanced down and spotted the source hidden behind the leg of a timeworn credenza piled high with clutches, gloves, and fur-lined hats. Kosena and her roommates had soaked cotton balls in peppermint oil in hopes of driving out the mice.

She slipped her hands into the pockets of her silk pajamas. "I suppose I could make some."

"That would be nice." He didn't wait for her, walking directly into the kitchen and rummaging through the cabinets for the percolator.

"Bottom right," she directed from the doorway. "You came alone?" She peeked into the hallway before shutting the door and locking it fully with the chain lock and a deadbolt.

"Haven't been able to get Kessler out of bed for a few days." He began filling the basket with coffee grounds from a Mason jar by the spoonful. "He's been a mess without you."

"I'm sure he'll recover. Broken hearts always heal in time." She grabbed the percolator and filled it with water from the tap.

Niklas placed the basket inside and topped it with the lid. "I'm not so sure. For some reason he's still madly in love with you."

"That's a mistake." A genuine sadness appeared in her eyes. He liked that, seeing her express a little authentic human suffering for a change.

He reached for a matchbook inside a jar on the counter. Half a dozen lay jumbled inside, all of them pilfered from local cocktail lounges, hotels, and department stores by the looks of the covers. Lighting the stove, he slid the percolator onto a burner and adjusted the flame. "Agreed."

Eyes narrowing, her lips tightened and pinched together as though laboring to hold back a flood of retaliatory insults. Instead, she simply said, "You have a cruel streak, don't you?"

"More of a fraternal protective streak." He shook his head reprovingly. "You know, Kessler would have died for you. Because he's honorable and naive and loyal to a fault. And he still doesn't suspect what you did. Still thinks you were some damsel in distress who needed saving that night at the train yard." They stared at one another defiantly, letting the accusation hang in the air. "How much did Barbieri offer you to turn on us? Or was it the promise of a life of luxury as a gangster's moll in Chicago that did it?"

"I don't know what you're talking about." She screwed up her face with a look of indignation, but her voice wavered—just a little—and betrayed her. "He hurt me. I had to tell him or he would have killed me."

"For someone who lies so often, you're shit at it."

Her lips quivered and tears flushed her eyes.

"Back at the train yards. The suitcase with women's clothes inside. Your clothes." Pulling his scally cap from his head, he swept a hand across it and straightened the bill, then tossed it on the countertop. "See, I know you. Better than Kessler does, I figure, because I'm not blinded by infatuation. I just see you for what you are, in plain light. Hell, I might know you better than you know yourself. You're not one to miss an opportunity, even if you have to debase yourself and betray your lover to take it."

"You don't understand." Her voice strained, the veins in her neck throbbing. "He followed me home. Demanded to know where you lived and waved a knife in my face. So I sweet-talked him. I told him if he let you both live, he could have me, too. In a way, I saved your lives," she added hopefully, as though that would redeem her.

"I'm sure the kid who bled out on our apartment floor after taking Barbieri's bullet to the gut is grateful you did that," Niklas said sarcastically.

"I'm sorry that happened. And I'm sorry you and Kessler got hurt. I just...." she looked away, wiping at her cheeks with her wrist. "It was the only option I had."

"No, it was the easiest option you had. A chance to move up in the world, nice and simple."

Her hands balled into fists. "You act as though you aren't doing the same thing by selling smuggled machine guns. You treat me as though I'm the only one at fault, but you both kept that from me. Lied to my face about it." Her voice dropped and she stepped closer to him. Her breath smelled like cigarettes. He had never seen her smoke. "Admit it: For all your sermonizing and lectures, you're just like me, looking for a way out. Scratching for a foothold so you can climb a little higher out of the mud. And even if you care about the people you hurt in the process, it's not going to stop you, is it?"

Suddenly feeling very tired, Niklas sighed and leaned against the cabinets. "Well, since we're so much alike, why don't you join us?"

"I don't understand," she said, her brow furrowed. "Just a second ago, you were accusing me of betraying you. Now you want me to, what, work for you?"

"That's right."

"Doing what? Selling guns?"

"Yes. I think you would be quite good at it."

"Why? Because I'm a seductress with no sense of morality?" she asked in a mocking tone.

"Morality is a bit subjective in this context."

"Do you hear yourself? You're selling guns to violent criminals who are going to use them to kill people. How is that at all subjective?"

"They already have guns. And knives. Baseball bats. Brass knuckles. Piano wire. They're killing each other every day. We're just selling them a more efficient way of doing it."

She smiled sardonically and shook her head in disbelief. "You're always so quick to answer the most difficult questions. That's how I know you're full of shit. You've thought about this. A lot. And you've worked out an answer that satisfies just enough to allow you to sleep at night."

"That may be true. But the facts remain, even if you don't like them. There are more criminals made every day. You can blame the war for it: running young men through a meat grinder and expecting them to just go back to an ordinary life afterward. Or you can blame Prohibition. The police who line their pockets with bribes to look the other way. Or the ordinary people who gladly exchange their honest money for a bottle of booze to take the hurt out of their lives for a moment. Regardless of who is to blame, reality persists: There's money to be had. A big, messy pool of it. And for once it doesn't belong solely to the businessmen and the politicians. Now, you can choose to sit on the sidelines and feel morally superior for it, or you can wade into the cesspool with the rest of us wretched, miserable people and get a piece of it for yourself. Either way, there will be agony and death. Because that's what life is: an exhausting saga filled with suffering and disappointment. You can't change that. But you can mollify it for yourself." The coffee began to perk. He grabbed a pair of ceramic mugs from the countertop and filled them, steam wafting upward and flooding over the rim in silver coils. He handed her a cup. "Kosena, I'm offering you a job. And you're going to accept it."

"You know, I usually find confidence attractive in a man." She crossed her arms. "But yours just reminds me of a snake oil salesman and it makes me want to punch you in the throat."

Ignoring the empty threat, Niklas pressed his attack. "You know your days in vaudeville are limited. Sleeping on the train to avoid paying for a hotel room. Lugging suitcases of props around the country with you. Performing the same act to the same audiences who love you when you're on stage and spit on you in the street. Seducing men like Julian in the hopes he'll give you more time in the spotlight. But every year that passes, your beauty fades and your body stiffens. Soon you won't be able to perform your act, assuming anyone is still showing up to see it. You'll be reduced to mending garments for the other performers or handling their accounting, surviving on their charity."

She held her mug to her lips, the steam bathing her face. "That's a bleak view of my future."

"It's a pragmatic one. If you were an unsightly hag you wouldn't have a single person at your shows. You sell your beauty every day. What happens when you don't have any more wares to sell?"

"I'll manage, just like I always have," she said sulkily, running a bare foot up her calf.

"What I'm offering you is an opportunity to not have to worry about that ever again." He gently wrapped his hand around her arm. Her skin was cold. Almost imperceptibly, she leaned into the warmth of his palm and looked away. "Come work with us. I need a salesperson. Someone who understands the psychology of men and how to manipulate them."

She shrugged away from his touch and looked at him as though he had pinched her. "God, even your compliments are just insults in disguise."

He sighed and sipped his coffee. "A talent of mine, it seems."

After a moment spent evaluating the peeling wallpaper in the small galley kitchen, she broke the silence. "How much would I get paid?" she asked, almost a whisper, as though she was ashamed and didn't want anyone to hear.

"Four thousand dollars base with additional commission for sales."

Her breath caught in her throat but she quickly forced a laugh to cover it. "I never took you for having a sense of humor." Her smile slowly faded as he stared back at her impassively. "I'm no good at accounting or math. And I don't know anything about guns other than I don't like when they're pointed at me."

"None of which are requirements."

Sweeping a finger thoughtfully around the rim of her mug, she mumbled, "I'll consider it."

Grabbing his cap from the countertop, he gave it a flick and placed it atop his head. "Let me know by the end of the week. By the way, we're moving out of the apartment. Thanks for the coffee." He slid his half-full mug onto the counter and stepped toward the door.

"Wait, where are you moving to?" she called after him.

Unlocking the deadbolt and chain, he paused, hand on the doorknob. The cold wept through the narrow gaps between the door and frame, chilling the handle. "Someplace a little more secure."

Lost causes

E vening arrived like an overeager dinner guest—too early to be welcome just yet. The dying sun cast its final aureate rays on the buildings lining St. Peter Street, which thrummed with life. Men staggered into the road from the many bordellos, waving back at topless women framed in the windows as the next wave of eager patrons made their entrance. Loud music—live and recorded—roared through the glass and opening doors, blending into a joyous cacophony punctuated by shouts and laughs. Niklas paused before one of the cat houses with only a single dim light coming from an upstairs window.

"Looking for a good time, fella?" a familiar voice said from behind Niklas. He turned to find Maya leaning against a streetlight, hands shoved deep into the pockets of her purple coat, a mischievous expression on her face. "If I didn't know any better, I would think you were following me, the way we keep bumping into one another."

"Just lucky, I suppose." He nodded his head at the nearby building. "Barbieri's joy house is looking rather empty for this time of night."

Her smile faded and she nodded. "Someone shot it up a few days ago. The police think it was a professional job—only Barbieri's security were killed. No money taken. And no one seems to have gotten a good look at the shooters." A look of recognition flickered across her eyes before she turned her attention back to the building. "Of course, it will be back." She sighed and shrugged. "As long as the women working there are consenting adults this time, it will be an improvement."

"But the girls?"

She nodded knowingly. "I've seen to their care. The Protestant Orphan Asylum said they would take them in for now. My friends in the St. Paul Woman's Club are working to find them permanent homes among good families in town, assuming we can't locate their families in Chicago."

Niklas palmed a roll of bills and slipped them into Maya's coat pocket. "To help with the effort."

She retrieved the money, looked at it in her palm, then shook her head and handed it back. "Feeling a bit guilty, are we? Wanting to do something decent with your ill-gotten gains?"

"Not particularly. But we did get this money from the man who kidnapped those girls. Only seems right that we should use some of it to help them."

She stepped beside him and wrapped her arm around his elbow, steering him down the street. "How about you and that handsome brother of yours come to our next bake sale or piano recital, instead? Show your support that way."

"If I can get him out of bed," Niklas mumbled.

"Is he unwell?"

"In a manner of speaking. Lovesick. Bad breakup."

"Oh, I'm sorry to hear that." An impish smile formed on her lips. "That said, once he's ready to start seeing people again, tell him I am interested in getting to know him better."

Niklas snorted and looked to the sky beseechingly. "Unbelievable. He can lie sorry in bed and still get more dates than me."

Giving his arm a playful shake, she rested her head against his shoulder and said, "You're plenty handsome and could get anyone you admired. But I know perfectly well that you're not looking for that. At least not from me."

"How do you know?" he protested.

She stopped walking and turned to face him. "Your body language. Your eyes, even. There's distance, like an emotional armor you put up between you and others. I could never be the one to breach it."

He looked away and grunted ambivalently. "I'll let him know you would like to see him. He'll be delighted." They resumed walking.

A man nearby waved cartons of cigarettes overhead and shouted, "Gaspers? Nickel each." Another man walking by scoffed at the inflated price. The hawker dismissed him, telling Niklas, "After a shot of whiskey and a roll in the hay, he'll gladly pay double that for a smoke—you watch."

The farther Niklas and Maya walked, the quieter and emptier the street became, until it seamlessly transitioned to a prosaic, working-class neighborhood filled with modest little clapboard-sided houses. Children in frayed, oversize coats shouted and laughed as they played broomball in the street. Dogs barked from their tie-out chains on the front lawns.

"So what's next for you?" Niklas asked. "More undercover work for your pal, Detective Stauss?"

"If he needs help, sure. Otherwise, there's always plenty to do around the city. The Temperance League keeps me busy."

"It will keep you busy until the end of time. You would have better luck convincing people to give up eating."

Smiling, she reached over and tweaked his ear. "I happen to like lost causes. So much more rewarding when you succeed."

They stood together and watched the broomball game until it became too dark for the kids to play. Following a chorus of shouted calls to dinner from their mothers, the boys disappeared into the welcoming light of the nearby houses.

A coup counted

Detective Stauss had never entertained even a passing thought of having children. Besides his lack of physical attraction to women, he knew his career would always take precedence over family. Still, he imagined he now knew approximately what it must feel like to fail at imparting a vital lesson to a wayward son. Instead of taking this near-catastrophe as a warning to change his ways, Niklas would no doubt focus on the outcome alone—he did get his money after all—which would only embolden him. The young Dane had proven himself capable, cunning, and motivated: a dangerous cocktail that, if applied without moral direction, could pose a grave threat to everyone in the city. Stauss didn't relish the thought of going head-to-head with him, especially given all the constraints with which the department had already shackled him. It would be akin to entering the boxing ring with an arm tied behind his back while Niklas clutched a roll of nickels in each fist.

He also believed that Niklas was, at his core, a good man. One who had deviated from the path of virtue and propriety, but a good man nonetheless. And on some level, Stauss still believed he could be saved.

The phone on his desk rang and he jumped. He let it ring again before picking up the receiver. "Detective Stauss."

"You Minnesotan cops are something else," Detective Bradford said with a slight chuckle.

"What do you mean?"

"I call you up with a warning that Barbieri is coming to your town, and a few weeks later his body rolls into Dearborn Station in a refrigerated train car like a slab of beef, all shot to shit. Hell of a thing. Here I am, thinking no one would dare touch this bastard, least of all the cops in Crooks' Haven of all places, and you guys just knock him off as easy as a dove on a power line."

"He was no dove. And we didn't kill him. You know that."

"Well someone sure did. And whoever that is had better be damn sure of themselves and their skill with a gun, because the Gennas are gonna see red when this gets out."

"You don't think they'll let this one go?" Stauss asked, already knowing the answer. "You said it yourself: Barbieri was a loose cannon. The Gennas must have known this would happen eventually."

"You're talking about the Sicilian mafia, Stauss. Someone killed a member of their family. They're obligated to respond, even if they hated him and secretly wished he would catch a bullet. It's a matter of honor. I just hope you weren't too closely involved."

"Close enough."

"Just watch yourself, all right? I'll keep my ear to the ground and try to give you fair warning when they make a move. But Stauss, if you know who did this, and God forbid they're one of your guys, you had better tell them to either make a whole lot of friends in a hurry or start making funeral arrangements. I foresee a massacre."

"I understand. Thanks for the warning," Stauss said, voice weary with sadness and acceptance. Bradford's warning was by no means a surprise, and in fact only echoed his own misgivings about the inevitable consequences of Barbieri's downfall.

The Chicago detective's tone softened. "Take care of yourself, Stauss. You're one of the good ones. One of the last good ones from where I stand. We can't afford to lose you."

"Likewise, my friend."

Stauss eased the receiver into its cradle and stared at it for a moment before putting on his coat and tugging the pull chains on the lights in his office. It was only five, but he hastened for the door. At one time he would have felt guilty about that, calling it an early night instead of eating a makeshift dinner while hunched over his desk, writing reports no one would read and evaluating boxes of evidence. But if the years had taught him anything, it was that there would always be more criminal cases awaiting him in the morning. Whether he drove himself to the brink of death with sleep deprivation or got a full eight hours each night, a new stack of casework would still be resting on his desk when he arrived the next day, just as it would long after he had taken his final breath. Better then, he reasoned, to take the longer view and preserve himself, holding out for as many years as his body and mind would allow.

When he arrived at his apartment, the detective began peeling off layers of coats and scarves, his hat, and his gloves, placing them neatly by the door, each in their place in little stacks or suspended from hooks on the wall. He stood for a moment by the radiator in the living room, letting the heat warm his hands and seep into his aching muscles. The siren song of a hot bath and an early bedtime called to him, and he made no effort to resist. Stepping toward the bathroom, he paused. Something felt off. Something out of place.

That's when he noticed it.

Wedged between two throw pillows on his sofa sat a thin rectangular package wrapped in brown paper. He approached it slowly, as though it might start ticking or suddenly catch fire. A small note had been folded in half and tucked into a seam of the wrapping. He opened it and read aloud, "A gift for you. A coup counted for me."

Stauss smiled and shook his head. He had to give it to Niklas—at least he had a sense of humor. The detective set upon the wrapping, tearing away the paper to reveal an oil painting. One that stole the breath from his lungs, his eyes fixed on the vivid hues of a French island village in springtime. Matisse's *Vue de Belle-île*. The painting that had been displayed for years in The Commodore's restaurant.

He sat back and sighed. He couldn't in good conscience keep it. It had either been purchased using ill-gotten money from a now-dead mobster, or it had been stolen outright. Still, at least for tonight, he would admire it for as long as he wanted, maybe even allowing himself to run a finger along its edges as he pictured himself there, leisurely strolling along the flower-lined cobblestone path on his way to the beach.

Open for business

T he bank had quietly closed down months before. The squat two story, built of rust-red brick and bone-white masonry block, stood flanked by a dozy hardware store and an auto repair shop that hadn't seen a new customer in weeks. A pair of concrete colonnades loomed like sentries alongside the front door. Iced-over pine boards had been hastily nailed across the front windows and a finger-thick logging chain, paired with a heavy padlock, safeguarded the door. Niklas recalled walking by and being surprised to discover a bank could go out of business. Seemed impossible given that they were the ones with all the money.

It had been a small one as banks go, with a confined atrium and a faded tile mosaic floor, only a few teller windows emerging amidst a fence line of black-painted iron bars.

"It would make a perfect retail space with a little elbow grease," the seller said, patting his protuberant belly as it draped between a pair of loud red suspenders. Insisting on guiding them through the building, he kept up a steady bombardment of creative uses for every begrimed corner while repeatedly using the word 'sturdy' to describe its construction. He appeared blind to the layer of dust on every surface and the persistent scritching of mice behind the plaster walls. The atmosphere smelled of age-yellowed documents and mildew.

"Upstairs has an office space you could use for bedrooms," the owner continued, pausing at the base of the stairs as if steeling himself for a mountainous climb. "Has a nice view of the street, but the alley out back could use some cleaning up. Got a couple of stray dogs living out there that get a little yappy at night, but they're harmless."

Niklas nudged Kessler, gesturing with his head toward the bank's interior. The owner's voice faded behind them as he slowly ascended the stairs, continuing to extol the virtues of the building with emphatic gusto between asthmatic wheezes and clomping footfalls.

As they turned the corner, they came face to face with the bank's vault door—tall as a horse and a foot thick, built of solid steel. It swung upon hinges that looked like they belonged on a battleship, fastened to the wall with bolt heads the diameter of half-dollar coins. The vault sat empty. A small table rested in the center, the walls covered in a grid of steel safe deposit boxes.

Niklas gazed upon the cavernous space admiringly. "What do you think, little brother? You could store quite a few guns in a room like this. Could even lock it up and leave for a spell without fear of someone stealing them."

Kessler breathed deeply through his nose, hands on his hips as he appraised the space. Finally, he gave a subtle nod. "I think this will do nicely."

If you enjoyed this novel, please take a moment to leave a brief review on Amazon and Goodreads. It goes miles toward helping promote an author's work and is appreciated enormously.

A Minnesotan outdoorsman, award-winning novelist, and editor, Nate Granzow likes the smell of gunpowder, the taste of gin, and the feel of leather-bound books. In addition to writing fiction, he's worked as a magazine editor for a Fortune 500 publishing company, copy-editor for a military news network, and editor-in-chief of a digital hunting magazine.

To discover more of the author's work, be sure to visit
www.nategranzow.com

Made in United States
Orlando, FL
17 December 2024

56024356R00174